The
Spruces

Pearl Collinson
Syd from

The
Spruces

REX HOLMES

CAITLIN PRESS INC.
PRINCE GEORGE, B.C.

Caitlin Press
Box 2387, Stn. B
Prince George, BC V2N 2S6 Canada

Layout and design by Warren Clark Graphic Design
Cover design by Warren Clark Graphic Design
Cover photo by Lenard Sanders
Author photo by Janet Robinson

Caitlin Press acknowledges the support of the Canada Council for the Arts for our publishing program. Similarly, we acknowledge the support of the Arts Council of British Columbia.

Holmes, Rex, 1923-
The spruces

ISBN 0-920576-79-6

    I. Title,
PS8515.O46S67 1999   C813'.54   C99-910685-6
PR9199.3.H5816S67 1999

THE CANADA COUNCIL | LE CONSEIL DES ARTS
FOR THE ARTS | DU CANADA
SINCE 1957 | DEPUIS 1957

"Some little talk awhile of Me and Thee
There seemed—and then no more of Thee and Me"

The Rubaiyat of Omar Khayam

Introduction

THE PLACE WAS CALLED THE SPRUCES BY THOSE WHO KNEW THE country in the years of the depression, although the same name could have been given to any number of such homesteads in the area. As the name suggests, it was one of those evergreen islands in the midst of the great northern deciduous forest. Presumably such islands existed because of the presence of an unusual amount of water, and they were referred to, with some exaggeration, as swamps. They were not swamps in the conventional sense of the word since there was no permanent standing water in them, and in the late summer and fall they appeared to be as dry as anywhere else in the surrounding area. Nonetheless, the water must have rested very near the surface because the evergreens, together with the lush undergrowth, bore witness to its presence.

In the one hundred sixty acres of land which made up the quarter section there was not one arable patch of ground except for the tiny hummock where the cabin was built. All the rest was heavily wooded with spruce, a few widely dispersed tamarack, and on the higher side, a good stand of jack-pine. The fact that the homestead was not suitable farmland explains why no one ever tried to take it over since it was abandoned in 1933. How any of the cabins could have survived is strange since other far more substantial buildings of the same era have disappeared entirely. Yet it is still there, a tumble of rotting roof poles inside what little remains of the walls. Broken and decayed bits of lumber in the debris, a window that seems to have fallen out more or less intact, and a rusting sewing machine indicate the building was never cannibalized, and that is strange because a building abandoned in those days was usually stripped by the first passer-by who coveted any part of it.

There was a restless stirring throughout the Dominion during the great depression. While some rural people, caught up in a more than usual grind of poverty, fled to the cities to swell the ranks of the unemployed, many of the city people moved into the country in their frantic search for security. Some of the more adventurous, seduced by the ancient Canadian lure of free land, turned north-westward to the Peace River country where the dream was still a reality. They came in wagons, on horseback, by freight, by passenger train, on foot, and even by car to file on a homestead and begin a new life. Those who were familiar with farming were lucky; those who were novices were in for some cruel disappointments.

One couple–numbered, surely, among the most innocent of all the new settlers–tried to make a home at The Spruces. They came in the spring of 1932, lived there one summer and one winter, and then were gone. Hardly anyone knew of their arrival or of there brief tenure, or would have cared even if they had known. No one remembers them now.

1

THEY STOOD SIDE BY SIDE ON THE STATION PLATFORM WATCHING the train disappear across the prairie. They made a handsome pair. He was tall, muscular, erect, his head a wire tangle of unruly black hair over eyes that looked out dreamily on a world he seemed to find unreal. She, a China figurine, was five-feet four inches tall, weighed one hundred and ten pounds and appeared to be much smaller than she really was. A slight stoop gave her an air of helplessness that was completely belied by her clear, determined eyes. Her dark hair was cut severely short in a boyish bob that should have made her look masculine, but instead made her more intensely feminine. Both of them were dressed in city clothes which had seen much service and, in Kevin's case, gave evidence of recent travel. Although he appeared slightly rumpled, Joanne was exquisitely neat from the top of her head to the tips of her high-heeled shoes.

"There goes our last link with civilization," Kevin commented, gesturing toward the departing train. "Here we are for better or for worse."

"It has to be better; we have seen the worst."

Except for the skeleton of a grain elevator still under construction, the station stood alone at the edge of the prairie. While the station house itself was freshly painted in the dismal red common to most railway property, the wooden platform had never been touched by a brush, and already the planks had weathered a driftwood grey. Beyond the jumble of cabins that was the town, a deciduous forest rolled away southward to evergreen-crested hills standing in a sentinel arc from the southwest to the southeast, while to the west and north more or less open prairie undulated to the horizon with only one cluster of farm buildings and the ubiquitous fences to mark the foothold of civilization. Although it was after five o'clock in the afternoon, the sun still stood high in the sky.

"Looks more like noon than afternoon," Kevin remarked, looking at his watch.

"Land of the midnight sun."

"Well, not quite."

"I thought it would be different than this. Wilder, I mean."

"Looks wild enough to me. Over on the hills anyway."

"I thought the station would be surrounded by forest, you know, like northern Ontario."

"The article spoke of miles and miles of empty prairie just waiting for the plough."

"Well, there it is, in that direction anyway. You got a plough?"

"Judging by the fences, I would say a lot of people have been here with ploughs already." Kevin put his suitcase down, took Joanne's and set it down beside his own and said, "We are here; shall we dance?" And they danced to music that only they could hear.

While they were dancing, a wagon drew into the yard and stopped. The driver stood watching their performance. After a few moments he called out, "Pelican Jesus, folks! This ain't no dance hall."

Kevin and Joanne stopped abruptly. "We were just celebrating," Kevin said sheepishly.

"Celebratin' what? Christmas or th' New Year?"

"Getting here."

"Most folks celebrate when they're leavin'."

"You going back into town?" Kevin asked, looking uneasily at the drayman, at his faded overalls, his unshaven face, and the tattered cigarette hanging from his lips.

"Yep. I got no place else t' go."

"Then how about a lift?"

"Got any money?"

"Yes, I've got money," Kevin snapped with a good deal more conviction than he actually felt, for the truth was he had precious little. The drayman studied Kevin for a second or two; then, he shifted his eyes to Joanne with considerably more interest. He turned again to Kevin, and the two men sized each other up. Something in the man's eyes broke down Kevin's usual reticence, and he found himself extending his hand. "Kevin McCormack," he introduced himself. "Here is my wife Joanne."

The drayman shook Kevin's hand with a firm grip. "Ed Reed." Turning to Joanne, "Pleased t' meet y' Ma'am. Yez look like city slickers t' me. Yez come up here t' see how th' natives make their livin' or did yez fergit t' git off in Edmonton?"

"We've come looking for a homestead," Joanne announced, holding Ed's gaze with pure blue eyes that made every man who ever saw them want to protect her from exactly what he had in mind.

Ed shook his head. "If yez don't mind m' sayin' so, yez're the most unlikliest lookin' pair of homesteaders I have ever saw, and I have saw a galore."

"Unlikely or not, that is what we are here for, and we are anxious to get started."

"We need somewhere to stay while we are looking for a farm," Joanne broke in.

"A farm? Now I know yez have lots of money."

"She means a homestead."

"Now I know yez must be broke. Anyways, they's two hotels in town. Hop on and stand up front and hing onto th' dray. This here'll be a wild ride when I get these two stallions fired up, and I'd hate t' see yez all beat up from jouncting around. Get up yez lazy good-for-nothin's"—the last comment directed at the horses as he snapped the reins. "I don't know which one of them buggers—excuse me Mrs. Mac-is th' laziest, th' black or th' grey. Not that I blame them," he added after reflection. "If I was a horse I wouldn't work any harder than I had t' either. I'd as soon be a dog, because they never do nothin' but lie around all day lookin' for somethin' t' eat or scr...., ur, chase. Chase. Some has to pull sleighs—I'll admit that— but all they got t' do is go someplace where there ain't any snow. Anyways, if I was a dog, they's a lot of people in this town would get mistook f'r trees."

Kevin flashed a glance at Joanne, saw her grin, and relaxed. "People not very nice here then?"

"Some is; some ain't. They's bastids wherever y' go. I take them as they come. Th' way I look at her is, if they was all as nice as me, th' charm'd be spread way too thin, whereas the way it is now I kin say I more or less got a copyright on her. Charm, charm that is. Like a goddam Englishman told me one time, 'Ed, you've got couth you haven't even used yet.'" He slipped the reins around the tie-post, withdrew a disreputable looking tobacco pouch from his pocket, and began making himself a rather wretched look- ing cigarette. "I kin not git th' hing of her," he complained. "No matter how I wrap these thin's, they look like a parcel. Prefer m' pipe."

"Why not smoke it now, then?"

"Because they say cigarettes is worse f'r y' than a pipe."

"Sounds as if you are determined to make yourself sick."

"No, ma'am, y' see not runnin' risks is like cheatin' somehow. Unless y' give God a chanc't t' do y' in, y' can't really say y' got Him mocked, now kin y'?"

"Oh boy," Kevin snorted. "That is what I would call complex reasoning."

"Much obliged." Just as they entered the main street, a democrat drawn by two brisk young horses crossed in front of the wagon with a sour looking man at the reins.

"See him?" Ed indicated the other driver by tipping his head so that his cigarette pointed at his target. "That fellow c'd've put this town on th' map. Railway was goin' t' end right here one time. They needed ground f'r their yards, but that sour old pr...uh, gentleman wanted too much f'r his prop'-ty so they just moved on north t' where somebody else was more reasonable. Leastwise that's what they say. It may be true; a fellow c'n make or break a town like that. It's been done before. Me, now, I never made or broke nothin' except for maybe a horse or a girl, an' I'm already too old even f'r that, more's th' pity. All I've got left is m' pride, an' even that's wore kind of thin."

Pride, Kevin thought, that is about all I have too. He remembered his father's refusal to lend him money to come up north. The old man looked on the whole project as a pipe dream, and he may well have been right. Nonetheless, there was no reason for him being so vehement about it and nasty in his refusal. Never again would he ask his father for anything. He had not quarreled with him; he had just let the matter drop, and they had come on a shoestring of their own making without any parental blessing. In any case, whatever happened to them could be no worse than the humiliation of the past year: begging in the city for work where no work could be found, surviving on the fifteen dollars a month Joanne earned as a housemaid, and the dreadful evening she had come home crying with rage because the woman for whom she worked had insisted on having her back massaged.

"There's th' hotel over there t' th' right—the white buildin'. Ain't she a palace? There's another joint as is cheaper, but she's got one minor drawback; namely, she's raddled with bedbugs, an' could be yez'd take exception t' that. Personal, I'd prefer t' do without them. I like eatin' out, but I don't like bein' ate out, so to speak. But don't let me influence yez in one way or another."

"We'll take the palace here," Joanne said decisively. "I love bed-bugs, but not every night."

"Thought y'd maybe look on her that way. Not that y'd be in much danger; y'r so thin the buggers'd have a hard time findin' somethin' to chew on. By th' way, if y're feelin' rich an' hungry, they's a dinin' room in th' hotel. If yez're just hungry, go to the Plaza; that's a Chink place. Food's lousy, but cheap; thirty-five cents f'r th' regular three course, or fifty-five cents fer th' deluxe."

"What's the difference between the two?" Kevin inquired.

Ed blew his nose noisily into a grey rag taken from his pocket. "Not much. Maybe yez'll get a clean plate with th' fifty-five center, or maybe a chopstick. Chinks have funny ways. Whoa, boys!"—drawing up on the reins. "This here's th' post office. I'll just drop off them two bags-since that's what they pay me f'r—an' then I'll haul yez over t' th' hotel."

"Oh, don't bother," Joanne protested. "We can easily walk from here."

Ed stopped and slowly ran his eyes down her legs. "In them shoes? With heels like them y'd steeple y'rself t' th' sidewalk in three steps." Then with real kindness he added, "Besides y'r too small t' be stompin' around haulin' bags of stuff. Yez both wait right here."

While Ed was in the post office, Joanne and Kevin looked around themselves. The main street, which had obviously been a sea of mud not too long before, had solidified into canyons and minor mountain ranges up heaved by iron-rimmed wheels. Already the process of erosion was at work; the mountains were being crushed down and the canyons were filling in. Here and there antic gusts of wind sent rooster tails of dust flying. Except for a fat woman pushing a baby carriage, the wooden sidewalks were empty. From somewhere behind the livery stable a stationary engine beat out a rough rhythm, a monotonous series of single bangs followed by four muffled drum strokes.

"I am afraid that I, like Moses, have brought you into the wilderness to perish," Kevin apologized again.

"Listen to me for one last time," Joanne answered. "Our coming here was more my idea than it was yours. I'll admit I am a bit scared, as I am sure you are too, so don't make it worse. We are here now and the past is gone forever. Let us make the best of it, come what may; let us have fun as we always have even when things were bad."

Kevin looked down at her, saw tears in her eyes, saw the fragility of her shoulders, and felt a familiar spasm of tenderness tear at his chest, or his stomach, or his heart, wherever it is that emotions flourish.

"All right, we shall do exactly that. No more whining from me. We are young, we are healthy, we have no one depending on us, and we have no money to pay our way back even if we wanted to go. Now smile."

Ed emerged from the post office, scrambled onto the wagon, and took up the reins. "T'gether boys. Let's make some rich folks richer than they already is."

A few people now converging on the post office lifted their hands in greeting to Ed and gazed curiously at the strangers. To each one Ed bellowed a greeting, "Fred boy! Jack boy! Jean girl!"

"Do you have to remind them of their gender?" Joanne teased.

"Remind them of what?"

"Their gender. Why 'Jean girl'? Might she think she's a boy?"

Ed stared at her for a moment. "Y' know, I never gave her a thought. Just a habit I fell into. Come t' think of her I never say, 'Get up there mare' now do I? Just a habit. Here we are at the Mecca of th' north. This here's a first-class establishment, though a wee bit wore." He jumped down and held out his arms to her. "Come on, I'll catch y'."

She hesitated, then let herself go. He caught her by the waist in his two massive hands and deposited her lightly on the steps. "Just like liftin' a bird. Nothin' but feathers. I shot a whisky-jack one time when I was young an' mean, an' damned if y' don't put me in mind of her: a puff of feathers, an' a body made of twigs. F'r the life of me I can't see y' swingin' a grub-hoe. If y'r as smart as I think y' are, y'll catch the next train back an' open up a hat shop."

"Don't put temptation in her path," Kevin intervened. "We are here to homestead and I need her to help pull stumps."

Ed extended his hand. "That's more like it. Nothin' I like better than a straight answer. When y'r gettin' y'r gear together don't forget a set of harness f'r her."

"I hope it isn't too expensive."

"Th' best of luck t' both of yez. Don't f'rgit yez've a lot t' learn, an' I'm more than willin' t' do the teachin'. I'm not what y'd call a college perfesser, but I do know a thin' or two. I'll help yez if y'll ast."

"How much do we owe you?"

"Agh, I was only foolin' about that. I was comin' down anyways. Fergit it."

"I don't want to be beholden..."

"Y'll be holdin' a sore ass if y' keep on about it. Remember I'll give yez a hand if yez want it. If y' don't want it, y' kin bite my arse. How's that f'r a deal?"

Kevin stood mute. At last Joanne broke in, "Kevin hasn't got very sharp teeth. We'll be grateful for any advice you can give us, and we thank you for being so kind."

"Aw jeez. Aw, it was a pleasure. Sleep as good as yez deserve. Come see me at the livery stable anytime. I'll be there unless I'm dead in the meantime an' that hasn't happened too often."

As the wagon moved off, Kevin turned to his wife, " 'What manner of man is this?'—to borrow a phrase."

"He is a truly gentle man."

Kevin nodded his agreement as they walked together into the hotel.

2

TO HER DISMAY JOANNE FOUND THE HOTEL HAD NO RUNNING water, and her dream of a hot, soapy bath after four days on the train vanished. Both she and Kevin washed themselves as best they could in the basin provided with the room, changed into casual clothes, and wandered out of the hotel past the curious eyes of the clerk, to look for supper. The town, they found, consisted of two streets, a traditional main street and a back street. There was a general store, a livery stable, a blacksmith's shop, a Chinese restaurant, one other hotel—a sleazy looking two-storey affair— a police station, a church, and a scattering of houses, some of them log, but most of them frame. The buildings on the main street had the false fronts peculiar to prairie towns, and the rest were rectangular boxes with no sacrifice of utility to aesthetics. Dogs wandering everywhere accosted the strangers noisily.

After a brief walk, Kevin remarked, "Well I guess we've seen all there is to see. How did you like it? How would you like to live here?"

"It would be tolerable, I guess, but I am glad we can't."

"Maybe we could if I can find work."

"You promised me a homestead, remember?"

"All right my love, a homestead it shall be. After all if one is going to live in a town, no matter where it is, life would be about the same. What we want is adventure, right?"

"Right."

"What if we get hemmed in by bears and water snakes?"

"As long as I don't have to massage their backs, bring them on. What price freedom?"

"Here here. Right now, what about some supper?"

"We should get some bread and bologna and eat it—them— in our room. We have to save every cent we can."

"Nuts. This is our first night in town, so let's live it up. We'll go to the Plaza and feast as Ed suggested on the fifty-five center. I am starved."

The Chinese restaurants right across the Dominion were pretty much the same, Joanne reflected, and the Plaza was no exception. Along one wall and down the cen-ter were two rows of high-backed booths finished in dark brown wood to which flickering twenty-five cycle lights merely added gloom. Along the left wall stood a glass-topped counter backed by wood-en shelves in which and on which were displayed a few faded chocolate bars, several brands of cigarettes, pipe tobacco, a cluster of dusty punch-board prizes, a card of pocket knives hanging loosely on strings, a box of Rowntree chocolates with an insipid girl's face on the top, two mouth organs, Copenhagen snuff boxes, and an array of aging pies. One innova-tion Joanne had never seen in the East was a gasoline barrel converted into a washstand on which was a wash basin, a pail of water and a soap dish. On the wall to the right hung a filthy towel and a toothbrush on a string.

"Look at that," she said, pointing to the toothbrush.

"Want to brush before supper?"

"If it is all the same to you, particularly since I just abluted, I think I shall forgo the opportunity. Thank you very much for pointing it out to me though."

"Don't mention it. Where shall we sit? Here?"

"Hold it." Kevin took her by the arm and guided her to the opposite seat.

"You can sit facing the window to watch the crowd go by." He had noted that from the seat she had chosen she could have seen directly down the aisle into the kitchen, and with sure instinct he knew that what she would see she would not like. The waiter, cook and presumed owner, an ageless Chinaman in a dirty apron, shuffled up and waited without com-ment while his clients studied a much fingered menu.

"I'll take pork chops and French-fried potatoes," Joanne decided.

"Me too," Kevin agreed.

From his vantage point Kevin watched the preparation of their meal, details of which he mercifully failed to communicate to his wife. First blowing some of the ashes off the stove, the Chinaman seized a blackened piece of bacon fat kept on a hook for the purpose, and proceeded to smear it about in the area he had blown clear. Next, taking a potato in his left hand, he hacked it into chunks, letting the pieces fall where they would amongst the ashes and smoking fat. Then he added two pork chops and let the whole mess simmer in a pyre of smoke.

"What on earth is all the smoke about?" Joanne asked, craning around the edge of the booth to see what was burning.

"He's having a little trouble with the stove," Kevin replied, not wholly lying.

A tiny, fox-faced little man came into the cafe, followed by a diminutive boy who was obviously created in his father's image. Both were dressed in ragged blue overalls, grey flannel shirts, and heavy boots. The boy had definitely not washed for a considerable period of time, nor had his father, although in his case a grey stubble of beard camouflaged to some extent what lay beneath.

"Howdie," the man greeted them civilly, taking a booth opposite the McCormacks. "Strangers, aren't you? My name's Kinney, Fred Kinney. You may have heard of me if you come from the East. This here is Floyd, one of my sons."

Kevin nodded distantly, not yet accustomed to western ways like being accosted by strangers.

"Hello," Joanne answered brightly. "We just got in from Toronto."

"Times are tough there so we hear. People dying in the streets from starvation and the like."

"It's not quite that bad. There is no work, but we didn't see any bodies lying around. Did you, Joanne?"

"Well not many anyway. How is it here?"

"For a good place to be, it's just dandy. For a place to work, well you can't because there isn't any. None. There is nothing going on now the railway is finished, and there is nothing in sight. Floyd here might just as well have stayed in school for all he is likely to make this year."

"Working? Why, how old is he?"

"Eleven, going on twelve."

"Merciful heavens."

"That's nothing. I started working in a bush camp when I was two years younger than he is now, but he'll just have to hang around until something turns up."

"My Dad's got a new gun," Floyd broke in without any particular relevance.

"He has?"

"Yep," Kinney confirmed. "Just got her from the Eaton's catalogue. She's an ex-army rifle, cost seventeen fifty."

Floyd nodded proudly. "Seventeen dollars and fifty cents for a goddamned gun."

Kinney beamed his approval. "He got that from his mother. He never misses a thing."

At that point the Chinaman interrupted their conversation with their plates. The McCormacks looked at their food and then at each other. Finally Kevin shrugged and began methodically chewing, while Joanne picked at the mess in her plate with her fork.

"Two slices of mince pie and two coffees," Kinney ordered. "I wouldn't mind tucking into a whole meal myself, but nowadays a man can't afford luxuries like that."

"I haven't done anything with mine except stir it around. Do you want it?" Joanne offered.

"Let me have her," said Floyd.

"Done. Take it—I mean her. Do I mean 'it' or 'her' Kevin?"

"When in Rome..."

"Now Floyd, you say 'thank you' to the lady."

"Thanks," Floyd muttered; then after he had sampled, he added, "Goddamn good meat Mrs. Lady."

"Are you a farmer?" Joanne asked, directing her question to Fred.

"Nope, homesteader."

"What's the difference?"

"Well, a farmer is a homesteader that has made good. I haven't made good yet."

"Interesting point. What does a homesteader live on hereabout?"

"About whatever he can shoot or grow or pick off a wild branch. Course you have to have a gun and cartridges and that takes a dollar or two from time to time. Course if you run out of cartridges, you can always snare rabbits. In any case there is always relief. We live on relief and I aim to stay on it. Last time I went in for the money, the agent asked me, 'How long do you intend to stay on relief, Mr. Kinney?' I said, 'Forever.' Made him mad."

The Chinaman arrived with the pie and coffee and for a few minutes the Kinneys were busy loading their cups with sugar.

"Some folks say coffee's no good for kids. It stunts their growth, but"—slapping the bib of his overalls—"I've drunk it all my life and look at me. What harm did it do me?"

"What harm indeed," Kevin agreed, looking at Kinney's five-foot, four-inch frame.

Joanne leaned across the table and whispered to Kevin, "Do you suppose there is a closet here?"

With no attempt to hide his curiosity, Kinney, too, leaned forward to hear what she was saying. "The outhouse is outback," he volunteered.

"As the name would imply," Kevin interjected.

"You go through the kitchen and out the back door, unless you want to go out front and around the building."

Choosing the front door to avoid seeing what she was sure she must see in the kitchen, Joanne walked out, her head held high, her steps light and confident. Kevin turned to watch her go, and his breath caught in his throat.

"Mighty pretty woman you got there."

"Just what I was thinking. Is Floyd your only child?" he asked in order to direct the conversation onto safer ground.

"I said before, no. We've got seven: two girls and five boys. Floyd here is the youngest."

"That's quite a family."

"You don't know the half of it. Had them all in ten years, and me with only one nut."

"What!"

"Thought that would shake you up. One nut. They hacked the other one out because of a tumour. Hacked it out while I was sitting on a chair in the kitchen—no anesthetic, nothing."

"A tumour, you say. Whatever became of it?"

"It's in a museum in Halifax and it's still growing. It was as big as an apple when they hacked it out, and the last time they wrote it was as big as a grapefruit, a monstrous thing."

"In a museum too! You'd wonder they would let a thing like that out of the province."

"They don't know any better out here."

"Incredible," Kevin remarked dryly.

"Isn't it though? Strange how little it takes to make a man famous. You talk to anybody in the medical field in Canada and they'll know the name Kinney. That's why I thought you might know me when I introduced myself."

"What about in Europe; do they know about it too?"

"Funny you should say that; there's supposed to be a delegation coming from Denmark as early as next summer to have a look at it."

"Oh, they'll be going to Halifax."

"Here too. It's the other one they are most interested in. I've proved I could still have kids after the operation, you see, that is what fascinates them."

"Any danger of the kids being half-wits?"

Joanne returned, looking a bit pale.

"Rough?" Kevin asked.

"Wonderful," she lied. "So colourful, and aromatic, and so many witticisms printed on the walls. Did you ever hear, 'Here I sit, broken heart...'."

"NO! And I don't want to!"

"Killjoy." She picked up her coffee cup, almost sipped at it; then, remembering, put it hastily down. "One thing I don't understand, Fred— can I call you Fred?"

"Sure, sure."

"One thing I don't understand: you say you are on relief and yet you just bought a gun. I thought relief was..." She paused in confusion and then floundered on, "For the needy."

"You are right, Missus, but you don't have to tell them everything. The trick is to go there hat in hand while you've still got a nest egg stashed away. The trouble with most folks is they wait until they are starving before they...Floyd, for Jesus sake if you are going to drink that ketchup, pour it in your cup! You never know who might have drunk out of that bottle before."

Calming, he wiped his mouth on the back of his hand and again addressed himself to Joanne. "What was I saying there?"

"About not waiting for relief."

"Oh yes. Well like I said what keeps most hogs away from a trough is foolish pride. If you are going to make a go of it here, I suggest you go for relief first thing tomorrow while you still have something left, if you do have something left. Bury your wallet and go in there sobbing. You're not known here, so if you want I'll lend you a couple of kids to make your case even more pathetic. Lay it on thick."

Kevin frowned and glanced at his wife. "Thanks for the offer, but here is one hog that is going to stay away from the trough and keep his pride intact."

"Until death do us part," Joanne volunteered.

"Suit yourself. Just one last piece of advice: when you go to the store, ask for credit as soon as you've placed your order. Because you are new, Old Fletcher will think you are rich and that way you can get away with a wagonload of stuff before he finds you're broke. The time to ask for something is when you look as if you don't need it. You going to stay here for a while or are you just looking around?"

"We are looking for a homestead."

"You won't have much luck. The good places are already taken, at least the close ones. You'll have to go back in about twenty miles or so to pick up something half decent, and your wife won't think much of that. She doesn't look like a country girl to me. The first coyote will send her running back to town."

Joanne fixed cool blue eyes on him and held him frozen. Kinney faced her for five seconds before dropping his eyes and mumbling, "Come to think of it, it'd more likely be the coyote that would come a-running."

"More likely," she agreed. The conversation died. Kinney snuffled at his pie while Floyd scooped sugar from the bottom of his cup with his fingers. The Chinaman came back, picked up the dishes and offered pie. The McCormacks shook their heads.

"These away back homesteads you were talking about," Joanne broke the silence, "are there roads into them?"

"Trails. You can get in even with a car in some places, but only in the dry season. Right now a wagon could get in. When it is wet, you sometimes can't even walk on them."

"Do you know of any particular place you would recommend?"

Kinney shook his head. "Go out towards the Cutbank country is all I can suggest. They say the soil out there is pure black and about four feet deep. Never been there myself. As I said, if I were you, I'd stay in town and go on relief."

"One last question, where does one go to file on a homestead?"

"Government office, back of the police station."

They said goodnight, stood up and went to the counter where the Chinaman seemed to be waiting for them to pay. As he was making change, Kevin said, "Look at those, Joanne."

"Those what?"

"Those mouth organs. Hohners."

"Just what we need most."

"Agh, when you get tired of staring down coyotes, you'll be glad to hear me play."

"You've got one now."

"Almost on its last legs."

"Legs on a mouth organ?"

"Figure of speech."

"Here is the deal: I will buy you one from the first ten dollars we make on our farm—read homestead."

"Promise?"

"Cross my heart and hope to die."

At the door Kevin stopped and went back to their table. "Listen, Fred, when those Danes get here, look me up, will you? I'd like to see that remaining testicle myself and maybe some pictures of that monster in Halifax."

Joanne called, "Come on, husband. Goodnight Fred. Goodnight Floyd."

Kevin looked back, catching Kinney and Floyd staring at Joanne, the father with his furtive fox face, and Floyd with his hooded old man's eyes.

3

ALTHOUGH THEY COULD ILL AFFORD IT, THE MCCORMACKS stayed in the hotel for two days while looking for a suitable homestead. Reason dictated that he should check the land carefully before he filed, but Kevin did not really know what he should look for and he hated to expose his ignorance by asking. Eventually he signed for a quarter section in the area Kinney had recommended, influenced by the agent's report that there was already a house on the property, and by the fact that they could not afford to spend anymore time in the hotel.

After filing, the young couple went to the general store to buy staples without being sure of what they needed. The storekeeper, Mr. Fletcher, greeted them warmly and introduced them to his wife. "These people are moving out to a homestead," he told her, "and they've come to pick up a few essentials."

The two women looked at each other and immediately flickered into mutual hostility. "How do you do," Joanne said coldly.

"Good morning," Mrs. Fletcher replied. She studied Joanne, looking for defects and finding none, grew colder still. "It looks as if you may need some, agh, sturdier clothing. You are hardly dressed for this part of the country. But then, I don't suppose you will be staying long. City people quickly find the hardships more than they can cope with."

"Do they? Well, I am a pretty good coper even if I say it–who should-n't? to borrow one of my mother's phrases."

"Oh, you have a mother still alive?"

"Yes and a dad too. Did you ever have a father?"

"Joanne," Kevin intervened. "We are straying from the subject in hand: groceries, remember."

"I was diverted. Mr. Fletcher, how are you fixed for bread?"

"Oh dear. We get bread in only once a week, and I am afraid this isn't the day. Most of our customers bake their own."

"Oh, well, flour then?"

"That we do have. It comes in twenty-five, fifty, or one hundred-pound bags. You know, of course, that many, agh, useful things can be made from the bags?"

"He means underwear, but you wouldn't find that fancy enough for you."

Joanne stepped around Fletcher and stood facing his wife at close range, hands serenely at her sides. "Mrs. Fletcher, I can see that you are one of those people who always say exactly what they think. What a pity you never think anything pleasant."

"Well!" Mrs. Fletcher flounced into the back room and slammed the door. With her departure peace descended as if dust were settling.

"We don't really know what to buy," Kevin admitted, sitting down on a nail keg looking helpless.

"I know how you feel. This is all new to you. Just let me lay out a few things I think you will need—practical things—if you disagree, just speak up. You will want flour, we already discussed that, salt, sugar, dried beans—that is the staple diet when there are no other vegetables available—vanilla, a pound or two of butter, but remember it won't keep long, lard, yeast cakes, baking soda, toilet soap, laundry soap, a big pail of Roger's Golden Syrup..." The list went on and on while Kevin grew bored and then uneasy as the pile grew.

"Do you have any stoves?" Joanne asked.

"We do not carry any, of course, but we can bring one in, and you'll have it in about two weeks."

"How much are they?"

"Kitchen stove, heater, or both?"

"Cook stove."

"As low as forty dollars."

Kevin winced, coughed, tapped the floor, and made faces.

Joanne looked at him, and getting the message, said, "Well we won't order one until we get settled in."

"Just so. Have you any tools? An axe? A saw?"

"Agh—yes. No, I mean we haven't anything."

"Here is a fine Swede saw, saw file, and an extra blade. Do you want a single-bitted or a double-bitted axe?"

"Golly, I don't know."

"Well the homesteaders seem to prefer the double-bitted as they feel it has better balance. The single-bitted are better for splitting. How about both?"

"No, no! Make it a double-bitted."

"In case you intend to eat rabbits, you will need some snare wire. Do you know how to make a snare?"

"A snare?"

"For catching rabbits. Here, I'll show you how it is done. Remember rabbits are usually quite plentiful, and you may be glad to have them if other game is scarce. You had better watch this too, Mrs. McCormack."

While he was demonstrating, Joanne gazed about the room. She would never have believed so many things could be crowded under one roof. There were bolts of cloth, packages of needles, spools of thread, axes, saws, grindstones, blocks of salt, bits of leather she assumed must be harness, a cream separator, an open case of dollar watches, shaving brushes, bars of Fels-Naptha laundry soap flanked by an equal stack of "P and G", Royal yeast cakes, knitting needles, fence hammers, shoes, dress shirts, coils of barbed wire, rolls of hay-wire, lanterns, liniments, dishes....

"Think you can make one, Misses?"

"Make what?" she asked. "Oh yes—snare—I think so," she lied, not having paid any attention to what he had been saying or showing.

"Whip up a couple just to show us, Joanne," Kevin urged, delighted at her confusion.

"When we get home I will." As she spoke she thought, we really are going home, to our own place. Our own house. We could never have done that in the city. Then in a burst of good feeling she looked right into Fletcher's eyes, smiled sweetly, and said, "You really know what you are doing, don't you?"

Fletcher blushed with pleasure. Kevin cleared his throat, bringing Fletcher back to the business in hand.

"Where will you people be living?"

"Way out back in a place called The Spruces," Kevin answered, adding defensively—he didn't know why—"There is a house already built on it."

"Oh, you've seen it then?"

"No."

"Goodness, gracious. That's only...." He stopped himself abruptly. "That's about twenty miles out in the valley. Have you got a rig?"

"A rig?"

"A wagon, horses. How are you going to haul your stuff out there?"

"We, ah, we," he looked at Joanne. "We've been thinking about that, haven't we Joanne?"

"All night long."

"Are you thinking of buying an outfit?"

"Lord no, not yet."

"Can we hire someone?" Joanne intervened.

"Well Ed Reed does that kind of thing. He is the drayman; you may have seen him at the station. There is no train now until next Tuesday, so maybe he can help you."

"We know him already. How much do you think he would want? What should I offer him?"

"You'd better ask him that. If you go over to the livery stable, he should be there. Meanwhile, I'll look after your little lady here. By golly, we almost forgot a lamp, or a lantern. Spare chimney, oil...."

"Okay, I'll go over to see him. If you get done there Joanne, maybe you'd better whip up a few practice snares."

"If I do any whipping, my lad, it won't be snares that are the recipient."

"Better throw her a chocolate bar," he suggested to Fletcher. "She gets mean when she gets hungry."

It was a dandy joke, but once he was on the street Kevin began to wonder if Fletcher would think he had been trying to cadge a chocolate bar. Perhaps he should go back to explain. Nuts. Surely the man had a sense of humour. Then it occurred to him that he should have stayed with her rather than leave the responsibility of outfitting up to Joanne. He would become the laughingstock of the whole country if word got around. He would have to be more careful of his actions and of what he said. What if Joanne ordered more than they could pay for? It would be awful if he had to admit he was nearly broke. He knew very well that she would be as careful as he would be himself, but she just might get carried away through inexperience. Talk about being the laughingstock if he had to go through and cancel items to make ends meet. They were off to a bad start. Why had neither of them thought about the cost of moving out to their new-found place? Such lack of foresight could ruin them now that they were on their own. Well, perhaps Ed would come to their aid. On to the livery stable. He would approach Ed firmly and with dignity, and let him set the price as he, himself, had no idea of what to offer. This was one more opportunity to make an ass of himself, something at which he felt he was all too adept.

4

KEVIN WANDERED OVER TO THE LIVERY STABLE, LEAVING JOANNE to finish the shopping. He found Ed busy shifting hay from a pile on the floor into the mangers.

"So y're still alive," Ed greeted him laconically. "Have yez found a place t' lay y'r heads yet—outside th' hotel that is."

"Yep, we've signed up."

"Fast workers. How did she look?"

"We didn't see it."

"Where's it at?"

"Way out. Some valley in the area Kinney talked about."

"Cutbank. I see y' done her scientific, studied her close before jumpin'. Well f'r oncet old Kinney ain't lyin', although he'd be upset if he heard me say that, him bein' the world's best liar. The soil is good out there, but she's a long way out. Yez won't be comin' in f'r coffee every day of th' week."

"Yes, even I can see that, but to tell you the truth we won't be having any coffee if we don't get out of that hotel today. I was wondering...we thought you might..."

"Might what? Run f'r parliament?"

Kevin took a deep breath. "We wondered if you could find time to take us out there?"

Ed smiled. "Y're a stiff-necked pecker as Moses used t' say. It near killed y' t' ast, didn't it? What would y' do if y' had t' ast a real favour?"

"I'll pay, of course."

Leaving his fork jammed in the hay, Ed led the way out of the musky silence of the stable into a clamour of sunshine. "I'll haul yez out there with all y'r gear, and I'll be glad t' do her. Five bucks, okay?"

"Of course it's okay if it's enough."

"When' ll yez be able t' pull th' pin?"

With a sigh of relief Kevin answered, "Anytime. Joanne is just buying the stuff right now, over at the store."

"Hardly thought she'd be buyin' it at th' church. How much gear have yez got?"

"Not very much: our two bags, a sewing machine, and a trunk plus whatever Joanne has purchased at Fletcher's."

Ed looked at the wagon and nodded to himself. "Stove?"

Kevin shook his head.

"No stove, eh? Not even a heater?"

"No. Fletcher said they started at forty-five dollars. That stopped me."

"Foller me an' I'll show y' how t' make a stove that'll start on a dime, or at th' drop of a match."

He led the way around to the back of the stable where an odd assortment of material had accumulated over the years. "Roll that there gas drum 'round t' th' wagon. It'll make th' best heater y've ever saw after I've had a whack at her. They's a tangle of stove pipes hid 'round here somewheres, can I just lay a hand on them."

First flipping the barrel over on its side, Kevin rolled it to the wagon, seized it with both hands, and threw it onto the dray. Ed, following with several lengths of stovepipe, watched the maneuver with obvious satisfaction. "So th' city boy's got a muscle or two he has scarce wore out yet. Y' look like a man who knows a day's work from a day's play."

"All I ever wanted was work," Kevin answered, "and it is the one thing I have never been able to find."

"Yeah, well I'll give y' some now. Take that barrel back off again. Y' ain't got enough stuff t' fill th' dray, so we'll take th' dray off an' put a box on instead. Dray's way too wide f'r th' road we'll be travellin'; we'd be scrapin' willers all th' way in."

An hour later Ed pulled the wagon up in front of the store and he and Kevin went in. "We're all set," Kevin announced. "Ed's taking us out."

"Y' buy out th' whole store?" Ed teased, looking at the pile on the floor.

"She has done very well," Fletcher interjected affably.

"Done well f'r y'r store y' mean. If y' want t' take a wheelbarrow an' run her money over t' th' bank, we'll hold th' fort until y' git back."

"Come now, that isn't fair at all." Then to keep the peace Fletcher turned on a weak smile and added, "Isn't he the one? Isn't he a card?"

"When y' git t' see St. Peter with all y'r money in a bag, on your way down, it'll be y'r conscience as' ll be all ate out, not mine. Let's git this stuff aboard."

All three joined in carrying the goods to the wagon, where Ed supervised the loading. "I'll kind of stack th' stuff so's y'r lady kin lie down if she gits wore out. We've gota bit of distance t' go, an' although she'll joinct around some this way, she'll be so tired she'll be glad she's got a place t' lay her pretty head. As f'r us two, Kevin m' boy, y' can ride up front with me an' share the mosquitoes—or let them share us. Whichever."

Kevin helped Joanne climb into the rear of the wagon and then took his place on the front seat beside Ed. "Thanks for everything, Mr. Fletcher," Joanne cried. "Say good-bye to Mrs. Fletcher for me. I know she'll be sorry to see us go."

"I'll do that. If ever you need anything, you know where to come."

Ed shook the reins, murmuring, "Th' son-of-a-bitch knows there is no place else for y' t' go. Get up y' lazy black bas...devil. See how I've quit th' swearin' Mrs. Mac?" he yelled.

"Very commendable," she yelled back over the uproar of the iron wheels. For a time they drove in silence, Ed hunched over on the seat, the reins slack in his hands, his body relaxed to the motion of the wagon. Beside him Kevin sat erect and tense, resisting each bump, while in the back, intoxicated with the newness of every experience, Joanne rested comfortably on a folded tarpaulin with her back supported by Ed's bedroll.

"What a perfect day," she cried, but the men could not hear her. Overhead a few woolly clouds grazed aimlessly across an otherwise empty sky. The air was tinted with the perfume of wild roses that flanked the route on either side. The sounds of civilization diminished as they moved away from the town, leaving only the restless breath of the wind and the occasional bird cry.

"Something bothering you, Ed?" Kevin asked uneasily, interpreting his companion's silence as annoyance.

"Eh? Me? What's that?" He sat up and shook out the reins.

"You mad?"

"Broodin'. I was just broodin' away there. Y'll get like that too after y've been here awhile. The place is so big. Look' t there"—gesturing to the west. "Them hills, see. Beyond them lies th' mountains, they tell me, an' past that they's th' sea. An' betwixt here an' there y' may not find a livin' soul f'r all that I know, not one. No matter what I'm doin' I can't fergit that, th' emptiness of her. Right now y' kin see out an' beyond, but soon we'll be closed in by trees, swamped by them, an' y'll think y'r bein' drownded in forest, or at least by willers, but always them hills will be waitin', standin' there f'r a million years. Makes a man feel he don't amount t' much."

They reached the bottom of a hill, crossed on a frail wooden bridge, and began the long slow ascent on the other side. There were a few houses on the creek flats hidden well back amongst the trees. Most of these were log shacks; a few were built with lumber. None of the homesites looked prosperous, except for one substantial frame house surrounded by a billiard table lawn and a well-trimmed hedge.

Ed lifted a laconic hand. "Fletcher's place. Palace. He rents it out t' th' government agent. No matter how tough times is, they's always some bugger either gettin' rich or gettin' richer. No justice."

After wrapping the reins around the post to free his hands, he withdrew his pouch from his pocket and began rolling himself a cigarette. "He's got this palace here, Fletcher, yet he an' his wife live back of th' store uptown. Th' craziest part is, an' it hurts me t' say it, is he ain't such a real bad guy after all. The whole countryside is after him f'r credit an' that'd be enough t' drive anybody nuts, but he sometimes gives credit t' those who needs it even tho' he knows he'll never git a red cent back. He's a sometime philangist."

"I suppose Kinney is one of the needy."

"Yeah, but he doesn't bother askin' no more since he already owes a piss-pot full. Anyways, he's all set up with relief now, an' Fletcher sucks that money in like a bee in a sirrup pail. They're in cahoots. Hey Mrs. Mac, how'd y' like that wife of Fletcher's?" he bellowed.

"Loved her on sight," Joanne called back.

"Thought y' would. One thirteenth of a coven, that's what she is. No one in his right mind would give her bed space. Fletcher has t' be f'rgave with a old broom jockey like that waitin' for him t' take off his socks an' jump in t' bed. I'd as soon bed a set of deer horns." The terrain leveled off just as Ed predicted and the road lost itself amongst the poplars that pressed in on each side.

"Poplars," Joanne called out, "poplars everywhere. It's a rain forest of the north."

Ed turned to look at her with quick approbation. "That's right; that's what I always thought. She's a jungle of popples. Them cannibals an' thin' in th' south has nothin' on us with their bamboo growin' like the Dickens. Y' whack off a field of popples an' think y' got y'rself a farm; then when y're not lookin', she closes back in on y' as good as any jungle. If I was a religious man, I'd have t' give th' Lord a straight talkin' to. If He'd of put half th' effort in t' makin' spuds grow as He puts in t' popples, we'd all be feastin' more often. Still I guess He favours popples an' that's His business. There is no accountin' f'r tastes as Shakespeare used t' say—when ast."

They drove on, each lost in his or her own thoughts. Kevin, with a familiar frond of anxiety stirring against the lining of his stomach, Joanne dreaming of the house they would find at the end of the road.

"Yez got a rifle?" Ed asked, rousing himself.

"Yes, thank God I had sense enough for that. It was my Dad's, a thirty-thirty. It is pretty old, maybe my Dad's dad's."

"Dad blame it. She must be well along in years, but like myself she's probably improved over th' years. No twenty-two, eh?"

"No. Will we need one?"

"Depends what y'r plannin' t' shoot. You hit a partridge with that thirty-thirty an' y'll be pickin' up pieces of meat f'r a half mile 'round, unless y' can pick its eyes out like one of them sharp-shooters in th' books. I'll tell y' what I have f'r y' because I figured y'd need it. I brought along my old twenty-two. I've got two, y' see. This here one kept mis-firin'—I mean it missed fire off an' on. So I ordered a new one, a beauty, an' then I found out it would do th' same damn thin'. Twas th' ammunition, no fault of the gun at all. An, t' be sneaky, I brought y' three boxes of th' old ammunition. What'll happen is y'll aim f'r half an hour at a bird, say; then, when y' pull th' trigger th' damn thin' won't go off and th' bird 'll fly away laughin'. She'll be better than nothin', but not very much."

"I can't pay..."

"At last y' admit y' can't pay f'r somethin'. I never seen a guy so anxious t' pay in my whole life. Y' should wear that wallet of y'rs around y'r neck before y' wear y'rself out reachin' f'r it. I don't want t' sell y' th' gun; it's a kind of keepsake, but I'll lend it t' y' f'r as long as y' need it. Y' got t' bear in mind that y'll need y'r money f'r Fletcher."

"Well, that is very, very kind of you. To change the subject, I don't know how to get to our homestead."

"It's about time we found out. I know where t' turnoff th' highway t' git in th' general area, but we'll have t' nail her down a little tighter than that. Gimme y'r paper."

He drew a pair of steel-rimmed glasses from the bib-pocket of his overalls, perched them on his nose, and peered at the paper. "She's north of— no, by God, that's the Allen's place—an old English woman with a shack full of potted plants—an' there's th' old Thompson place—he killed hisself about ten years ago. Y're south—Jesus Christ! Whoa boys!"—grabbing the reins and jerking the horses to a stop.

"What's the matter?" The sudden stop had almost sent Kevin over the front of the wagon and under the horses' heels.

"Is this, honest t' Christ, th' homestead yez've filed on?"

"Yes, that one there with the cross on it."

"That government son-of-a-bitch. That there's The Spruces an' I know it well." Crossing his arms on his chest, he looked around furiously as if he expected to find someone he could attack. "I knew I should of gone in with yez. I told y' I could help, but no, y' were too damned proud..."

"What's the matter with the place? What's all the uproar about?" Kevin felt resentment flaring, feeling his judgment was in question, and knowing that there was every reason why that should be so. He had, indeed, been precipitous in his choice.

"What's the matter with it is it's a evergreen swamp; that's what's th' matter. Why, man, y'd have t' have real genius t' pick a place like that. In a half-million miles of clean popple y've gone an' picked one hundred acres of evergreens all jammed t'gether an' harder than hell t' cut down an' uproot. Why there ain't even enough ground there t' even put in a garden. Almost. All y' got is spruce, pine, tamarack, willers, a creek..."

"I didn't know," Kevin said miserably. "The clerk told me there was a house on it, and we were glad because we need someplace to stay right away."

"A house! Dear God we could of built yez a better house in a couple of weeks."

"I never built so much as a chicken house in my whole life and wouldn't know even where to start."

"I told y' an' I told y' I'd give yez a hand..."

"That's enough!" Kevin snapped. "Let's get on with it. I've filed and that is that."

For a moment Ed studied him over his glasses; then he removed them, shoved them back into his pocket, handed Kevin his papers, shook out the reins and bellowed, "Giddap!"

After a few hundred feet of silence he began whistling tunelessly through his teeth. Finally he started chuckling to himself.

"What's so funny?" Kevin asked morosely.

"Y' got mad at me—bit my head off. I was afraid all along y' were one of them Biblical fellers that was always wearin' out their neck turnin' th' other cheek. Then y' snap at my ass, and as long as y' kin snap an' snarl there's hope f'r y' yet. Here take these lines an' see if y' kin keep this rig betwixt th' ditches whilst I light up m' pipe. Y'r about th' sorriest homestead picker I ever seen' but y'r goin' t' make her as long as y' kin learn t' put y'r pride in y'r pocket an' hang on t' y'r wallet." Whereupon he began singing, "When I look back on th' years behind/ Th' tears they fall and blind me/ When I dearly think of th' pretty little girl/ Th' one I left behind me."

"Very cheerful," Kevin groused.

"Says in th' Bible, 'Oh be joyful unto th' Lord an' come before His presence with a song.' Christians don't pay much attention t' that; they prefer t' go 'round hangdog an' frettin' over sin."

"I wasn't planning to come before His presence for a long time yet. Never mind, though, you are right. Joanne!"

"What is it?"

"Rejoice."

"I am; I am. But why?"

"Biblical injunction, and because we are on our way to our new home."

"That," Ed approved, "is th' way t' do her."

"I will play 'Money Musk' on my old mouth organ. Joanne wouldn't let me buy a new one."

"When y'r done with that one, play 'Hummerskew'."

He did and they rejoiced, all three.

5

FOR THE FIRST TEN MILES THEY FOLLOWED THE HIGHWAY, A narrow grey ribbon, graded but unsurfaced, packed hard from iron-rimmed wheels. In the whole distance they met only one other wagon, and once a Model-T touring car. "The traffic isn't exactly fierce," Kevin remarked.

"She's thickenin' up a storm. Come late summer y'll see a lot more auto-mobiles hangin' 'round. One day last summer I seen three in the space of four hours. She's still a bit early in th' year f'r the really heavy traffic like that. By then th' roads will be dry and solid. By times."

"This one looks pretty good to me right now."

"Looks ain't everythin'. She's not bad f'r th' time of year, but don't fool y'rself. Five minutes of rain an' she'll be a quagmire. In th' meantime, never f'rgit she's thin and a wheel kin drop right through her. That doesn't matter much with a wagon an' a team of horses, but with one of them auto-mobiles a dropped wheel kin mean she'll scratch herself in like a dog diggin' f'r gophers. Ever seen gumbo when she's wet?"

"Wet, no. We saw some on the street in town, but it was dry and hard as a rock."

"Just so. See them tracks there where th' wheels has wore her smooth? Smooth as a baby's arse, wouldn't y' say?"

"Smooth, although I have never had much of a chance to test out your simile."

"Be that as it may, two minutes after th' rain starts she'll be slick and sticky. Sticky like y' never seen before. She'll pack on the wheels an' John The Baptist hisself couldn't pry her off. Like I said, I've saw car wheels drop right through without any warnin'—drop right t' th' axle an' there she'll sit, th' wheels spinnin' an' neither th' car nor th' driver gettin' no place."

About ten miles from town they turned off the highway onto a narrow trail cut through a tangle of overhanging willow and alder. The snow was long gone, but still the route was soft under foot, and in the low places the water stood in deep pools. The iron rims of the wagon cut into the wet soil, twisting and yawing the chassis and the box as the horses plunged ahead. Wherever there was an appreciable hill, the spring freshets had cut canyons in the centre of the road, and when a wheel dropped into one of these, it seemed as if the wagon would turn completely over or break in two. Somehow it recovered each time just in time and their slow progress continued.

Once they passed an abandoned homestead where a deserted shack stood with the doorway gaping and the door hanging from one hinge.

"There's th' place y' should of grabbed—the old Myhren place: good garden, easy clearin', southern exposure. Trust a Scandihoovian t' pick th' best. Swedish fella. He was supposed t' marry one of th' Horsley girls— within a month of marryin' so they said. Then her dad fell into th' river back there, and this crazy Swede jumped in t' save him. Well, her old man come out downstream aways none th' worse for wear, but th' Swede was drownded dead. What in Sam Hill would he want t' save the old man f'r anyways? This Myhren wasn't fixin' t' marry him was he? Just like a Swede t' show off like that. I never yet seen a Scandihoovian who wasn't stark-starin' crazy. Yet I never met one neither who wasn't a good feller at heart. It's th' cold weather does it t' them—makes them crazy, I mean— they have fearful cold weather wherever they come from, so they say, and that's what turns them crazy."

"Is it as cold there as it is here?"

"Well, maybe no. This here is th' coldest place in Christendom, or wherever. There is some people..."

"Don't tell me, some people are coming over from Denmark to check it out."

"Well now, just how in hell did y' know that?"

"Kinney must have told me."

Kevin waited vainly for some further comment. "Well?" he demanded. "Well what?"

"Finish the story."

"How much finish do y' want? I told y' Myhren drownded."

"But what became of his fiancée?"

"Oh her. I don't know—I think she married a Traves from over Beaverlodge way. Yeah, Jim Traves. Just two months after Myhren threw hisself in th' river."

After a moment's reflection, he added, "She had to; she was in calf."

"Who did it?"

"They say 'twas Traves, but I always figured Myrhen had th' major hand in it. More than a hand."

"See," Kevin interrupted joyfully, "that's why we didn't file on the place: there was a legitimate heir."

"Illegitimate y' mean. Baw! Haw!"

At last the willows came to an end and they broke out into another poplar forest that went on and on all afternoon. As soon as they were free of the willows Joanne's spirits rose. "My turn to ride up front," she called. "You guys seem to be having all the fun up there."

"Fine by me," Kevin agreed, "I'm going to get off and walk for a stretch. Sitting on a board is not the most comfortable position in the world, especially when it is thrashing around like a raft at sea."

"Quit complainin', look what I've got t' put up with ridin' up here all afternoon with y'r wife. I won't even be able t' swear at th' horses."

"Sure you can," Joanne comforted him. "Listen, not only can you swear; you can teach me how."

"Say, that's fair. It was my mother who taught me."

At six o'clock in the afternoon they drove down the bank of a gulley into a small clearing amongst the willows.

"We could make her tonight easy," Ed commented. "But she'll still be there in th' mornin', so why kill ourselfs? Th' horses will be tickled pink, thinkin' of th' water an 'th' green pea vine. They will have t' be hobbled, but they f'rgit that each time th' silly fools. And, to tell y' th 'truth I could do with some rations myself."

"What time does it get dark here?" Joanne asked, looking warily about.

"This time of th' year she scarce gits dark ay-tall. She doesn't bother t' git dark until it's almost too late. Some nights y' could read a newspaper at midnight if y' was silly enough t' have one. In th' winter she'll be dark enough t' please th' devil, tho' he's supposed to be th' prince of darkness hisself an' this an' that. In midwinter she'll be black at five in th' afternoon, give or take a half hour either ways. In th' mornin' yez'll be eatin' y'r pancakes by moonlight, at least on clear days." While he was talking, Ed unhitched the horses. Why don't y' make a fire whilst I look after these nags. There's wood a plenty, an' y'll find water in th' spring if y're not careful. She may smell like an Ay-rab's armpit, but she's reasonable clean foreby a dead rabbit or two."

"A dead rabbit!" Joanne protested.

"A dead rabbit never hurt nobody. One spring I was visitin' this family way back in, an' they was talkin' about their well. T' hear them tell her, she was a piss-cutter even though she smelled a bit off, y' know. So just t' show off, I bailed her out with a bucket, an' y' know the bottom of that well was a six-inch layer of decayin' rabbits, all a mass of slime. Appetizin'.'"

"A few dead rabbits never hurt nobody, much," Kevin repeated.

"Y'd think them homesteaders would of caught th' dengue or at least yellow fever, but not them. They flourished."

"Where will we sleep?" Joanne asked.

"Wherever it pleases y'. That's one big advantage of this country: there is lots of space. Yez kin make a bed in th' wagon' if y'r so minded. Me, I'll sleep on th' ground. She's none too soft, but she's warm. Another thin', if y' sleep on th' ground th' mosquitoes kin git at y' from only three sides."

"Maybe the ground will be better for us at that," Joanne agreed, thinking of the smell of the wagon box and her dark suspicion of what had been hauled in it in the recent past.

By the time the campsite was ready to everyone's satisfaction, and they had eaten their supper, even though it was still broad daylight, there was a distinct feeling of evening closing in. A flock of partridges in one of the taller trees made much ado about settling in for the night. Some evil bird swooped through the campsite, a half-seen flash—menacing—while mosquitoes hummed in high cadence where the willows fringed the clearing.

After the dishes were cleared away, Joanne touched Kevin on the shoulder and whispered, "Can you come with me for a minute?"

"Okay."

"Bring the suitcase."

Kevin obeyed. "Where are we going? Are we running away?"

"Dressing room; I want to change. Let's go over there where the woods look thick."

"Lead the way."

"No, you. You go first; you're the man and I know my place."

"Oh ho! Discipline at last."

"Take my hand."

"This gets better and better. You are unusually friendly tonight. Is it resurgent love?"

"No it is the possibility of surgent bears to coin a phrase."

Kevin laughed and then subsided. In amongst the willows it was much darker than in the open and somehow the presenceof bears seemed a distinct possibility.

When they returned to the fire, Ed looked at Joanne with open admiration and some surprise. "Pyjamas! Night-gownd, rather. Man I ain't seen much of that."

"One never sees too much of nightgowns," Kevin volunteered.

"Don't you wear a nightgown?" Joanne teased.

"Who, me?" Ed responded. "Hell no. I scarce got time t' wash m' socks, let alone a mess of night-gear. An if y' ll allow me t' say so, Mrs. Mac, even if I did I wouldn't look so darned pretty as y'rself. Besides, these overhauls is so comfortable I can't bear t' take them off. When y' spend a lot of time sleepin' on th' ground, y' need all y' kin git twixt y'rself an' th' rocks. Not that there's all that many rocks around here, but there's sticks an' lumps galore. I mean galore."

With a casual boot he kicked the fire together, releasing a cone of sparks. Kevin and Joanne drew closer, and all three stood in companionable silence.

After a long period of brooding, Ed lifted his head and, still lost in thought, fixed on Joanne. As he became aware of her, his face softened. "I keep wonderin' how yez'll make out away out here, city folks. Is thin's really that bad out in civilization?"

Kevin nodded. "Bad enough. I could not find work anywhere, and God knows I tried. It was just hopeless and getting worse. Joanne worked for a while as a housemaid..."

"Well, hell, I don't want t' discourage yez or nothin'—I mean hell—innocents. Do yez know what yez'r up against here? Do yez know what it's like here in winter? Do yez know how t' live off th' land? Do yez know what y' kin eat an' what y' can't eat? Aren't yez afraid y'll git cabin-cranky out here all by y'rselfs? It ain't no picnic."

"It will be a picnic if we make it one," Joanne intervened.

"What are y' goin' t' eat?"

Joanne waited impatiently for Kevin to answer, but he hesitated so long she finally answered for him. "We planned to come up here and raise turkeys. People always want turkey meat."

"Turkeys! German Jesus, girl, what're y' goin' t' do with turkeys?"

"Sell them, of course."

"Who to, before God?"

"Well, town people. In the market."

"The market? The MARKET! Aw God girlie—aw God!"

Savagely he yanked his tobacco pouch from his pocket, chumbled himself a cigarette, jammed it into his mouth, yanked it out again, spat, jabbed it back in, lit a match with his thumb, burned himself, yelled, "Shit!" and murmured disconsolately, "Market, Jesus. There ain't any market this side of Edmonton if they even got one there. No market ay-tall, and even if they was, turkeys is th' hardest buggerin', thin' t' raise this side of hell. Turkeys is all th' time tryin' t' commit suicide, even worse than rabbits in that respect. Even worse than rabbits. A turkey would sooner git some horrible disease an' up and die before he'd face th' axe. Y' have t' be one of them psych'rists t' git a turkey t' use any sense. I knew a feller tried raisin' turkeys. He started out with twenty an' he raised them t' school age in spite of themselfs. Then they took t' dyin' until he had only two left. Well by that time 'twas mid-winter, there had been a chinook an' when it died down th' snow froze into a hard crust. Well, these last two turkeys got th' idee they was goin' t' Venezuela, an' they took off just a-runnin' acrost th 'snow. Poor old Pete—he was th' damn fool tryin' t' raise them—he took after them an' he follered them for five miles. Doesn't sound like much, five miles, does it? The thin' t' remember is that th' crust on th' snow was too thin t' hold him up an' he had t' creep on hands an' knees. At th' end of those five miles he was wore out an' so was th' knees of his pants."

"Did he catch them?"

"Oh sure, but he was so mad he wrung both of their necks an' that was the end of his herd of turkeys. Like I said they ain't easy t' raise, turkeys."

After a few tense minutes of shifting his cigarette back and forth with his tongue, he turned to Kevin. "We won't talk no more about turkeys. Have y' ever used a axe or a saw?"

"A little bit. You don't run into much of that in town, but I did do quite a lot of splitting."

"Figures. Y've got a axe an' a saw. How about a shovel?"

"Did we get one, Joanne?"

"No, I didn't think of it."

"An' old Fletcher must of forgot too. Kill him if he found out he might have sucked out another buck. Course he may have been afraid if y' had one y' might come back an' bury him with it. Well, no harm done; I always carry one in th' wagon. Y' kin borrow that one f'r awhile. Y'll find her a mite wore down at th' lip as she's turned over a snide of dirt in her time, but I never yet seen a shovel that wouldn't work, as long as there was a man t' help her along, that is."

"That is very good of you. I'll pay..."

"I figured y'd do that. When y're enterin' heaven—if y'r slated f'r that destination—y'll be haulin' out y'r wallet."

He hawked and spat in the fire. "And if old St. Peter is like most of th' Christians I've met, he'll be gladder than hell t' take it. Nothin' lights up a good Christian's eyes like a dollar bill, or even a shinplaster. We'd best be gettin' some more wood; that was a sorry pile y' put together before supper. First rule about gatherin' wood is, when y're absolutely sure y've got enough t' do th' job, go back an' git twice as much more. It's somethin' like money in that respect."

He floundered and cursed amongst the willow bushes until he found a blackened stump which he brought back to the fire. To Joanne there was comfort in the uproar he created, for surely, she thought, no living creature would dare to come around after such a tumult.

"That stump 'll burn like a piece of that Caledonian cedar that Hiram skidded out of Tyre," Ed shouted joyfully. "She's jam-packed with gum."

"Ed," Joanne asked in a small voice, "are there any..."

Ed looked at her quizzically. "Are there any what, little lady?"

"Bears?"

"Bears? Why sure, there's doz..." He stopped abruptly and glanced at Kevin. Then with an absurd attempt to undo the damage, he added, "Oh bears! I thought y' said hares—ugh—no bears. None. Never seen a bear in m' whole life' round here—practically."

Both Kevin and Joanne laughed. "Nice try anyway, Ed."

"Put my gawd-damn foot in her, didn't I? Well, anyways if y' must know," speaking to Joanne, "they's maybe a one-two, little black fellers that wouldn't hurt nobody that I know of. Any black bears I ever seen was too busy runnin' t' go 'round bitin' people's ar—arms or anythin'. It just seems when a bear decides he wants t' be somewheres else, he just goes an' can't think of nothin' else. Th' only animals y' needs t' fear is moose. They can be mean. Most times they'll take off like a brace of blue geese when they see a man—especially a Christian—but sometimes if y' hurt one or y' come on him sudden, he'll get ugly. Don't y 'worry y'r pretty little head about bears, honey; watch f'r moose an' worry about starvin' t' death; that'll keep y'r mind off bears."

After a few moments of silence he asked Joanne if all she had to wear were the high-heeled shoes she had on at the station.

"Didn't you see the moccasins I had on today? I got them at the store and have been wearing them ever since. Didn't you notice?"

"Well now, by golly, yes I seen them. What I'm after is wouldn't y' say they was a tad on the large side? Why a girl y'r size could put t' sea in them."

"Fletcher advised me to get them big enough for heavy socks."

"What he meant was he had a whole bunch that size an' couldn't sell them fast enough. Ah well, at least they'll be warm, an' oncet y' git th' hing of them, y'll be able t' do th' two-step in them: two steps in each." He slapped his hip and guffawed.

"In the bush," Joanne replied, "it might be more appropriate to learn the fox-trot." She slapped her hip and tried to imitate his laugh

"What will you do for moose-sic for all the dancing?" Kevin chimed in.

"That's enough of that. I am all in, and I want to go to bed while the fire is still on and you guys are still up."

Earlier Ed had explored the banks of the gully and had come back with several armfuls of dead hay which he had then arranged in two piles at a safe distance from the fire. While supper was cooking, Joanne had spread their blanket on one of the piles, and now she was glad she had done so, for she was suddenly too tired to do more than crawl into bed. Although when she first sank into the soft hay she thought she would be asleep in a second, she had not counted on the effect of late daylight, nor was she prepared for the night sounds around her: small creatures rustling in the grass, some birds settling in for the night, the crackling of the fire and its echo from the surrounding trees. Within a few feet of her bed a mouse stood up and cut down a weed which fell with the sound of thunder in the mouse's ears. Something of the emptiness of the country around her, of her aloneness in spite of the presence of the two men made her aware of her vulnerability.

She looked over at the two men standing by the fire, glanced uneasily toward the darkening trees, heard the nervous stirring of the horses, and almost cried out for Kevin. She stopped herself abruptly, remembering that she was there by her own choice. No sissy stuff now, she told herself. You are now a pioneer. No blubbering. Resolutely she snuggled under the blankets, shut her eyes, and eventually slept.

Sleeping, she dreamed that she and Kevin were back in her mother's house; they were expecting company, and as usual in her dreams, she was wholly unprepared. She opened the cupboard only to find no food; the laundry had been left undone and lay strewed all over the kitchen floor; the clock had stopped and she did not know when her visitors would arrive; Kevin was shouting at her....

On hearing her cry out, Kevin hurried over and stood for a moment listening anxiously. From time to time she whimpered and made a small scratching sound with her foot, sending shards of tenderness through him. She depends on me, he thought. On me, the last person on earth that anyone should depend on. It seemed impossible that this small, living thing, breathing ever so gently, so exposed, so fragile, should be his responsibility.

Back beside the fire, he crouched down and gazed into the flames with troubled eyes, while Ed sat nearby, calmly puffing on his pipe.

"She sleepin?" Ed asked.

"Yes, but I think she is having bad dreams."

"She's wore out. She ain't used t' rattlin' 'round in a wagon, and she ain't exactly built' f'r skiddin' logs. She's just a little lady through an' through, an' by Gawd y're lucky t' have her."

"You are right."

"Y're goin' t' have y'r hands full, my lad; no doubt about that. She won't make it none th' worse f'r y' tho'. She has enough spirit f'r th' two of yez."

Kevin picked up a stick and began poking aimlessly at the fire. Normally he hated to talk about his own affairs to anyone else, yet there was something about the older man that drew his confidence. "I'm lucky; I know that. I have nothing to worry about as far as Joanne is concerned; she is stronger than I am. What I do worry about is me. I am so useless. I don't know anything about this kind of life. You can call me helpless Hannah."

Ed was silent so long Kevin began to regret he had spoken and revealed his own weakness. Finally Ed shifted uneasily, his face visible in a sudden flare from the fire where a century old pine knot blazed up in a tiny supernova.

"Well, I wouldn't be too sure, now, about this strong business. This here is a rough country way out here where nobody really belongs, y' know. She'll let some of us stay, some of us, an' even prosper, an' it ain't always th' strong ones. Sometimes I think that nature hates th' strong. Y' can't necessarily git nowhere meetin' nature with a club; sometimes y' got t' creep up on her gentle, slow an' sneaky. Us westerners ought t' listen t' them heathin' Chinese oncet in awhile. Y' don't hear them braggin' an' boastin' about how they conquered th' wilderness. When a Chinaman does git a bit of rice t' grow, he hollers, 'Bad Rice!' just t' keep th' gods from hornin' in on th' profits by snatchin' th' crop back, lock, stock an' barrel. Maybe there aren't no gods, but why take a chancet? Now it strikes me y're not th' type to provoke what might be out there, an' maybe even y' kin fergit y'r pride long enough t' holler 'Piss poor wheat' if y' happen t' grow some an' suspect th' gods has got a hot eye on y'r crop. Doesn't cost y' nothin'; just look on her as insurance. This country might just take a likin' t' y' if y're careful."

"And Joanne?" Kevin's voice was almost a whisper.

Ed stirred uneasily. "I don't know. She may be too strong, y'r wife—I don't know—she may snap instead of bendin'. All y' kin do is keep that arm around her, and beyond anythin' else be joyful with her. She needs joy t' run on, like a car needs gas." He tapped his pipe on a log and shoved it in his pocket. "Now I'm goin' t' hit th' hay. All this philosophizin' has wore me out."

6

IN THE LAST FEW MILES TO THE HOMESTEAD THE ROAD DEGEN-
erated into two scarcely discernible ruts choked with dead leaves from the
previous summer. Obviously whoever had made it had simply chosen the
easiest route rather than cut down a tree more than he had to. Now it
descended slightly and the deciduous trees gave way to spruce and tamarack, to long open spaces that had once been beaver meadow, to acres of
Labrador tea. There was no sign of surface water, yet the ground underfoot
was springy with wet moss.

The shack stood on a hummock of slightly higher ground surrounded
by a heavy growth of spruce trees, some of which actually touched the rear
wall of the cabin.

As they approached, the wagon twisted and heaved as the wheels sank
into the marshy ground, but as soon as the weight had passed, the moss
rose slowly and the ruts disappeared. Then the horses gained the higher
ground and the wagon rolled free.

"Whoa, boys, hold up now." Ed sat for a minute, looking around crit-
ically. "Shack's still in one piece. It's a wonder somebody hasn't stole th'
window. Usually y' leave a place two weeks and she'll be stripped naked,
an' she'll be all gone except th' walls. Guess nobody's silly enough t' come
all the way out here even for a ginuine window."

Kevin and Joanne went up to examine the house, and were struck
dumb. Although they had not discussed the subject, they had both imagined a rambling old farm house of the kind seen in rural Ontario, not made
of stone of course and probably weather-beaten, but a real house for all of
that. Instead they were looking at a shack not more than sixteen feet long,

fourteen feet wide and about seven feet high, built of spruce logs from which the bark had never been removed. It had a slanted roof of spruce poles covered with shattered tarpaper held in place by more small poles.

There were no partitions, just one room with a rough board floor, a door of the same material hung on leather hinges, and one window not quite two feet square with four panes of glass. In the corner stood a bunk made from spruce poles with thin poplar saplings laid in it side by side to form makeshift springs. A combined table and bench was fastened to the wall beneath the window, while a washstand in the form of a shelf was secured to the wall to the right of the door. An arrangement of apple boxes served as the only cupboard. In the roof the stovepipe hole was plugged with a rusting lard pail. "Dear God," said Kevin, looking about him in dismay.

Joanne stood in the doorway, her back to the sun, peering into the dim room. She saw the crude furnishings, the dry bark peeling from the walls, the dead leaves stacked in the corners, the filthy glass panes in the window, the rat excreta sprinkled liberally about the floor, and felt a lump gathering in her throat. All her hopes fell apart at one blow, and she stood in desolation.

Ed blundered into the room and stopped, blinking his eyes to adjust them to the dim interior. "She's not exactly what y'd call y'r every day Taj Mahal, nor is she too similar t' Buckin'ham palace, but th' packrats seem t' have taken a shine t' her, y' can't deny that." He made a slow tour around the walls, now peeking through the gaping chinks between the logs, now stripping off pieces of dead bark. "Look at th' roof—a sieve. Now yez know why we stopped last night. I didn't think y'd be in shape t' face her."

"Now we'll have to get roofing," Kevin said in despair.

"Tarpaper, y' mean. Roofin' is too expensive."

"Does it rain much?" Kevin asked, hoping for a negative response.

"Off an' on. Some years she rains cats an' dogs; others she's dry as a bone."

"Maybe this will be one of the dry ones."

"I doubt her. I never yet saw a time when a leaky roof didn't just natcherly draw th' rain. The Lord can't stand a wore out piece of tarpaper."

For the first time since he had entered the shack, Ed looked directly at Joanne, saw that she was crying, and immediately broke up himself. He said, "Aw honey..." Then he patted her on the head with one great awkward paw, sniffed loudly, said, "Jesus." Murmured, "Little fellow," took out a much used handkerchief, made to offer it to her, saw its condition and wound up by blowing his own nose.

"Joanne," Kevin began and then stopped in confusion. It was not often he had seen her cry. He turned and left the cabin, helpless and defeated.

When they were alone, Ed said gently, "I can take yez back straight away if y' can't face her, little lady. There's no disgrace in gettin' out before th' fight starts; no disgrace whatsoever. Y' just give th' word and we'll have yez both back in town so fast y'll think th' bears is hot on y'r heels—oh now I have put my foot in her—bears! Why can't I keep my big mouth shut?"

Joanne pulled herself together, forcing herself to smile. "Thanks Ed, but the battle was joined the day we decided to come here. We won't run away just because we didn't find your Taj Mahal."

"Good f'r y'. No more cryin'; I can't abide t' see y' cryin'. Y' got Kevin t' care f'r y' already, an' now y've got old Ed f'r whatever that's worth. Now what kin I do f'r y' that's decent?"

"Well, I guess you can bring me the broom." As he turned to go, she added, "And Ed, I deeply appreciate your kindness."

While Joanne busied herself cleaning out the shack, the men began unloading the wagon and stacking the goods just outside the door.

Having brought the broom in, Ed commented, "At least y've got a table an' a bed, an' th' most important thin' is they're paid f'r an' y' don't have t' share them with nobody else. Somebody could easily have cleared everythin' out complete. As it is, it's as good furnished in here as a hotel—pretty near. Now, Kevin, come over here an' cut out th' broodin'. Stand that barrel on end there an' I'll show y' how t' make a stove out of her. I'm th' champeen maker of barrel heaters. Every man has a natcherel talent, or so they say, an' this here is mine, makin' stoves out of barrels. I brung a box of tools so you'll notice; I carry them wherever I go, because y'never know when somebody might need a stove. We start th' festivities by cuttin' a door in th' end, square of course, after I have drew a pitcher."

Using a carpenter's square and a thick pencil he drew a square on the end of the barrel and began chiseling it out, his hammer blows ringing echoes all through the forest.

"I get a great satisfaction," he shouted, "out of cuttin' steel. Don't know why, unless it's because it seems impossible when y' start. Look in my kit there f'r some bolts an' nuts, an' a couple of hinges. Bring them over, an' th' drill too, an' th' centre pop."

In a short time he had cut the door free, the only accident occurring when it finally broke loose and fell inside the barrel beyond the reach of his arm. He put his head through the hole, cursed hollowly and in a rage lifted the barrel in the air and shook the offending piece out.

"Got the hoor! We'll put th' hinges on th' door first. Y' kin drill th' holes if y' ain't too wore out watchin'. Fasten th' hinges t' th' barrel first when y're ready. She'll be pretty."

Once the door was finished he began cutting a circular hole in the side of the barrel at the far end. "This here hole's f'r th' pipe. Th' flange of th' pipe 'll keep her from slidin' through, but t' play safe we'll put a wire through her as well. Y'd not want t' wake up some night an' see th' whole pipe ay-cordeened through th' hole. Th' filler hole there with the screw-in cap is y'r damper. Does she burn too swift y' slap th' cap in an' tighten her enough t' calm her. Seen a family one time lost th' plug, lettin' th' fire go hog wild, darn near burnt down their shack. They couldn't find th' cap, so they used a turnip t' plug th' hole when required. Y' ever smell burned turnip? Not what y'd call incense or incest, whatever. If we had a car rim now, we could cut her in two t' make laigs, but since car rims is few an' far between, we'll have t' use a dirt box t' set here in. Didn't I say she'd be pretty?"

"It's decent of you to go to all this trouble," Kevin apologized during a pause in the uproar. "You've got to be getting back, I know, and we'll just have to manage."

"I ain't in no tearin' hurry t' get back. I ain't leavin' no babes in th' woods without seein' them settled in. Th' onliest thin' is, could y' get that little girl of y'rs t' ease off on th' broom an' rassle a pot or two 'round th' fire. If I don't eat soon I'll be like one of Kinney's cows that up an' died after a hard winter. My gut is stove right in." He stopped abruptly. "Stove in—see—buildin' a stove an' I'm stove in! Baw Haw!"

Kevin, shaking his head in mock dismay, went to call his wife, while Ed went on with his work still chuckling to himself.

Joanne handed her husband the pail. "Water."

"Hey," he shouted to Ed, "where do I get water?"

Ed stopped pounding. "They's a meander betwixt th' island an' th' swamp there. This time of year she'll be full t' bustin', but later on in th' fall she'll be drier than a year-old heifer. Fellow was here before just dipped her from a hole in th' swamp, bugs an' all, th' way y'll have t' do now until y've got a well dug. Th' bugs'll be fierce. Pay no attention; they slide down y'r throat real easy after y' git used t' them."

The creek wandered through the swamp and across the meadow, now running straight and now doubling back on itself. The water moved sluggishly in the narrow places, while in the broader pools it did not seem to move at all. In one such pool a pair of ducks floated idly, watching Kevin with suspicious eyes. Blackbirds, busy about the overhanging alders, called liquidly, while dragon flies, flying double with the tail of one attached to the head of another, clattered over the marsh grass.

"Here you are my pride and joy; don't look in it or you may lose your appetite," Kevin called, bringing the pail to the fire.

"Your 'pride and joy', my condescending spouse, does not know what to make for dinner. We have no bread, no canned food, no meat, no fresh vegetables. We have dried beans, rice, flour and a few other staples, all of which will take hours, if not days, to prepare. What will I make?"

"You are the cook," he snapped, feeling that she was somehow blaming him for the shortage of necessities.

"Fine," she flared back. "You're the breadwinner. Where is the bread?"

Instantly contrite, he muttered, "Touché. How about flour porridge; I did win some flour."

"Flour porridge! Ed will have a fit."

"Well I like it."

"All right, flour porridge it will be."

Fifteen minutes later she called, "Come and get it."

Ed looked dubiously at the pallid mess on his plate. "What's this here delicacy?"

"Flour porridge. Kevin loves it. I was going to serve T-bone steak, but this is what he insisted on." She passed him the pail of Roger's Golden syrup.

"Syrup too! By George this is goin' t' be a feast. Any coffee?"

She handed him an enamel mug. "One spoon or two? Sugar that is."

"Three; I'm weakenin' fast and need all th' help I kin git." He took his meal and sat on a log near the fire where he began noisily slurping it up. After the third spoonful he paused, "Kevin loves this stuff, eh?"

"Adore it," Kevin agreed.

"Well, chickens have the gout, as they say in French."

"Do we have any neighbours?" Joanne asked, taking a place on the log beside Ed.

He shrugged. "Well, we come by th' Johnstones' place aways back—a five six miles maybe. Mannie an' Annie Johnstone. Some folks'll tell y' they have a second kid just f'r company f'r th' older ones—y' know, somebody f'r little Johnny t' play with. Well old Mannie an' Annie fixed the earliest ones up with about thirty-four brothers and sisters."

"Aw, come on, Ed."

"Okay, six perhaps. Them kids is so shy y' kin never git them in sight long enough t' count them. Mannie there is th' limit. Y' know what he done when he first came here?"

"What?"

"He found his homestead'd been partly burnt over, see. So instead of cuttin' some nice green logs t' build his house, he used th' half-burned ones. That house is a sight t' behold."

"They are our nearest neighbours?"

"Not quite. Away back t' y'r right there—tho' y' couldn't go there straight—maybe four miles as th' crow flies—is Froman, rest his soul. Dirty? Oh he's dirty. Lives all by hisself. Long hair right down t' his knees, last washed about nineteen eighteen or thereabouts. Crazy as a cut cat they say, though how anybody knows f'r sure I can't say since nobody ever sees him hardly."

"Well, you've seen him. Is he?"

"Is he what?"

"Crazy."

"Crazy is as crazy does. All I know about him that is a mite peculiar is that on moonlight nights he goes around firin' into th' treetops. I seen an' heard that." He paused to fill his mouth with the last of the porridge. "Yez won't want f'r company."

Kevin laughed. "Who used to live here? You spoke of an Englishman..."

"If y' mean who came here first, God knows. Th' last feller t' live here was a Englishman, as y' just said. He was crazy too. Everybody comes here is a bit nuts—present company excepted of course. Burns was his name, Tony Burns. Here he was livin' in th' bush with enough work t' keep five men goin' full blast night an' day just t' keep th' house equipped with wood an' water. Y' know what he done?"

"Started shooting at trees?"

"No, he done worse than that; he put a pole twixt two trees—y' kin still see it over there—so he could exercise. Wanted t' keep fit, he said, an' him so played out with root twistin', wood cuttin', an' water carryin' he could hardly get hisself out of bed."

"What became of him?"

"Y'll never believe this in a hunnert years: he stayed out here f'r three years, an' then one day he went into town an' run off with th' butcher's wife. They wound up in Claresholm, I heard said. 'Twas Andrews met them out there when they went there t' do some thrashin'." He shook his head in wonder. "Just think on that; he was here f'r three years out in th' bush, never got t' town more than twicet, an' even so he manages t' charm the a...panti...—oh boy, I'm gettin' in up t' th' hocks—I mean he runs off with another guy's wife. Y' can't trust no bloody Englishman, never. If y' ever see one hangin' 'round th' bushes here, Kevin, y' better rush this little lady of y'rs right in t' th' house an' lock every door in sight."

"I'll certainly bear that in mind. You hear what he said, Joanne?"

"How will I know it's an Englishman?" she queried.

"Easy," Ed replied. "He'll be wearin' breeches, talkin' a blue streak, an' lookin' bored as old hell. Y' can't mistake them."

"Thanks," Kevin replied. "I'll keep my eyes open and an ear out, and if I see one..."

"What will you do?" Joanne asked sweetly.

"Lock the door on you as Ed suggested if it's daylight. If it's moonlight, I'll send for Froman."

"Who fires only at treetops."

"Tree th' son-of-a-bitch first," Ed advised. "Come t' think of it, if I was ten years younger, I'd advise y' t' do th' same thin' if y' saw me comin' 'round." His porridge finished, he peered hopefully into the pot. Seeing that it was empty, he lit his pipe. Since he was obviously still hungry, Joanne offered to try her hand at some bannock.

"No thanks, Mrs. Mac. I ain't used t' livin' high on th' hog like that. Never overfeed a willin' horse." He guffawed, choked on tobacco smoke, and fell to coughing.

When the spluttering had subsided, Kevin asked again about work prospects.

"Y're about a year late. Last year most everybody was workin' on th' railroad, but that's all finished now. Besides if y' did find a job, just how in hell would y' come home nights away out here? If y'r goin' t' stay here an' be a homesteader, y'll have t' forgit about work."

The McCormacks were silent. "If y'd settled nearer t' town, y' could maybe sell a bit of wood. Y' could never haul her in from here. It sells f'r three dollars a cord if it's dry, split, an' piled in th' customer's back yard. Two-fifty green. None of y'r Ontario cords neither; a cord is a pile twenty-four foot long by four foot high an' in sixteen inch len'ths. Even then there's one guy in town counts th' sticks; then he figures out th' empty spaces between an' deducts accordin', an' y' accepts that or y' load her all back up an' take her back t' where it come from. Anyways, it seems everybody is tryin' t' sell wood. More guys sellin' than there is buyin'." He belched. "An' that's God's truth."

"Have you any other suggestions of what we can do to make ends meet?" Joanne asked.

Looking directly into her eyes, Ed nodded slowly. "Yep: y' kin eat what y' brought; y' kin try f'r a garden after y' clear a bit of ground an' grow a few radishes an' spuds—altho' th' frost will git her, or th' bugs will make short work of her—y' kin pick a few berries; or y' kin pray Jesus that a moose or two will come callin'. Oh yes, partridges an' rabbits come under th' headin' of delicacies. Last of all, y' kin put y'r tails between y'r laigs an' head back t' civilization where y' kin starve in company. Probably that last is th' thing y' would be wisest t' do."

"I can't," Joanne responded. "Mrs. Fletcher would say she was right."

"An' we sure can't have that," Ed agreed as he stood up, leaned over and rapped his pipe smartly on the log he had been sitting on. The stem broke and the bowl rolled into the weeds. "I'll be bitch-bound; I broken more pipes that way like y've never seen."

7

IN THE AFTERNOON WHILE THE MEN WERE INSTALLING THE barrel heater, Joanne took the laundry down to the creek. It was her first chance to wash all their clothes since leaving the city and it was long over-due. Though the day was warm and sunny, the water was still cold enough to numb her hands after the first few minutes. For a tub she had only the water pail for washing, and the creek itself for rinsing, a scheme that worked quite well, except that there were so many small creatures swim-ming in the water she wondered if she were actually accomplishing any-thing. But to paraphrase Ed, a few dead insects in amongst the sheets "never hurt nobody."

Winding its way through the flat marsh, the creek was completely aim-less in its course, and there seemed something dark and secretive about the slowly moving water. All around the woods were filled with the faint sounds of insects, a peaceful background broken occasionally by a bird's cry to accent the peace. There was an atmosphere of eternity, as if these trees, this creek, the moss itself had existed since the last tectonic upheaval had shuddered into stillness. "As it was in the beginning, is now and ever shall be" took on a new meaning.

As she bent over the pail, she heard a twig snap and looked up into the eyes of a doe not ten feet away on the other side of the creek. They looked at each other, the doe and the girl in mutual astonishment, each lovely in her own way, the animal all grace and with wistful brown eyes, the girl slim and equally graceful. For a few astonished seconds they studied each other, two casual strangers, neither one quite belonging where she stood; two females whose gentleness was wholly out of character with the idea of wilderness where violence was supposed to be the way of life.

Joanne called, "Kevin," and immediately felt she had broken a trust. At her cry the deer started and sailed away in high, graceful bounds deep into the swamp.

"What is it?" Kevin shouted, as he and Ed came running.

"A deer, a live deer."

"Too bad," Ed commented. "We could of used a dead one, but they don't usually make them like that."

"I'm glad she got away."

"Deer's even gladder no doubt. Say, I'll tell y' one thin' f'r sure, all this whoopin' an' hollerin' has gave me a appetite f'r meat that is fearful, an' 'it's gave me an' idee where we kin git some.

"Now," pointing at Joanne, "don't get no idees about flour porridge an' th' like. I'm gonna scare up somethin' f'r a man t' sink his teeth into."

"Not the deer please!"

"That deer is just now skirtin' Winnipeg. I've got somethin' else in mind." He turned on his heels and strode back toward the house.

Kevin watched Joanne for a moment, stirred by her excitement and by the open V of her blouse. "Now that we are alone, what do you think of it, the house and the place?"

She picked up her newly washed clothes and held them out to him. "I think it's all lovely, and I think it is exciting."

"Why did you cry then? As if I didn't know: the house isn't a house at all; it's a shack. The whole place is a swamp—even I can see that; there is hardly any place fit for a garden; the water is full of bugs."

"Help me carry these things back to the house and don't be so miserable. The house is already cleaned up, and soon it will feel like a real home to us. You'll soon plant a garden somewhere, and there are enough bugs to makes sandwiches for days. Look at me. Am I blubbering now?"

At her cheerful response, Kevin too brightened up. Suddenly he swept her up in his arms, laundry and all and ran with her to the house. She was right; all it would take was courage and work. He would build the place into a ranch, a place of plenty.

Once back at the house, however, he could not think of anything further that needed doing. The stove was installed, the wagon was unloaded, Joanne had the house under control, what else was pressing? He wandered aimlessly about for awhile, tried to help Joanne, was dismissed firmly as being supernumerary, went for water, and finally decided to try his hand at cutting some wood. Fortunately their predecessor had left his sawhorse intact. Secretly pleased that he was alone, Kevin brought out his saw, placed a short log on the horse and took a few tentative strokes, awkwardly at first, but soon he caught the rhythm and he became a part of the saw. At last he had found something he could do well.

A half hour later Ed reappeared carrying the twenty-two in one hand and a cluster of dead birds in the other. At the sawhorse he stopped and watched for a minute; then, nodding approval, said, "Looks as if y' got th' hing of her. Stay with her until y' have enough f'r winter."

Appearing at the door, Joanne clapped her hands. "Partridges!"

"Not partridges, young lady; these here are called spruce hens because they hing 'round spruces. Others call them fool hens because they're too stupid t' fly away even after y've started shootin'. Seems like they like t' git shot. I almost had t' disappoint this bunch tho'—th' blasted gun wouldn't fire. I don't know whether it's the rifle or th' ammunition as I said before. I'll check th' firin' pin before I go."

Joanne picked up one of the birds to stroke its sad head with her finger. "Why does everything we eat have to look so pretty? Do I fix them up like chickens?"

"Nope; I'll show y' how t' peel them." Taking hold of one of the birds by the head, he snapped off the body, seized it by the wings with one hand and by the feet with the other, and with a quick jerk ripped it apart. The internals stayed with the leg section, leaving the wings and the breast as a separate unit. He then broke the wings from the breast, tossed the legs and the wings aside, and held the breast out to Joanne. "Y' don't never need a knife with birds, y'r hands is y'r knife."

Kevin watched his wife out of the corner of his eyes, expecting a violent reaction. Instead she looked on calmly, storing everything she saw for future reference.

Now, young feller, just y' throw them breasts in th' pan with a bit of lard, or put them in th' water t' boil with a bit of salt."

"What about the legs?"

"F'rgit them; they's not enough meat on them t' waste y'r time on. Bury them."

"Any fish here?" Kevin asked when he came up to see the action.

"Not so's y'd notice. Creek dries up, y' see, an' would leave th' poor fish flounderin' 'round in misery. What I can't figure out is how th' fish knows that th' creek won't be there f'r long. Oh, y'll see a one-two maybe. Some will come up in th' spring an' get caught in one of the pools until deep summer, an' that's a mistake will cost them their lives. Th' majority, tho', are smart an' they either don't come or clear out as th' water begins t' narrer down." While he was talking, he prepared the rest of the fool hens before passing them on to Joanne.

Kevin resumed his woodcutting.

"I like the stove," Joanne commented, making Ed blush with pleasure.

"Glad y' like her." He looked around inside the house. The dishes were stacked in the apple box cupboard; pots and a pan were hung neatly on the wall behind the stove; a red table cloth covered the table; the new wash basin sat side by side with the water pail on the stand, and the skunky smell of packrats was fading.

"Well now, she looks like a house."

"It is a house."

"Hey don't git y'r shirt in a knot f'r cryin' out loud; I said it looked like a house, didn't I? Are y' plannin' t' go on cookin' in here?"

"Where else?"

"Outside. I'll fix a fireplace f'r y'. Y' go on usin' that stove in here, come summer y'll be roasted alive. Besides th' smoke outside'll be a comfort t' y'."

"A comfort? Why?"

"It'll chase away th' mosquitoes from time t' time. I don' t know where th' beggars are t'day, but they'll be along in due course, don't y' worry y'r head. Y'll be so ate out by midsummer they'll be a mite cautious f'r fear they'll fall into th' holes they made in y'r skin earlier." He wandered around the shack, looking idly at everything, until he noticed the bed made up with blankets lying on the bare poles underneath.

"What do y' intend t' do f'r a tick?"

"A tick?"

"Yes, a tick—aw, I forgot yez easterners was poorly spoke. A tick—a straw mattress."

Joanne hesitated. "Well, we've a blanket to put under us as you see."

"Now there's a comfortable idee. Might be all right f'r Kevin, but a skinny feller like y'rself is apt t' fall right through th' poles an' be left hingin' there till mornin'. You got an extra pair of sheets?"

"No. We've just one pair; we don't have extra anything."

"Thank God f'r small mercies as m' mother used t' say, poor soul. If y' kin git that machine of y'rs to work, make me a sack out of them two sheets. We'll fill her with dry grass that'll be soft an' snug, though noisier than hell. Baw Haw!"

Proudly Joanne opened her machine and sewed the sheets together on three sides. "How's that?"

"Not bad. Kevin an' I will fill her in a flick of a lamb's tail."

"As your mother used to say."

"God bless her."

He went out to Kevin and roared, "Put down that saw. D' y' want t' wear her out th' first day? Come give me a hand with some serious hayin'."

Along the edge of the creek tall grass still stood from the previous year, dry now and easily torn out. The two men worked side by side, ripping out handfuls and dumping them in the sack. It was pleasant in the bright sunshine and the gentlest of breezes. Kevin's hands, soft from long idleness, were quickly cut and bleeding, but he didn't care as long as he was accomplishing something. Ed worked with a long-extinguished pipe clenched between his teeth.

When the improvised sack was stuffed to the limit, they took it to Joanne who closed the open side by hand. After another tour of inspection, Ed called out, "She's even washed th' winder."

"Not exactly a Herculean task since there are only four panes in the one window."

"Never mind," Kevin comforted her.

"As soon as we get rich we'll have a window in each wall."

"Provided th' walls haven't fell down in th' mean time," Ed offered with great encouragement.

"When you put in the new windows, I'll make curtains that hang right to the floor—out of Mrs. Fletcher's flour sacks, of course."

Ed sniffed. "Never could see no sense in havin' a winder put in if y'r goin' t' cover her with rags. No sense ay-tall."

"That's because you are not a woman."

"They's times when I'm glad I ain't. If I was a woman, I'd have a awful reputation—worse than th' hoor of Babylon. Baw Haw!"

"Baw Haw!" the other two agreed.

8

ED STAYED THE NIGHT, ELECTING TO SLEEP IN HIS WAGON instead of sharing the cabin.

"Youse folks has been on the road, so to speak, for near on two weeks now, and last night in th' open. They'll be so much thrashin' 'round on that tick tonight a feller'd not get a moment's sleep, let alone a night's rest. I'll just roll up in m' rig and mind m' own business like m' good mother told me t' do." With a now familiar bellow of laughter he slammed the door behind himself and strode off, whistling, to his wagon.

Though the sun had finally gone down, it was still broad daylight when Joanne and Kevin went to bed. Nevertheless, as they were both exhausted, they fell quickly into a heavy sleep. Sometime in the night, Kevin woke with a start, finding Joanne already awake listening. "Kevin, do you hear that?"

"Hear what? Oh!"

Somewhere deep in the swamp a lone coyote yapped querulously. Then from farther away a chorus of its friends, as if in hot pursuit of something wretched and frightened, yapped and snarled. The silence that ensued was filled with the sinister conception of a prey torn apart in agony.

"Are they getting closer?"

"No, but did you ever hear anything so ominous in your whole life?"

"Not only sorrowful, but sinister. How would you like to be out there in the deep forest and hear that going on close by? Oh please, Kevin, do not ever leave me here alone."

"Take it easy, honey. Ed says they are coyotes, not wolves. Both are harmless, he says."

"He lied about the bears."

"He's telling the truth this time. In any case we're inside and safe as bugs in a rug."

"Bugs sometimes get stomped on, even in rugs."

As he lay there in silence, Kevin became acutely aware of the space around them, of their absolute aloneness. It was as if he were high in the air, looking down on their house, a tiny fortress, the only sign of humanity in a sea of wilderness. It was a sensation he would not forget.

The scent of the swamp seemed heavier at night, more oppressive. Long after the coyote chorus was silent, he lay there thinking: here we are and we'll soon be all alone. Joanne thinks she is safe because she has me, and she thinks I can protect her, though why she should have any confidence in me, I do not know. As for me, I have no one to lean on but myself, and I have no faith in me at all. I am all there is between her and all the fearful things—real or imagined—around us: like animals, forest, hunger, and, eventually, the cold. And what can I do? Even if I had the equipment, I would not know how to use it; I don't know how to raise a crop, or where to sell it if I had one. We have enough food for only a few weeks; we have virtually no money left; there is no work for anyone, and even if there were, I could not leave Joanne here alone. This was a stupid move, just as Dad said, a pipe dream. Tomorrow we will go back with Ed and wire home for the fare back.

Ed said to rejoice, to keep Joanne rejoicing. What have I to rejoice about? Well, I have Joanne, and we both have good health. We have a roof—of sorts—over our heads and no rent to pay. When it gets cold we have fuel a plenty and a Jim-dandy stove to burn it in. There is food in the forest, Ed has already shown us that. There is ground that can be dug up for a garden, and Joanne bought seeds. We have no children to care for— yet. There is some water on the place even though it is full of bugs. We have everything we need; we should be able to survive. He would not quit. "Joanne," he whispered, shaking her. "Wake up."

"I am already awake and have been for a long time."

"I have been lying here thinking of all the things we have to be thankful for."

"That's funny; I've been thinking along the same lines. There are coyotes here—maybe wolves, bears, moose, mice, packrats, and things we haven't even heard of. We could have a fiesta of worries, but there are far more things that we don't have to worry about, like: rent, fancy clothes, fuel bills, keeping up with the neighbours, going to church, buying meat..."

"You hit it exactly. You know what?"

"What?"

"Hand me the mouth organ and we shall dance." Joanne got up, marveling that daylight had already returned and it was only two o'clock in the morning.

"Here, take and play this."

Without another word Kevin got out of bed, put one arm around her, and announced "Redwing" to which they shuffled around the floor, tripping over the warped boards and laughing. Back in bed he went through his limited repertoire with Joanne singing where possible. Once the coyotes joined in the chorus. Eventually they fell back to sleep, but not for long. Soon the mosquitoes came visiting, first by twos and threes, then by the hundreds. In the grey light Kevin counted twenty on his hand when he held it free of the blankets. Joanne stirred restlessly. Soon they were wide awake and slapping. If they put their heads under the blankets, they felt they would suffocate, and in any case at least one foolish insect always managed to get trapped in with them. It would hum frantically and pip, pip, pip to and fro. If it rested for a moment, the two humans would brace themselves for the needle which might or might not be inserted. The cabin was filled with the hum of massed insects. Finally, in disgust, both people crawled out of bed just as the sun broke over the swamp.

"Chock that little experience up as one of the reasons not to rejoice," Joanne complained. "What we have to do is make this house impervious to insects. I'll make that my first job: fill up the cracks with mud or whatever so that it will be absolutely bug proof."

"I would not be at all surprised," Joanne declared, "if they have bored through my shoes." She picked up her town shoes, shrugged and put them under the bed, before pulling on the moccasins that Ed had so admired the day before. Kevin went outside, lit the fire, and stood there coughing in the smoke, his eyes watering, but at last free of mosquitoes. By the time Ed had dragged himself from the wagon the coffee was boiling, and the flour porridge bubbling.

"What's f'r breakfast?" he asked, fumbling with his tobacco and coughing spasmodically.

"Surprise! Flour porridge, brown sugar, coffee," Joanne replied.

"That's a nice change. F'r an awful moment there I thought y' were goin' t' say sausages, toast, an' fried aigs. Say, what was all that uproar in th' shack last night? I expected some straw thrashin', but I didn't expect no music an' hootin' an' hollerin'."

"Come now, Ed, it wasn't that bad. We were just counting mosquitoes and blessings, and Joanne got me up to dance."

"How about that? You were supposed to have long faces, thinkin' back on Toronto and all them lovely streetcars."

"Did you hear the wolves?"

"Coyotes mainly, though one of them singers did sound like a wolf. Friendly creatures carousin' with no danger t' man."

"If you say so. Of all the sounds I ever heard in my life," Joanne replied, "that—those—were the eeriest."

"And the mosquitoes, their music sad too?"

"Fierce! Awful!"

"All yez heard an' seen was just a practice; wait 'll th' whole orchestra tunes up."

"How come we weren't bothered so much the night before at the spring? We heard them by the million, but they did not attack."

"God knows. Mosquitoes is peculiar. When y' hear them dronin' away like they done that night an' not bitin'. I really believe they are there just to give the night hawks a chance t' pitch in."

"Very obliging of them, don't you think?"

"Maybe it is just th' way this country is: she pours on all th' misery she's got f'r days an' days 'til y' think y' can't take her no more; then f'r no reason ay-tall she quits, lets up, and right away y' start thinkin' this ain't so bad after all. Same thin' in th' winter. Just when y'r ass—pardon me—when y're froze blue, along comes th' chinook an' in no time y'd think 'twas summer. If my good mother was still here, she'd say 'twas a caution an' just one more case of God's sense of humour."

He pushed his pipe into the right side of his mouth, and with a grimace spat out of the other side squarely into the fire. He stood there, hands deep in his pockets, grey stubble on his face, eyes half-closed.

"Guess I'll have t' be gettin' along this mornin'. Wish I didn't as I kind of enjoy y'r company, but I've got work t' do what with them hordes of people arrivin' day by day. Anyways, barrin' any dirty tricks of fate, I believe yez are goin' t' make a go of her. Anybody kin git up in th' middle of th' night with th' wolves a-howlin' an' snappin' at th' very door, an' sing an' dance amongst the mosquitoes is crazy enough t' win."

"'Those whom the gods love, they first make mad,' or something like that," Kevin quoted.

High in a spruce tree a tiny puff of feathers asked querulously, "Do you like the parcheesi?" Another whistled the opening bars of "The Rock Candy Mountain," faltered, missed the tune and began again. A whisky-jack swept down from a high perch, gazed arrogantly at the people, then hopped around the fire hoping for scraps until as another bird, all blue, swept in with a raucous cry and usurped what the whisky-jack had claimed as its territory. After vociferously stating his intention, a squirrel, highly agitated, scurried down a tree at a safe distance from the fire expressing angrily his displeasure at intrusion, while near at hand some insect successfully fired his engine and let it run in a high-pitched whine like a miniature chainsaw at a time when chainsaws were yet to be invented.

"Caesar's Augustus," Ed burst out, plucking an ant from his porridge and throwing it in the fire. "If I was God, I would never've made ants—or" —meditating—"any other bugs neither. I'd a spent my whole time makin' women. I'd of made four women f'r each man."

"Did you ever think of getting married?" asked Joanne.

Closing one eye and tipping his head onto one side, he squinted at her, nodding slowly.

"I thought about it, an' thought about it, but never did nothin'. They was precious few girls around when I first come here, an' those that was here smelled like milk, y' know, from th' cows, an' from operatin' th' separater an' such. That kind of smell takes th' edge off a feller's enthusiasm. But that ain't all. I had a buddy one time, a real nice feller, even though a Englishman. Clean feller; kept th' neatest shack y' ever seen, just like y'd expect a woman t' do—though not as house proud as you, Mrs. Mac."

"Call me Joanne."

"I thought y'd never ast. Anyways this friend went an' got married an' right away, of course, she started calvin'. Th' last time I seen their house— not that I associated with them much after th' kids came because y' know how people are, once the first calf hits th' deck they go all t' pieces an' are no good f'r nothin' except makin' more—an' it was an absolute shambles their house. A shambles an' dirty t' boot. Stank! Half-naked kids runnin' all over th' place, bawlin' like heifers, dirty dishes on th' table, an' dirty napkins strewed all over like cow flaps on th' prairie. Th' final straw was she went an' papered th' whole house with newspapers if y' please. I'll never f'rgit that; leastwise I never have."

"Well it isn't always like that," Kevin interjected.

"No but it could of bin. If I could of found somebody like," he paused, "Joanne here, I'd be hitched up right now."

"And we could be pasting up newspaper here together."

"While a host of tubercular children would be out feeding the chickens," Kevin added.

"Could be," Ed agreed, "although I don't see no more chickens than is necessary out there right now."

"Speaking of putting up newspaper, I want to fill up the cracks in the walls to keep the mosquitoes out. How is it done? With mud?"

"Y' won't have much luck with mud tho' there will be plenty of that around. Y'd best gather moss an' pound her in between th' cracks; it's called chinkin', an' moss is th' best chinkin' there is. Th' mud'd dry out an' fall off every time y' slammed th' door. Well, I guess I'd better do like the beggars, 'eat an' run'. I'd better hit th' road."

"Here's your five dollars, Ed. I wish it could be more after all the extra things you have done..."

Ed looked at him, pretending not to understand. "What five dollars?"

"The trip—bringing us out here; that was the deal."

"I don't remember nobody sayin' nothin' about no five dollars. I've been meanin' t' come out here anyways, an' I'm plannin' t' pick up a few poles on m' way out."

"Come on now; a deal is a deal. You need poles like I need lace underwear. You know very well I can't take charity."

"Now listen," Ed replied, pushing the money away. "Y're an easterner an' as such y've got t' be forgave f'r ignorance. Charity is somethin' y' have t' kiss ass f'r—excuse the language—a helpin' hand is what one neighbour gives another. If I needed th' five dollars somethin' sorrowful, I'd snatch her an' run. Fact is I've got so much money right now that one of them Rockerfellers—from Denmark—is buggin' me every week f'r a loan. Right now it's y'rselfs that needs th' money t' git started on. I've done yez a couple of favours. Okay. Time will come when y'kin do me a one'r two, an' in th' meantime I don't want t' hear about it. I bid yez both a good day."

Kevin's secret relief was overwhelming. Five dollars was desperately needed. When the team was hooked up, he shook Ed's hand. "We thank you with all our hearts. I will return your kindness; I promise you that."

"Good enough," said Ed, before turning to Joanne."Mrs Mac—I mean Joanne—if they's any nicer girl in th' world, I don't want t' meet her. When y' feels sad or upset, just remember old Ed is thinkin' of y'." He clambered into the wagon, took the reins, shook them and shouted, "Come on now"—adressing the horses—"the quicker yez git home, th' quicker I kin find yez somethin' harder t' do. Git on now."

A few yards down the road he stopped the wagon, motioning Kevin to come forward. When Kevin came alongside, Ed spoke quickly. "Listen, I got t' speak quick so there's no time f'r backin' an' fillin'. This homesteadin' is goin' t' be maybe harder than y' think, an' y' could maybe get into some serious trouble. If y' start starvin' t' death or break a laig, that don't matter too much; that is what men was made f'r. What I can't bear t' see is f'r y'r little lady t' git hurt. I can't stand it. If y' git into real trouble, come git me if y' kin. It's only a day's hard walkin'—do y' good. F'rgit that pride of y'rs; just remember I'll give y' all th' help I kin. Remember it ain't just y'rself y' have t' look out f'r—tho' I don't have t' tell y' that. Tell y'r wife she makes th' best flour porridge I ever ate, an' it won't be worth my while t' eat anymore before I see yez again—it was that good."

As the wagon disappeared at the edge of the clearing, Joanne came up and slipped her hand into Kevin's, and they stood there until the wagon was out of sight and sound.

"What was his last secret message?" Joanne asked.

"He said if I didn't take good care of you, he would come back and hammer in my head."

"You know he wouldn't say a thing like that. He is too gentle."

"He is that indeed and we are lucky to have met him. Goddamn gentle man."

A capricious gust of wind fluttered a ribbon of decayed tarpaper on the shack roof just as a bird, matching their mood, lamented, "Oh dear, dear dear." Overhead a hawk, in the guise of hunting, swam the blue sky in a giant orbit, from time to time releasing concentric circles of sound.

The McCormacks turned back to the house, walking slowly, not speaking—subdued.

9

THE SHOVEL BIT EASILY INTO THE RICH BLACK SOIL. HERE, AT least, Kinney had been right, for the soil on the creek side of their island was pure loam which even Kevin, inexperienced as he was, could see would be excellent for his purpose. The patch he had chosen was along the edge of the creek where it entered the meadow. It was completely free of even the smallest bushes, would be near the water, and was not very far from the house. He had decided to postpone the plastering of the cabin until he had the garden planted.

At first the digging went quickly so that by evening he was sure he would have a huge patch ready for the seed. He had not, however, taken into account the ravages of soft living. His hands quickly blistered, the blisters broke and filled with dirt, his back shrieked, and his shirt was soaked in perspiration. His hair, already long, fell into his eyes, and when he brushed it back with an impatient arm, he streaked his forehead with grime, while the perspiration in his eyes made him thoroughly miserable.

Remembering his father's vegetable patch, he had laid out a fairly large square which he thought would be adequate for their purpose. From the seeds Joanne had selected they should produce peas, beans, carrots, turnips, lettuce, radishes and parsnips. He wasn't sure how long all these delights would take to grow and mature; all he was sure of was that he wished they were ready now. With each thrust of the shovel, visions of vegetable dishes flashed on the screen of his mind until he grew too tired even to think of food.

When Joanne had offered to help, he had firmly refused. She was far too slight for manual labour, and in any case he would not, he resolved, have her become a workhorse like some farm women he had seen. Yet, as he grew more tired, he began to resent her not being there. It wasn't fair for him to be doing all the hard work while she stayed in the house, fiddling with the dishes. Well, he would show her; he was killing himself for her as she would realize after his heart attack. Then he pulled himself together, remembered that she had offered to help, that he had refused her offer, that he was supposed to be a man. Some people got a bit weird in the wilderness they said, and here he was going squirrely already.

Too bad that Ed had gone home; it had been so good to have someone experienced around to show him how things should be done. Still, he was gone; they were on their own, and he had better get used to it.

From time to time he paused, leaned on the shovel and gazed around. Behind him and to his right stood the house, small against the evergreens that grew close behind it. Where he worked, he was below the edge of the island that dropped off onto the meadow they had crossed coming with the wagon a few days before. To the right of the house the evergreens slowly gave way to a deciduous forest stretching far to the right out of sight beyond the meadow, across which the creek meandered. How much of what he saw lay on their property he did not know. He should have asked Ed to help him establish the boundaries before he left. But why? There was no one around to dispute his claim; he had a world to himself and where he planted what was his own business. Right now it was only necessary to take one step at a time: thrust, stoop, turn, crumble the soil and press on with the next insertion. He had been there since time began; he would be there forever.

At last when Joanne called him to dinner, he lay down his shovel, straightened his back and started for the house. Halfway there he stopped, remembering Ed's cautionary about being careful not to lose his precious tools, went back to the garden, picked up the shovel and drove it into the ground in an upright position where he could not fail to see it.

Dressed in a polka-dot blouse, a trim black skirt and her town shoes, Joanne met him at the door with a dish towel in her hands.

"What happened to you? Did you hurt yourself?"

"Nah! I'm a bit stiff that's all. In case you don't know it, you're even prettier than Sleeping Beauty." He dipped some water into the wash basin and doused his face and hands. "Here I am dressed like Louis Hebert, while you look like something fresh from the store."

"Something fresh like Mrs. Fletcher? Don't answer that. Do you think you will go around all bent over like that for the rest of your life?"

"What you are observing, dear lady, is adaptation. What you have here is a city boy in transition between a life of unbroken leisure and a rugged

northern boy accustomed to strenuous labour. In a day or two I intend to
take up bear wrestling."

"Oh. Well, don't expect me to entertain your antagonists. How doth
the garden grow?"

"Inasmuch as you are still hoarding the seeds, neither seeding or ger-
mination has yet taken place."

"Surprise. Can I help?"

"With the planting, yes. You may be able to start tomorrow morning."
He squeezed his long legs under the table while Joanne brought the bean
pot. After she had spooned out the contents they looked disconsolately at
their plates.

"There is richness for you," Joanne quoted.

"Thank you, Mr. Squeers."

"Only this isn't milk, it's beans."

"That's food, I guess. Haven't we got any bread or something?"

"How the devil could I make bread without an oven?"

"What are we going to do? Surely we can't just eat beans forever."

"This afternoon I will try my hand at making bannock in the frying
pan. Do you suppose we could find some berries in the bush?"

"Search me. Listen, you will admit you are always right, nasty-paws?"

"Correct."

"Well, isn't that a box of Royal Yeast on the shelf there?"

"It is."

"You bought it?"

"It was certainly not a gift."

"Now if you can't make bread because you have no oven, what are you
going to do with the yeast?"

Joanne looked at him for a moment before turning on her slow, sweet
smile. "I intend to mix it with the beans."

Kevin looked around as if he expected to find something else that was
edible. "I guess that's dinner. I'm going to have to shoot something, or we'll
starve to death." He stopped. "You know, that is literally true."

"Before you go back to work, show me how to use the twenty-two.
This afternoon I shall go in search of prey. Perhaps I will run into a flock
of fool hens."

"Bravo! Come for your first lesson, bearing in mind your teacher is
only slightly more familiar with weapons than you are yourself."

He showed her how to load the rifle, a simple operation as it was a single shot. "Here is how you cock it, but do not carry it cocked, ever. Don't
shoot until you are sure you will hit your target—that is rather pompous.
I mean try not to waste ammunition. Cocked or not, always have the barrel pointing away from you. Promise me that."

"Promise. I am a little reluctant to shoot myself, too, you know."

"Always treat your instructor with the utmost respect. Now aim at that tree over there and see if you can hit it."

She fired and missed. "I must have aimed at the wrong tree."

"Never mind, you put a hole through that cumulus cloud almost directly overhead."

"You will eat those words when I come back laden with steaks and chops."

"And sausage."

"I may even bring down a full roll of bologna."

"Good luck. You look gorgeous, but you had better put on some old rags if you are going bushwhacking. Don't forget your moccasins."

"Yes, Dad. Kiss me good-bye."

As the afternoon wore on, Kevin found to his amazement he was growing less tired even though his muscles were still sore. He began to enjoy the sun, the fresh smell of newly turned earth, the day sounds from the swamp. Three little brown birds landed in his garden and ran to and fro looking for worms. He was comforted by the idea that he was doing something necessary and important without interference of a boss. He experienced a warm rush of joy that came very near euphoria.

Around three o'clock Joanne came back empty-handed. All she had seen was a whisky-jack and a woodpecker. Nonetheless, she, too, was ecstatic. "It's lovely in there, all shade in places, sunshine in others. I braved the wilderness, and have returned unafraid. Mind you, I had the gun."

"A lot of good that would have done if you had been attacked by a bear."

"Don't shatter my illusions of security. Having failed in the hunt, I shall return to a woman's place and try my hand at making bannock. You will adore it."

The following day both of them went to the garden patch, Kevin to continue digging and Joanne to seeding, aggravating Kevin to distraction by reading every word on each seed package and nervously insisting that they be followed to the letter. He, on the other hand, had no patience with such details, pretending to believe that it would be just as effective to throw the seeds in helter-skelter. He snapped at her for being so meticulous even while admitting to himself that she was right.

Later in the afternoon she came to stand idly at her husband's side while he went on digging until, aggravated, he stopped. "What's up?"

"Nothing yet; don't you think it a bit early to ask?"

"Well, Miss Sarcasm, why have you stopped seeding?"

"There are no more seeds."

"Good Lord, and here I have been working away for nothing. You have used up about a tenth of what I dug. Why did you let me go on killing myself?"

"You seemed so happy at it. Anyway I thought maybe you were going to plant maybe a hundred acres of wheat."

As if in reward for their labour, two partridges burred in out of nowhere and lit on a tree close to the house. Kevin ran for the twenty-two, resolving that from that time forward he would always keep it at hand. For no good reason the partridges waited. Fool hens, indeed, Kevin thought. Kneeling, he took careful aim for what appeared to Joanne to be an eternity. At last he pulled the trigger. The gun clicked, but did not fire. The partridges, consumed with curiosity, studied his every move, although growing more restive by the minute, clucking and crouching for flight. Kevin cursed and tried again. On the third try the gun fired. One partridge fell as the other one took flight.

Joanne ran to the fallen bird, lost her courage and waited for Kevin. "Boy, you'll have to stop being so squeamish if you are to turn into a rugged northern girl."

"Boy yourself. Wait till you look into its eyes before you criticize me. It was a living creature, you know."

"Forgive me. But we have to eat and that means we will have to be ruthless."

"Are you going to tear it apart the way Ed showed us?"

"Yes. Turn your back."

Later when the partridge had made the transition from creature to meat, they sat down to a supper of partridge and creditable bannock.

"When the garden grows, I'll make a stew of partridges, peas, turnips and baby carrots."

" 'If wishes were horses, the beggars would ride.' For now let us take quiet satisfaction in the fact that the garden is in. Tomorrow I shall direct my talents to plastering the house. Tonight may well be the last square meal for about a million mosquitoes."

"You said 'plaster'. Ed said to 'chink' it with moss."

"Ed doesn't know everything. That moss business sounds a bit shaky to me. Note that the previous owner used mud only; you can still see it in places."

"Very few places."

"Be a little more adventurous. When you see the finished product, you will be overwhelmed. Trust old Kevin."

"Whatever you say," she answered, unconvinced.

"In Mexico, I have read, they plaster their houses with cow manure."

"Mm, I don't know whether to say I am glad we are not in Mexico or simply happy there are no cows here."

"Cows produce things other than manure. Think of milk, cream, cheese, butter."

She studied him for a minute, her interest aroused. Thoughtfully she dipped some water out of the pail. "Maybe you—Good God!"

"What bit you?"

"Look what we've been drinking!"

"Let me see," snatching the dipper from her hand. "Holy smoke, this isn't water; this is a swimming pool!"

The water in the dipper was seething with tiny red dots all too obviously alive, accompanied by other bugs of various size, some with feathery feelers, some with sets of oars, and flipping about amongst them were wrigglers like miniature whales.

"Did you get the water out of the creek, Joanne?"

"No," in a small voice. "There was a pool in the swamp that was much closer. The creek water is not much better."

"And will probably get worse as the summer progresses. In the meantime we will likely die of the dengue or yellow fever."

"Pray God that we go together."

"Pray God we don't go at all. This settles it; tomorrow I start digging a well, and the plastering will have to wait."

"The mosquitoes have been reprieved."

"Only for a night or so."

"Now for some good news."

She had found a rusty old pail in a dump of cans in amongst the trees and had made of it a miniature stove. "You see, spouse, we fill this with wet stuff, get it burning and then we bask in the smoke whenever the mosquitoes get nasty."

From that time on, their summer days and nights were passed in a haze of smoke. In time they no longer even noticed its presence, nor, they often suspected, did the mosquitoes.

10

KEVIN COULD HARDLY WAIT TO START DIGGING THE WELL. AFTER rushing through his breakfast, he dashed outside, picked up his shovel and set out on a quick tour of the island on which the house stood. Conditioned as he was by his session in the garden, he was sure that the work ahead would be child's play. His muscles felt firm and supple, and already the slight folds of fat built up in days of idleness had almost completely disappeared. He felt fit and in high good spirits.

At first he was tempted to dig close to the house for Joanne's convenience, but he realized that the well would have to be much deeper at that level. In any case the distance only mattered if he were away from home, an unlikely event. At creek level therefore and not too far from their garden, he started his operation.

Selecting a small dip in the ground, he started with a circle some four feet in diameter. In the first layer he was hampered by roots that ran in every direction and had to be chopped out before he could insert the shovel. Then he hit a layer of grey gumbo that was dry and extremely hard. Again he had to use the axe this time to break up the gumbo before he could scoop it out. The whole operation took on a new dimension that should have discouraged him. Instead he rather enjoyed inching his way down even though it meant much slower progress than he had expected. Any task that could be measured pleased him immensely. From time to time he would stop to savour the fresh air and to listen to the bird song all around him. Where else on earth could he find such peace and contentment?

By noon he had gone down about three feet where it began to dawn on him that the worst was yet to come. It had not occurred to him that as the hole deepened it would become more and more difficult to throw the dirt out. Furthermore it was clear that his hole would have to be enlarged to permit more maneuverability. All he could do was go down as far as he could and hope he would hit water before it became impossible.

When Joanne called, he went joyfully into the house and sat down at the table.

"Go and wash."

"What for? It's only mud and I will be going back to it in a few minutes."

"Look at me."

"Okay, I'm looking." Slowly he raised his eyes, taking in every well groomed inch of her. "You look like a city girl," he remarked with growing interest.

"Yes, and that is the way I am going to go on looking. It would be easy to let myself go, but I will not. We must go on being people. Do you want to look like the prototype farmer John, or even Ed?"

"I would be glad to look like Ed if it meant knowing everything he does. I can recall no farmer named John and therefore can not judge his attire."

"I do not want you to grow away from me. Let us resolve together always to wash, always to dress, always to be the people who came here. We must not decay."

He grinned. "Lead me to the wash dish, and lay out my tux for lunch. You have reformed me."

She paused in the doorway on her way to get the kettle. "I am not reforming you; I am merely trying to keep you as you were." She brought the kettle in and filled the basin. "There, my little man, wash thyself."

"Even so wash, Lord Jesus." Later in the afternoon he found he could no longer throw the dirt from the well without a tremendous heave on the shovel, and each time he tried, some of the load showered back into his face. Taking a blissful break, he leaned on his shovel pondering the problem. Suddenly through his mind there floated a cartoon about the war in which a character called "Ol' Bill" and one of his buddies were digging a trench. The man in the hole held a shovel to which was attached a string, and when the shovel was full, presumably Ol' Bill would haul it up by the rope. It was a silly thought, but just possibly there might be some sense in it. Could he fasten a rope on both ends of the shovel so that the dirt would stay on it on the way up? Nonsense. A pail perhaps? The water pail on a rope. Joanne should be able to pull it up if he did not fill it too full. He would see what she thought of the idea.

The following morning they tried out the new plan with Kevin doing the digging and the filling of the pail. Hauling the loaded pail out of the well may not have been the easier of the two jobs, but Kevin could not face the thought of having Joanne go down the hole; it had begun to dawn on him that the well might collapse. The work went slowly even though the digging was becoming easier all the time.

Late in the afternoon Joanne called down, "Time's up; I have to get supper."

"Okay, you go ahead. I'll just loosen up the next layer before I join you."

Loosen it he did, but to no purpose as Joanne had drawn the pail out of the well. He decided that since he had to climb out for it in order to fill it, he might as well quit for the day. Then to his horror he found he could not get out of the hole as he was down so far he could not reach the top. Since Joanne had withdrawn the rope there was nothing to take hold of. He tried jumping high enough to catch the rim. After several tries he stopped to take stock of the situation. Although Joanne knew where he was, she might not come to his rescue until supper was ready. He tried calling out until he realized it was hopeless. She could never hear him from the house. For a second he panicked. What if the well caved in?

"Joanne!" he roared. "Joanne!"

He took out his watch. Five-thirty. "Joanne!"

"What is it? What's the matter?" her blessed face appeared against the sky.

"Thank God. You took the rope away; I can't get out."

"Oh boy!"

"Is the rope still tied to the tree?"

"Yes."

"Solid, solid? Don't forget I am a lot heavier than the pail."

"It is tied solid."

"All right, untie the pail and drop the end down to me."

"Here it comes."

He caught the end, tested his weight and then scrambled up the wall of the well.

"I thought I was in for it. It was horrible down there when I realized I couldn't get out."

At the end of the third day Kevin struck a rock and could go no deeper. Fortunately as it was not very large he was able to dig around it, break it loose and lift it onto the pail. As it was too large to fit inside he jammed it under the handle where it seemed secure.

"Haul away," he shouted.

Hauling with all her might Joanne was just able to bring it to the surface, but she could not swing the pail out of the hole. When she freed one hand to reach for the pail it tipped and the rock fell back down the well.

For Joanne it was the longest minute in her life. Hearing no sound, she leaned over and looked down into Kevin's startled face.

"It's all right," he said shakily. "It's all right. Just hand me the rope; my digging days are over. It just missed me by an inch."

"Oh Kevin, I am so sorry."

"It's all right honey, let us go and sit down. It was my fault—I should have realized you couldn't handle a thing like that."

"Oh what would we have done? What if it had hit you on the head? How would I ever have gotten you out?"

"There would not have been much point in bothering."

Gently he guided her to the campfire, stirred the fire and moved the coffee pot where it would get hot. "Well, I wasn't hurt; that is the main thing. Let us forget it except to resolve to redouble our care in everything we do from now on."

He lay awake for a long time that night giving thanks to the gods or to God for having escaped. He also pondered on ways of removing the rock from the well without endangering themselves. He decided he would go down, put the rock in the pail, climb back out and lift it up himself. Fine, but they had, he thought dryly, almost come to the end of their rope. In another foot it would not reach and he needed slack to pull himself up. The well would have to be abandoned. What a waste of time and effort.

The next morning while Joanne was preparing breakfast, Kevin strolled out to have a look at his plan. He hated the thought of starting a new project without having finished the first. He climbed to the top of the dirt surrounding the well, picked up the pail, reattached it to the rope and dropped it in. The pail struck bottom with an unusual sound. He peered into the hole, and as his vision adjusted to the darkness he began bellowing, "Joanne" at the top of his voice.

"What is it? What's happening this time?"—flying from the house in her nightgown. "We've hit it!

We've hit water! Holy cow! We've hit water."

She peeked in the hole and cheered. They grabbed hands, jumped off the mound and spun in a circle.

"How do you like that? Our very first well and it's a gusher!"

"Down boy, down! There's water all right, but I can see little gushing."

Sobering, but still overjoyed, he drew on the rope, bringing up the pail full to the brim. Cautiously he inspected the contents before lifting it up and guzzling.

"Cold, by the Lord, cold and clear. You never tasted anything like it in your life. Think of it: no more bugs, no more green stuff—pure."

"Not bad," she admitted, "although it smells a bit like sulphur."

"That is because we had to go through hell to get to it." Again he lowered the pail into the well. "You know something?" he said with an air of wonderment.

"Many things."

"I think we are going to make a go of it. That chap that was here before, the Englishman, he survived didn't he? The difference is, though, he never accomplished anything. We have barely started and already we have a garden and a well. All it takes is work."

"He put up an exercise pole; that's something."

In a rare gesture of intimacy they walked back to the house, hand in hand, Kevin with a pail of fresh water in his free hand.

"If that stone had fallen on you last night, even if it didn't kill you, may have made it impossible for you to get out."

"And I would have had to spend the night at the bottom of the well."

"Yes, my dear, but you would have drowned."

"True. Then you wouldn't have had to listen to my mouth organ anymore."

"Do not joke about the unspeakable."

"A little black humour never hurt nobody."

"Ed said."

11

EARLY IN THE MORNING JOANNE AWOKE TO THE SOUND OF RAIN. While the pole roof muffled the patter of drops on what remained of the tarpaper, gusts of wind flung invisible pebbles against the window. A dismal trickle of water trailed down the stovepipe and spilled onto the stove. All around the room tiny cataracts emptied through the shattered roof to join the flood gathering on the floor. The corner where the bed stood, by some miracle, was still dry although the blankets already had a clammy feeling.

Woefully she clambered out and sloshed across the floor in her bare feet to see what could be done about a fire. They had not bothered to store any wood in the house, thinking they would never need any heat until fall. There were a few scraps of paper in the stove, but nothing to sustain a fire. A quick examination revealed that the food in the apple box cupboard was safe, but the flour bag sitting on the floor showed where the dampness was creeping upward; already a quarter of the meagre supply was soaked.

While she stood there in shivering uncertainty, a mouse dragged itself through the water and crept on to her bare foot, where it sat enjoying her warmth. She hated to shake it off even though the touch of its tiny feet made her uneasy.

By this time Kevin was awake. "What's up?"

"I am and the rain is coming down."

"Well for God's sake hop back into bed before you drown."

"I can't; there is a mouse on my foot."

"A mouse on your foot!" He sat up abruptly. "Kick him off; he may be rabid."

"Whoever heard of a rabid mouse? He'll go in a minute; he's just getting warm."

The mouse, as if on cue, hopped onto the floor and made off almost swimming.

"Look out for wet feet," Joanne cried, springing back into bed.

"Wet and cold."

"The floor is a lake."

"Fright eye! What next? Are we to sit here and drown?"

"It will be all over in a half hour; then, we can make a lovely breakfast and bask in the sun. Today is a holiday."

It was not all over in a half hour nor in two hours. At noon Kevin reluctantly eased himself over Joanne and slid his feet onto the floor. "No wood in the house either; I should be taken out and shot."

"Don't take all the blame; I didn't want the place cluttered up with wood, remember?"

"Well, it doesn't much matter whose fault it is; there isn't even any kindling, and Ed warned me about that." Grimacing, he picked up his pants. "Even these are soaked."

Outside he was relieved to find the weather quite mild in spite of the rain. In a few minutes he was thoroughly soaked and somehow that felt better. It was, however, dreary and a bit depressing. All around he could hear the patter of rain on the leaves, no other sound.

The small stock of wood he had cut was long gone. For the past week or so he had been using pieces of fallen branches and other debris. Now he needed stove lengths and something good and dry to get the fire going in the barrel heater. With axe in hand, he picked his way in among the trees, selected a dead spruce, and began to hack it down. The very first blow brought down a heavy shower of water onto his already soaking body. He chopped on doggedly, resolving never again to be caught without a supply of wood in the yard and a good supply of kindling in the house. Still an indifferent axeman, he took a long time to cut down the tree. Then he had to go for the saw to cut it into lengths he could carry back to the sawhorse. He then tried his luck with a dead poplar and was a lot more successful for it was far easier both to chop and to saw.

When he finally had a few armfuls cut and split, he carried them into the house. With a little luck he soon got the fire going while Joanne watched from the bed, wondering what she could do to help. Almost immediately the cabin began to warm up. Kevin brought in the kettle and the coffee pot and balanced them on the stove.

"How is that for service, my lady?"

"Stunning. You'll find a tip in my purse, my good man."

"The tip can wait while I remove two soaking shoes and as many socks. I had to use the breast stroke to bring in the fuel."

"You look as if you were doing some high diving too. Are you frozen?"

"Not as bad as you might think. Once I got working the old body, quickly heated up. Say, if old Noah had been exposed to this much water, he would have abandoned ship."

"That is precisely what my mouse did. He never came back."

They spent the whole day sitting on the edge of the bed, keeping their spirits up by drinking coffee, playing the mouth organ and singing from time to time. At noon they ate fresh bannock. Kevin had hung the flour bag on a spike driven into the wall by their predecessor, perhaps for the very same purpose. Unfortunately it was already too late as much of it had been soaked. They should have been thoroughly miserable, yet they were quite happy, enjoying a respite from the previous weeks of strenuous activity.

The following day it was still raining, the house was wetter, and they were not quite as happy as before. By this time two leaks had sprung in the roof directly over the bed, and that night they had to sleep, or try to sleep, with a lard pail and the wash basin balanced on the blankets. On the third day not even Joanne sang. The downpour had given way to a relentless drizzle. Grey clouds, heavy with water, hung low over the trees, and look where they would, there was never a sign of a breakup. The wind had died completely away and with it any hope of the clouds' removal.

Life for the McCormacks settled into a new routine adjusted to the constant drizzle. Once a day Kevin went out to cut wood. He soon found that dry poplar, though it was easy to cut, burned away far too quickly. Dry balm of Gilead was like burning fluff, while spruce, strangely enough, was in short supply as the forest, at least in the immediate area, was not decadent, and dry trees were few and far between. Each day he ventured a little farther afield in his search for the perfect fuel. It was on one of these excursions he discovered pine stubs.

Years before a fire sweeping across the countryside had killed off the evergreens, most of which had blown down and decayed; new trees had sprung up and now almost all trace of the original forest had disappeared. A few of the original pines, however, lost their branches to the fire, died, but did not fall. The bare stubs, offering little resistance to the wind still stood like gnarled fingers pointing to the sky-dry, hard, and sound.

Kevin found these first growth stubs made an excellent fire-starter. They were a bit harder to saw than the softwoods, but the blocks split easily and evenly. Being so dry, they would have burned beautifully in any case, as they were loaded with gum that would convert them into a roaring torch. Over a period of time he sawed up a thirty-foot log of this type

and split it into kindling which he kept in a special pile. Never again was
he to be caught trying to make a fire with soggy blocks the way he had to
do the first mornings of the rain.

For her part, Joanne sluiced the water out of the house with the broom,
thinking wryly that at least she would not have to scrub for awhile. So that
Kevin could dry himself as soon as he came in, and in order to dry out the
blankets, she kept the fire roaring in the barrel heater. It depressed her to
see the bedclothes steaming, especially since she knew they would be
damp again by nightfall if, indeed, they had a chance to dry at all. Still she
could not just leave them to mildew on the bed. Rain or no rain, leaks or
no leaks, the house had to be maintained according to her standards.

Rather than waste the wet flour, she made pan after pan of bannock,
stacking them on the shelf one on top of the other in neat towers. Whether
or not they would keep or for how long she did not know. Nor did she
know what she would do when they were all gone.

On a Friday morning the rain stopped, though clouds still hung low
over the trees.

"It has stopped," Joanne announced.

"The calm before the next storm."

"Don't be a pessimist; the sun will be out in a minute." Kevin got out
of bed and pulled on his wet socks with an air of determination.

"I am going into town."

"What for?"

"Roofing—tarpaper. Whatever." He gestured towards the roof. "I am
going to get this place watertight before it fills right up and drowns us both.
Although it won't make much difference really. If we spend the last of our
money on tarpaper, we will starve to death even if we are dry."

"That doesn't make too much sense. If we are going to starve to death,
there will not be anyone left to keep the house dry for."

"Maybe the Englishman will come back."

"With the butcher's wife. Well, we must keep things shipshape until
they arrive."

"I don't know how long it will take me to walk there and back."

"I am coming too."

He grinned and ruffled her hair.

"Do you honestly believe you can walk twenty miles over a muddy
trail?"

"Twenty miles there and twenty miles back."

"Verily. That is a long way."

She paused, remembering the seemingly endless wagon trip, the gullies they had negotiated, the freshet-scarred miles of road.

"I guess it wouldn't be too great an idea," she surrendered. "I would be a burden."

"Not a burden, but it might be quicker if I go alone."

"What about bears and—things?"

"You'll be all right," Kevin comforted her. "I will leave the rifle all set up for you, and the twenty-two as well if you wish it."

"Don't worry about the twenty-two; I know more about it than you do."

"Bears will not come knocking at the door, and you sure as the devil won't be bothered by people. Nothing will bother you."

Nothing, she thought is a sinister way of putting it. " 'Nothing' makes me think of something too awful to mention. You mean no animal or human."

"What else is there?"

"Horrors of the night. You've felt it too as it starts to get dusky."

"Come now, you are supposed to be emerging as a rugged northern girl. Keep the door locked and stay inside if you are scared. There is nothing to worry about."

But there was, for it was then she found the remaining bannock befouled by mouse dirt and ravaged by tiny teeth. The mice had held a hoedown during the night.

"You see," Kevin admonished. "The one you saved asked all his friends in to celebrate."

"While you are gone, there will be a *ravage des mice*; not one shall survive."

Kevin set out for town sans breakfast, sans lunch, sans Joanne.

12

FOR THE FIRST TWO MILES OF THE TRIP INTO TOWN KEVIN scurried along feeling sorry for himself having to walk twenty miles in the mud on an empty stomach. It was a long way to go and at the end there would be nothing more exciting than the endless attempt to make one or two dollars do the work of four. How was he to bring back what he could purchase? Where was he to spend the night? At any minute the rain might start again... He was a poor little man; there was no doubt of that, and Joanne had not seemed very upset when he left. There was no justice.

Then, subtly, there grew in him an awareness that he was starting to enjoy himself. As always a little physical activity warmed him and raised his spirits. He forced himself to lift his head to look around with eyes that had already grown in experience since the trip in by wagon. Walking, he could take more time to observe. For the first time he realized how really unique was their homestead. Nowhere else were there any significant stands of evergreens. To be sure there were individual evergreens and even a few isolated groves, but in the main the forest was deciduous: alder and willow along the creek banks, balm of Gilead here and there, poplar everywhere. Since the only trees that had any commercial value, according to Ed, were spruce and pine, they had a sort of monopoly on their own place, albeit far from market.

Although the road was muddy everywhere, walking was not all that difficult except where the road had been flooded and the water still stood. The only way around some of these miniature lakes was to leap from moss hummock to moss hummock and try to keep his balance. Fair enough. Unfortunately not all moss hummocks are the same and several times he plunged into the water flat on his face. On such occasions he learned to ease his distress by shouting four-letter words while wringing out whatever could be wrung out.

It began to dawn on him that on the homestead he had become a little too dependent on Joanne, and that he was becoming a bit of a crybaby. After all he was supposed to be the leader. Seeing a stretch of navigable road ahead, he took out his mouth organ and marched along to the tune of "Onward Christian Soldiers."

At the five mile mark—or what he thought might be the five mile mark—nature called urgently. Forgetting that he was alone in the universe and was therefore free from observation, he retired modestly behind a willow tree, lowered his trousers and....with a roar of anguish burst from the trees with a million mosquitoes swarming around or already attached to his external genital organs.

"This," he cried, "passeth all human endurance!"

Under heavy pressure from both his bowels and the mosquitoes, necessity became, once again, the mother of invention. Using experience gained at home he lit a fire, half smothered it with grass and squatted perilously over the cloud of smoke so generated. Then in default of paper, he used moss and felt himself one with nature.

"I am now," he mused, "a true northerner."

Ed had said that the Johnstons' place was six miles from The Spruces, although how he knew that so precisely Kevin was uncertain. He suspected that for want of naysayers Ed had established distances between points in accordance with his own whimsy. In any case shortly after the incident with the smudge Kevin came upon a road leading into the trees to a house constructed of burned logs which he assumed to be the Johnstons' place. His first impulse was to walk in and introduce himself as a quasi-neighbour, hoping that he might be offered something to eat and perhaps a blissful cup of strong coffee. As usual his natural timidity stopped him. He reasoned that if he did go in and introduce himself, the people might think he had just come in to sponge off them for a meal. That being too near the truth, he turned back onto the road and continued on towards town.

His next point of reference was the Myhren place where the unfortunate Swede who drowned had lived out the last part of his life. The place fascinated Kevin because of the tragic story, because of the appearance of the house and because it could have been the homestead for himself and Joanne. What intrigued him about the house itself was the height of the door; it was only about five feet tall. Why would anyone have such a short door unless he was a dwarf, and even then he would have to think about other people dropping in. Inside, the appearance was much as it had been at their own homestead except that the bed and other meagre furnishings were better built. Here, too, the packrats had taken up residence, as testified by a huge store of debris that rats deemed to be currency, such as leaves, fragments of tinfoil, bottle lids, and even a ball of yarn. All such fragments they brought in trade for whatever it was they removed, or so Ed had told him. Insofar as the homestead itself was concerned, it seemed at a glance to be a far better proposition than The Spruces. Some of the fencing still remained in place where there was evidence of a one-time garden. In spite of his loyalty to their own place, Kevin wished he had looked before filing.

There were no more stops until he reached the highway where he hoped he might get a ride. There was no traffic, however, and he set out on the last ten miles. He immediately wished he were back on the bush road for on the open highway the gumbo was still thoroughly soaked and in minutes his shoes weighed, or seemed to weigh, about a hundred pounds each. He found that he could make progress only by stopping from time to time to scrape the mud off with a stick. Eventually he discovered that if he walked along the bank at the side of the road he was much better off. Unfortunately the embankments were not always free and were in other places inaccessible. Nonetheless he managed to make fairly good time.

Then the gods relented: he came to a stretch where the highway had been moved and the old route, grassed over, made a perfect walking trail. There to his joy, he came upon wild strawberries by the thousands deep in the grass just waiting to be eaten. Eat he did until he could not poke anymore into his system.

Late in the evening he finally reached Fletcher's store which was, as far as he could ascertain, closed for the day. He knew that he could go to the back to arouse someone, but as he was as usual afraid of a rebuff, he decided to try his luck at the livery stable, reasoning that if there was no one there to give him directions to Ed's house, he might at least find a place to lie down. At the door of the barn he was greeted by a wizened little man with a leathery face and mean little eyes.

"What do you want?" the dwarf asked suspiciously.

Instantly affronted, Kevin replied carefully, "I want Ed Reed."

"He ain't here."

"Then where is he?"

"Home minding his own business."

"And where, pray, is his home?"

"What do you want to know that for? He'll be in bed."

Kevin clenched his teeth and his voice grew thin and hard. "I asked you where he lived. I suggest you tell me."

"Over there behind the hotel."

"Thank you very much for your kindness and forbearance."

"My 'for' what?"

"Foreskin, if you have one." How on earth, Kevin asked himself could a man so mean work for someone as kind as Ed. After a few steps his anger began to calm down as he thought, I am as bad as he was. Who am I to speak of forbearance?

Knocking at the door of the house indicated, he noted there was still a light on. After a few shuffling noises Ed opened the door, stood for a second, then exploded into a warm greeting.

"Pelican Jesus," he shouted, "if it ain't th' city boy from Toronto. I thought th' coyotes would of ate y' by now. I guess they must be more fussier than I thought. Where's that little girl of yours?"

"Home holding the fort. It was too far for her to walk."

"Well y're welcome anyways. Come in an' we'll shut th' door. I don't want t' let any of these mosquitoes out; they've already bin fed. How've yez bin?"

"Okay at first. Sort of wet in the last week or so."

"Roof leaked some, eh?"

"What roof?"

"I saw she looked like a sieve, though I didn't say nothin' f'r fear y'd git upset."

Kevin was struck immediately by the tidiness of the place; he had expected a shambles, thinking Ed would have no time for such niceties as neatness. The floor was clean, everything seemed to be in place, and even the lamp chimney was clean (although there was electrical power in town Ed was not one to embrace modern technology.)

Kevin sat down at the table, tired through and through.

Ed watched him for a moment without speaking.

"Y' come straight here?" he finally asked.

"No, I went to the store, but it was closed and I didn't want to disturb them."

"Y' needn't have worried about that none; old Fletcher'd open up his coffin t' sell a five-cent chocolate bar. He'll not rest easy if he finds out y' passed his store with a quarter in y'r pocket that he missed out on. Come t' think of it, did y' have a quarter in y'r pocket?"

"Yes, I did, but I kept a strangle hold on it."

"No doubt y've ate at least three square meals on y'r way in?"

"Well...no...I had a sandwich on the road of course."

"Oh, of course. Only it kind of beats me how y'r Joanne—smart an' all as she is—managed t' bake bread on a barrel heater. Course maybe th'

bread man has bin callin' regular. Those must have bin great little sandwiches y' had there."

As he talked, he busied himself about the stove, shoving the coffee pot
over the front lid, and taking a frying pan from the top. "How'd y' like t'
fasten y'r teeth over a few spuds an' a aig 'r two? That is if y've got any room
left after all them sandwiches."

"There is room," Kevin acknowledged, "for two sacks of potatoes, two
dozen eggs, and three chickens if you want to know the truth. We have
not, in the past few weeks, been overeating."

As he spoke he shut his eyes, and waves of fatigue started at his feet
and swept upward, each one breaking behind his eyelids in a burst of
mixed colours. A vision of their cabin drifted across his befogged mind.
Joanne might at that very moment be going to bed, seeming extra vulner-
able in her nightgown. Homesickness and anxiety crested the fatigue
waves. What if...but he better not let himself think of things like that.

"You ready t' eat? First call, as they say on th'railway. Don't y' go fallin'
asleep on me 'r I may have t' tuck into y'r supper myself even tho' I've
already ate. Nothin' like a mass of aigs slathered over spuds I always say,
especially when ast. After that see what y' kin do with some bread an'
syrup. Th' bread's a tad on th' heavy side, why I don't know. I made her
exactly accordin' t' th' receep—yeast an' all. When I dropped th' first loaf
she went clear through th' floor."

He placed the loaded plate on the table, advanced the salt and pepper
shakers, threw down a knife and fork and then began rummaging through
the cupboard looking for the syrup pail. "Take all the syrup y' want—well
them Jesus mice!" Flicking a suspicious black speck from the open pail, he
muttered, "Y' can't leave a lid off nothin' 'round here."

At that stage Kevin could have cheerfully eaten the entire mouse itself,
although he tried his best not to look too ravenous. Though the bread was,
indeed, grey and leaden, it was the first he had tasted since the day they
had moved to the cabin. As he ate he thought again of Joanne sitting down
to beans and battered bannock. It was not fair.

When it came syrup time, Ed watched for a moment; then, he said, "Y'
remind me of a real dirty story that'll make y' laugh. This travellin' salesman called on a farm couple out on th' prairies there. All they had t' offer
him was bread an ' syrup like y're lickin' up there right now except y' had
somethin' t' run her up and th' salesman didn't so he was a bit more eager,
y' see. Well, he pitched right in, slappin' th' syrup on a slice of bread, stuf-
fin' it in an' then reachin' for another slice, over an' over. Pretty soon th'
farmer got a bit worried.' Listen, my man,' he says, "don't eat th' whole
works now. We ain't rich yet."

So th' salesman he lays down his knife. Then all three of them goes t' bed in th' same bed—th' husband in th' middle f'r obvious reasons. Around midnight th' missus prods her husband an' hollers, 'John! John! There's somethin' after th' horses in th' barn!" Of course old John grabs th' rifle an' runs outside. The missus turns t' th' salesman an' says 'Now's y'r chance.' So th' salesman he jumps out of bed an' lays into th' last of th' bread an' syrup. Baw! Haw!"

When he had recovered from his own joke, Ed leaned back in his chair and lit his pipe.

"I like t' watch th' smoke risin' when I puff her out, watch her go way, way up, spread out an' sort of disappear. Seems like nothin' matters very much when I'm smokin; not th' price of wheat, nor barley, nor who is prime minister. Th' smoke makes livin' seem like a sort of dream. Y' know what I mean?"

"Well, not really; I don't smoke, you see."

"An' now how's that little lady of y'rs? Damned if I ain't missed her ever since I come back."

"She's fine except when I beat her."

"I kin imagine. Y' couldn't manage t' git y'rself drownded or ate out by a bear so's I could look after her, could y'?"

"Not if I can help it."

"Don't imagine I would neither. Anyways give me a rundown on how yez're doin' out there in th' sticks."

Kevin shrugged. "Not too badly, I guess. We've got a well dug, and the garden is in. The shack still has to be plastered, the roof needs paper—that's why I am here—we've shot enough partridges to keep ourselves in meat—what more could you ask for?"

"I c'd think of a thin' 'r two, like a kitchen stove, canned stuff, a team of Percherons... Y' ever put tarpaper on before?"

"Not so you would notice."

"Y' have t' be careful is all. She'll rip on y' if y' don't treat her careful, but most of all she likes to ay-cor-deen if y' try t' straighten her out. Other thin' is on a pole roof y' have t' allow a good overlap and y' have t' put a layer of poles on top of her so's th' wind can't get at her. That's why she's mostly blowed away like she is now. That Englishman didn't burden her down enough. Probably wanted t' spare th' poles f'r his gymnastics."

"How many rolls will I need?"

"I sh'd think one will do her. What y' gotta remember is leave plenty of overlap. She's a pole roof an' th' paper ain't goin' t' want t' lie too flat, an' then when y' put th' top poles on her she'll press down here an' there somethin' scandalous, and if y' don't have th' overlap, y'r goin' t' have a space.

That's why she's mostly blowed away like she is now. That Englishman didn't leave enough overlap, an' the wind caught th' edges, like I said before. If one roll ain't enough, y' kin always walk back an' pick up another. It's only twenty miles, give or take."

"One way."

"If y' have a bit leftover y' kin put her on y'r outhouse."

"If we ever have an outhouse."

"Y' got t' have one. Folks goin' by an' seein' no outhouse'll think y'r poverty struck in good earnest. Y've a garden in an' no outhouse; shame on y'. Now we come t' th' hard part: how're y' fixin' t' git that tarpaper back t' th' ranch?"

"On my back, I guess."

"Some tote that'll be. We got t' think of somethin' else." He got up, lifted the stove lid and spat into the fire. Then he sat down and cogitated for awhile.

"I'll tell y' what we'll do: I got an awful old horse outside there in th' livery stable. Old but wise. Wiser than a lot of people I know—present company excepted." He stopped and considered. "I take that last part back—no exceptions. He's wiser than yourselfs, because y' don't see him livin' in a shack in th' midst of nowheres, nor do y' see him bustin' ass diggin' no wells or th' like. In fact y'd have a hard time seein' him doin' nothin'. Horse sense; that's what he has, which is not surprisin' him bein' a horse an' all. Anyways, y' kin tie y'r stuff on his back an' take him along if he's willin' t' go. One time home y' just unload him, slap his arse an' bid him, 'Go home!' He'll come back by hisself providin' it suits him. If th' bears gits him, well, serve him right f'r bein' a horse an' not a bear."

For several seconds Kevin struggled with himself, trying to control his emotions. He could handle fatigue and he could handle kindness, but he could not handle both at once. He broke down and that broke Ed down.

Ed sniffed, took out his handkerchief, blew his nose, recovered himself and said, "Aw come on now, y're goin' downhill. A couple of weeks ago y'd have bin shakin' y'r wallet at me. Y' gettin' stingy in y'r old age?"

"Not stingy; just broke. I'm sorry to have made an ass of myself. We have to have tarpaper and some food and then I might just as well throw the wallet away."

"Of course y're broke; I knew that th' day we met. Who isn't? Th' whole country's broke flatter than piss on a plate. We've got t' help one another; we can't all be like Kinney an' live on relief. Y're workin' y'r place and tryin' t' pay y'r way. If I kin help a little, well and good. Here, dry these here dishes whilst I wash, provided y're not too stove up. Y' look all in."

The dishes done, the two men sat by the fire, Ed whittling, Kevin with heavy eyes trying to fight sleepiness. After a few fruitless efforts to sustain a conversation he stood up.

"I think I'll turn in."

"Good idee. Take th' blanket off th' trunk there an' hop into th' top bunk. I hope y're not apt t' piss th' bed, because I'm in th' direct line of fire."

"It happens only when I am very tired."

"Oh God! Well, I guess I'll just have t' wear my gumboots and slicker t' bed."

Kevin went outside, came back in, took off his pants and heaved himself into the upper bunk. With a deep sigh of satisfaction he stretched out, feeling fatigue pressing his body full length into the mattress. Below, he heard Ed rustling around getting ready for the night, heard the door latch click into place and the rattle of the lamp chimney as he put out the light.

Out of what seemed to be complete silence the ticking of the clock gradually became audible, growing in intensity as his ears adjusted to the new sound.

In the bottom bunk Ed turned over, his heavy body crushing the straw in his tick with the crackling of a brush fire.

"Kevin, you asleep?"

"Almost," Kevin replied returning reluctantly to full consciousness.

"Joanne makin' bannock out there?"

"Sure."

"I was wonderin'..."

"Wondering what?"

"I was just wonderin' see—wonderin' if she...Nah, best fergit it."

"Best forget what?"

"I was just wonderin' —see if maybe y'r Joanne would try a loaf of my bread. She might—oh hell—she'd think it wasn't up t' snuff—there might be a trace of mouse shit I missed. Best f'rgit it."

For once Kevin got it right.

"Joanne," he said, "would be tickled pink, just tickled pink."

"Well, all right then; I'll send her two. If I see somethin' suspicious, I'll just pick her off."

In spite of his fatigue Kevin did not fall asleep at once. Each tick of the clock, he mused, marks off a time we are separated, and when we are separated, it is as if each one of us were dead for the other. I'm lying here, warm and comfortable with a full stomach, while twenty miles away there is a girl, or, rather, the memory of a girl, in a shack all by herself. If she were to cry out now in mortal danger, I could not reach her for eight to ten hours even if I could hear her calling. He was heartless to have allowed her to stay behind. By doing so he had lost some of their precious time together. If the tarpaper and the horse had been ready, fatigue or no fatigue, he would have gotten up and started home that very instant. As it was, all he could do was·lie there and wait for the earth to turn into morning. He dreamed he was walking toward the cabin and that he could see a line of white shirts blowing and billowing in the wind.

13

FOR A FEW MINUTES AFTER HER HUSBAND'S DEPARTURE JOANNE stood watching him go across the meadow, thinking of the day they had stood in the same place while Ed disappeared. She tried to visualize the twenty miles of road. In the wagon they must have come through a dozen gullies, a thousand willow runs, endless acres of poplar; just thinking of the distance made her weak at the knees.

The house, tiny as it was, seemed extraordinarily empty with Kevin gone. He had such a way of filling a place. Often when he was underfoot while she was trying to do her housework, his presence irritated her, and she wished he would take his long legs outside. Now she would cheerfully have tripped over him a dozen times rather than be left alone in an empty cabin.

Still, she told herself, she couldn't start moping or she would be in a real state by the time he got back. Guiltily she thought of food. Famished herself, she could not help thinking of Kevin with a twenty-mile walk ahead of him without even a piece of bannock to keep him going. Reason however dictated that she would accomplish nothing by starving herself in sympathy other than to ease her conscience. Although she knew the contents of the cupboard by heart, she went over the stock once again: dried beans—which would take all day to cook; baking powder—useless now that the flour was spoiled—syrup too sickly sweet to be eaten by itself; yeast cakes—untouched and likely to remain so—and a few staples such as salt, pepper, and a little, very little, coffee. There was nothing that could be made into breakfast.

"Well," she decided, "the idea is that we live off the land. I'd better start seeing what the land has to offer."

Dressed in her oldest woollen sweater and a heavy skirt, she took the twenty-two down from the wall, loaded it, slipped a few extra cartridges into her pocket and went outside. At first, fearful of getting lost, she kept to the ill-defined road across the meadow. Within minutes her moccasins were soaked. Not an animal of any kind stirred and even she, inexperienced as she was, could see that she would have no luck in the open. She stopped, turned about and plunged resolutely into the forest. The swamp, still hushed from rain was heavy with the odour of wet moss and the remains of needles underfoot, bringing back to her mind a poem from her school days:

"The woods decay, the woods decay and fall;
The vapours weep their burthen to the ground."

All about her was the sound and feel of weeping: rain tears from the higher branches spattering on the needles below; clouds trailing disconsolate tendrils amongst the treetops; little brown birds hunched in silent misery where a few leaves failed to provide shelter; moss hummocks sighing underfoot as they gave way to her step. Once a woodpecker landed on a stub nearby, scurried about, rapped half-heartedly on the rotten wood and then flew off discouraged.

The instant she was in among the evergreens, Joanne's spirits fell, crushed down by the silence and the atmosphere of eternity. The trees around her had stood for perhaps a hundred years while before them other trees had grown in the same place had fallen and decayed leaving no trace. Yet there she was peeking out at the world through the slots of her eyes, concerned with food for her stomach to preserve a life that was meaningless in the history of the world. And now mosquitoes came in to attack, mosquitoes whose minuscule lives were of less significance even than her own.

She paused, hearing a pattering sound like heavy rain on dead leaves. Moving cautiously she rounded a huge tree, and there in a small clearing a flock of partridges were busily feeding on something on the ground. For a moment she stood still, fascinated by the scene before her; then remembering why she had come, she dropped to one knee, cocked the twenty-two, aimed and pulled the trigger. The bolt clicked, but there was no explosion. The birds, nervous now, stopped picking to peer at her with bright little eyes, seeming more curious than concerned.

Muttering, "I'll get you yet," she recocked, rested the barrel in the crotch of a small tree, aimed at one lone partridge in the branches above the rest of the flock—posted there no doubt as official watchman—and pulled the trigger again. This time the gun fired and the bird fell onto the moss where it fluttered about spasmodically. Still the remaining birds failed to take flight. On each of the next two shots a bird fell. Then the gun failed to fire once again. Disgusted, she stood up, rifle in hand pointed downward as she had been instructed, took two steps forward, and the gun fired.

Everything went into slow motion. For a moment she stood transfixed, gazing down at a neat hole in her right moccasin. Very slowly she sat down, laid the gun beside her, and began to undo the moccasin laces, while one of the downed birds struggled in the moss. She pulled off the moccasin and stripped off her sock. The bullet had passed between the big and second toe, leaving nothing worse than a burn mark, nothing more.

Aloud she said, "I am damned," and went on sitting, looking at her bare foot. It came to her that she was not damned, that she was a very lucky little person indeed, perhaps the luckiest in the entire north. She could have been seriously injured, could have bled to death and be damned indeed. Kevin might never have found her. She had every reason to thank her lucky stars, the gods, or God—whomever. If feeling intense gratitude for being saved is a tacit prayer, Joanne prayed there in the moss.

Danger lurked in everything she touched, and the slightest mishap could well mean disaster. She remembered the rock falling into the well, the awful moment when she thought Kevin had been struck down. She thought of the long, grey nights, the wolves howling—and yet, each adventure made them stronger, more sure of themselves. It was a good life they had chosen if she could just hang on to it.

Moccasin back on, she gathered up her three dead birds which she then dismembered just as Ed had shown her, a distasteful process made even worse by her own narrow escape.

She must not think like that; she must learn to be ruthless.

With great care she picked up the twenty-two.

"You are in disgrace," she told it, "but I will take you home and teach you some manners."

By the time the birds were ready to be eaten it was well past noon and she was starving. Nevertheless, she spread the table cloth and set out her dishes, the incongruity of her preparations all alone in the wilderness not even occurring to her. She changed her clothes, put on her shoes and sat down daintily to feast on wild fowl. Throughout the afternoon, although she tried to keep herself busy with the house, she could find little to do, and no matter how she fought, her eyes would turn to the road lying empty across the meadow. She knew Kevin could not possibly come back the day he left, yet she still hoped for a miracle. As the afternoon advanced she grew increasingly nervous, fearful of the oncoming night. In daylight her surroundings were sinister enough; in the darkness she knew it would be worse. But there would be no real darkness, she comforted herself, just three hours of poor light. Perhaps it would not be so bad after all. What did one do if fear became unbearable? One endured.

At supper time she again sat down to a formal meal, this time of cold partridge washed down with hot water.

Once the few dishes were done, feeling somehow that outside the house where she could watch for any approaching creature would be better than crouching inside, she went out and walked back and forth between the well and the house. The clouds were still lowering, bringing the twilight well ahead of its normal time. Slowly the outline of trees dimmed, the surrounding swamp grew darker and the far side of the meadow faded into obscurity. Stumps took on weird shapes, while in the forest darker foliage formed sinister silhouettes that upon close scrutiny seemed to move towards her. Several times, convinced what she saw was surely a bear, she raised the rifle, but managed each time to restrain herself, and each time the "bear" faded into nothingness.

If the outdoors was terrorizing, the thought of going into the house frightened her even more. She had left the door wide open in case a hasty retreat became necessary, a move she now regretted since who knew what might have gotten in while she had been prowling around outside? Moose, Ed had said were the only animals that need be feared, and even then only if one surprised them. Could one have blundered into the house without her noticing it? Was it in there now with its monstrous head swinging slowly from side to side? How on earth would she ever get it out of there without surprising it? She thought of the quick rush of hooves...

Something in the swamp crashed through the trees. There was a moment of silence. Then a raucous voice, like a parody of a witch, cried querulously, "WHAAT? WHAAT?" Joanne fled for the house while behind her clumsy wings floundered amongst the branches.

Slamming the door behind her, she dropped the bar into place and flew to the lantern with her hands shaking so badly she could hardly lift the chimney. She wasted two matches lighting the wick. In the pale yellow light the room was suddenly friendly and obviously free of moose. Now the window threatened. By contrast with the lantern light the dimness outside seemed black dark although she knew it was still just late dusk.

"Pull yourself together, Joanne. Pull up your socks."

The sound of her own voice comforted her though even to her ears it was a bit weak and squeaky.

"Ablution time. Teeth." She then discovered she had forgotten to get water; the teeth would have to wait, for nothing on earth would get her outside again. Perhaps she should light up the stove, warm the place to boil off a little anxiety. Fire at night, last thing before bed? What if the roof caught fire? She would then have to not only go out; she would have to stay out.

All the time the window was very much on her mind, ominous and dangerous. If she dared to look out it, something might look back in. An absurdly discomfiting sentence formed in her head as if she heard it spoken: "Lynx have pointed ears."

Hastily she undressed, slipped into her nightgown, checked the door for the tenth time, and carefully not looking at the window, carried the lantern to the bedside. If she left it lighted, a creature from outside would appear suddenly at the glass, its evil eyes glistening; if she put the light out, that something would appear as a shadow against the grey square of the pane. She decided she would extinguish the light, and sleep with her back to the window. But what if she awakened in the night and could see no light at all? She had to make a decision.

A lighted lantern could be a danger. The house was secure. She had the twenty-two and the thirty-thirty, both loaded. She made up her mind she would face the darkness and blew out the lantern.

The first squadron of mosquitoes came whining over the bed and peeled off for the attack.

Sometime during the night, startled awake by the sound of shattering glass, she lay there trembling until, summoning all of her courage, she raised herself cautiously from the bed, glad now of the grey light coming through the window. The room was empty; the glass was intact; the worst of the night was over. She had been dreaming. For some reason beyond her comprehension, happiness swept over her in long slow crests of euphoria. She would not have traded those moments for any others she had ever experienced.

14

ED WAS UP AT SIX O'CLOCK, BUSTLING ABOUT EFFICIENTLY, clashing the stove lids, clattering the frying pan into place, rattling the dipper in the pail, all to the accompaniment of cheerful but tuneless whistling.

In his bunk, Kevin lay listlessly, staring at the ceiling. His very first thought was of Joanne, wondering how she had passed the night. Since their marriage, they had never been separated, and he could not help feeling uneasy as if he had set a new pattern that would go on repeating itself. Remembering his resolve of the night before, he seized the side of the bed and swung himself to the floor.

"Y' made her, I see," Ed greeted him, flipping the pancakes in the air and catching them with the pan.

"Survived," Kevin agreed laconically. "I still feel as if my legs need amputating."

"Y' was a sorry lookin' sight last night I can tell y'. City fellers don't have too much stamina; they're not built f'r bush roads. Hung too low. Baw! Haw!"

Kevin limped to the window and looked out on another dismal, grey day.

"Isn't it, for Christ's sake, ever going to clear up again?" he asked in despair.

"Quit belly achin'; just be glad it ain't rainin' yet. Anyways, like I told y', she'll clear up like a shot as soon as y' gits that tarpaper on, guaranteed." With an exaggerated flip of the wrist, he cracked an egg into a second frying pan. "I broke a aig once't had a chicken in her. Put me off aigs f'r near a year. Smelt bad, almost like a calf born dead. Y' ever smelt one?"

"I have not had the pleasure."

"Y' didn't miss much. Damnedest stink like thick an' bitter. 'Twas an evil smell that made a man feel guilty, sort of. Somethin' Biblical about it, as if a man was interferin' in th' birth process, makin' some of God's decisions. Yeah, it smelt like sin."

Stooped over the wash bowl, Kevin sloshed cold water onto his face with cupped hands, feeling a stubble of beard. If Joanne could see him, she would not be pleased; yet neither of them had thought about a razor when he was preparing to leave. He would be an impressive sight at the store.

"First call!" Ed warned. "Aigs an' hotcakes made by th' best cook north of Edmonton. Fill up on these here condiments an' y'll be able t' face th' world like a man."

"A rugged northern man."

"Be that as it may."

With an uneasy conscience, thinking again of Joanne faced with the inevitable beans, Kevin folded his long legs under the table and fell to with gusto.

"Listen here," Ed interrupted. "I've had t' make a change of plan. Y' know that old horse I offered t' lend y'? Well, I had a word with him this mornin' an' he doesn't want no part of th' deal."

Kevin's grimaced in disappointment.

"Y' see, he's pretty old, and his self-respect don't allow him t' go wanderin' along th' highway with a roll of tarpaper on his back. Other horses would laugh at him, give him th' horse laugh so to speak. Baw! Haw! So th' upshot was I ast him if he'd mind pullin' a wore out democrat if I put shafts on it. Well, he would much rather just hing 'round th' barn, but I talked him into it. With th' rig to do y'r haulin y' kin buy out most of Fletcher's store an' take her with y'. What say?"

"I guess all I can say is, 'God bless you and the horse.' That way I can bring the outfit back as soon as we unload it. Joanne could come back with me, and then we could walk home together."

"I never thought of that there, but why not? Yez kin stay here an' we kin go t' a dance. I'll dance with y'r wife. But look here; if f'r any reason y' can't come back in, y'd better let th' old feller go back home by hisself, but without th' democrat like I suggested before. I kin always pick up th' buggy next time I come f'r tea."

A mouse, perhaps made hilarious by the plan he had overheard, emerged from a hole in the corner of the room and whisked across the floor, passing right under the table.

"Go, y' bastid," Ed shouted, narrowly missing it with a flung fork. "I read a book one time"—getting up to retrieve his fork—"about these here elephant walks in Africa. Seems them animals stake out a trail an' they keep usin' it year after year. You know what I figure? This house is built smack dab on a mouse run t' wherever the silly buggers want t' go. A sort of a mouse main street, y' might say."

"Very likely. I think we are on one too. The first morning of the rain, a mouse sat right on Joanne's bare foot in the middle of the room. He had to almost swim to get there."

The moment he had spoken he wondered why he had said what he said.

"She holler?"

"Joanne doesn't holler, except at me sometimes when I am deemed to be obstreperous. She just let it sit there until it got warm; then, it left."

"That figures, especially th' obttripper—the strep bit. Anyways I noticed that little lady isn't afraid of nothin' except bears, coyotes, moose, and chipmunks, t' name a few. Anyways y're lucky t' have her. But"—shrugging—"y' probably don't realize y're lucky t' have her. All th' same, I bet y'd go a hoorin' after a stray skirt just like th' worst of us."

"No, not I."

"I never yet met a man wouldn't go for a outside piece if he had a chancet. Dogs an' men are alike; all bullshit an' pecker."

"Now listen..." Kevin began in quick denial; then, he stopped in some discomfort.

"See?" Ed chortled. "Y' just thought of one, didn't y'? With a face like y'rs and y'r donkey riggin'—not that I've seen it mind—an' them long legs of y'rs, y' must of bin chased 'round like a billy goat in a she-goat harem, an' them all in heat."

"I have never..."

"All it would of took was time. Y'r safe now though. There is nothin' f'r y' t' chase way out at y'r place."

"What about the pole vaulting Englishman that had The Spruces before we did. He scored in a big way, according to you."

"Y're not an Englishman."

"Changing the subject, that fellow Kinney..."

"Yeah, we was talkin' about him before."

"Is it true—any part of it—about his testicle?"

Ed lifted his shoulders expressively. "Now just what gives y' th' idee I would go 'round peekin' at guys' weddin' tackle? How'd I know whether he's got one nut or thirty-two? He says he had one took out and it's still growin' an' I figure that's his business. Look here now,"—filling both coffee cups—"ever'body has t' have somethin', see. Take y'rself now, y're young, happily married an' about t' git rich on that farm of y'rs. On top of that you look like one of them there Adonises, whatever that is—supposed t' be somethin' good. An' y' kin probably hump th' castors right off a bed. Me, I got years of experience an' am just natcherly charmin'. But take a runt like Kinney; what's he got? He's nothin' but a underhung dwarf, the poor little fucker, with a host of tubercular kids that most of his neighbours had a hand in. If y' was him, wouldn't y'be inclined to guild th' lily a bit too? Of course y' would. Leave him be with his dream of that great knocker of his growin' away in a mus-ee-um back east. It's all he'll ever have t' boast about."

Kevin laughed. "For crying out loud, Ed, I wasn't criticizing; I was just asking your opinion of a rather bizarre claim, and I guess I got it. Speak to me now of 'relief'. What do you think of that business?"

Ed reached across the table for the tin of Ogden's tobacco, filled his pipe thoughtfully, lit it and leaned back in his chair.

"I dunno. I dunno what I think of it. F'r myself I'd rather starve than kiss ass f'r charity. They claim it ain't a gift, that y'can work her out afterwards on th' road, but I seen guys 'workin' her out' and, man, it's th' sorriest sight y'ever seen. Them guys don't work; they just lean on their shovels. And y' know why? Because th' work they're supposed t' be doin' don't need t' be done, an' nobody, but nobody, can play at workin'. In th' long run what little they git amounts t' charity, an' that's always bin a dirty word. An' yet, y'know, if I had a wife, say, an' a bunch of kids an' I seen their ribs startin' t' stick out, I s'pose I'd be in there hat in hand strugglin' t'git ahead of Kinney. When a guy goes gettin' hisself hitched up, he is just settin' hisself up f'r trouble, an' it's his own damned fault. I never felt I had the right t' take on somethin' I couldn't be sure t' handle, an' I can't see yet where I was too far wrong."

As he spoke, he tilted his chair away back so that he could watch the smoke from his pipe rise to the roof where it wreathed amongst the yellowed planks like a gas cloud rolling across an already poisoned battlefield.

"I won't say I ain't been lonely," he continued dreamily. "Batchin' can be a lonely business. Which reminds me of one of th' saddest thin's y' ever heard of. There was a young feller in here took a homestead out about ten miles an' he was off t' an awful good start. He had a cow, a team of horses, an' chickens by th' galore. He had barely started an' he was already makin' her go. Well, my old dad was with me that year an' he an' I used t' go huntin'. I don't know why, but that Sunday we went out past young Hatwick's place—he was th' young feller I am talkin' about.

"We was prowlin' through the bush back of his place when we heard a cow-bell a clangin' t' beat forty. No let up, just yingle yangle as a Scandihoovian would say. 'Somethin's up,' I said t' Dad. 'Let's go see. Maybe a bear has got a cow cornered.'

"We broke out of th' bush near a little clearin', and thereby God was th' loneliest cowboy anybody ever seen. He had that cow tied t' four trees, one f'r each laig, and he was on th' milk stool behind her just a whangin' away at her.

"I was f'r gettin' out of there fast, cause it embarrassed th' hell right out of me, but Dad was a rough old bugger who didn't care nothin' about nobody. He lifted his rifle, fired it in th' air and bust out with a great beller of laughin'.

"Well, young Hatwick looked up, fell off th' stool an' run away like as if he was bein' chased by old Nick hisself. Man did he run."

Kevin, open mouthed, waited for the finish, but as usual, Ed left him hanging.

"For Pete sake, what happened?"

"Nobody knows. Hatwick just disappeared an' no body ever seen him since. I knew he wouldn't want t' see me, so I sent th' dwarf out. After a few days we had t' bring in his stock, an' I sold most of it. Th' money is still sittin' in th' bank waitin' f'r him."

"Nobody saw him leave?"

"Nobody. I often think maybe he drownded hisself; who knows? But y' see th' tragedy of it. If th' silly ass had just stayed in that mornin' an' beat his meat th' way any respectable person would of done, he'd be with us now an' probably rich as that old Creases in th' Bible.

"I won't say I ain't bin lonely," he continued dreamily, "batchin' can be a lonely business, but m' conscience is clear, an' that is the main thin'. I got nobody on m' conscience, y' see; no other person's life. I can't help thinkin' how nice it'd be t' have a little lady like y'rs a-chirpin' 'round th' house; I can't help thinkin' about that. But, y' see"—dropping his chair forward and hitting the table in his anguish—"I couldn't bear t'see her gittin' hurt.

"I've been a hunter an' a trapper, an' I've a good many animals' lives t'account f'r. I'll not deny that, an' I suppose I'll have t' go on killin' if I want t'eat, but I don't want t' hurt any person or thin' any more than I have t'. I can't abide t' see thin's hurt by somethin' that's in my control; I just can't abide it."

He put down his pipe and stood up.

"So y' kin keep y'r homes and families, everyone of yez. When it comes t' women an' children, I've bin a cow bird all m' life, an' a cowbird I shall remain. Th' family men 'round here kin count theirselfs lucky th' fire in m' belly has about gave out."

"So endeth the lesson," Kevin concluded.

"Amen. An' now" —stretching himself—"unless y're fixin' t' rest up f'r another day, we'd better git over an' see if that horse survived another night. He's gettin' on an' I wouldn't be surprised none has he threw in th' sponge."

"Hey, how could he be dead? You said you were talking to him this morning about the cart."

Ed looked at him over the top of his glasses. "This mornin'? Oh, yeah. Well, that was late last night. I woke up and went over t' see him just after y' fell t' sleep. He's had plenty of time t' defunct since then."

"I dare say. What puzzles me is that you were snoring to beat the band before I fell asleep."

"Agh...well, I snored m' self awake. I was wonderin' how y' could sleep through th' uproar. That's when I went over t' talk t' th' horse. He was most unwillin', until I told him there was another way out, an' he wanted no part of that. That's th' saddest part of bein' a animal, they don't know that if th' goin' gets too tough they kin polish theirselfs off."

The two men strode across the town to the livery stable, where Ed led the way into the office. The same wizened little man who had given the surly directions the night before stood warming himself at the stove.

"Kevin McCormack," Ed introduced, "this here is Jack Powers."

Powers did not look up or extend his hand.

Instead of roaring, Ed said in a kindly voice, "Never mind; y' might as well git th' old dray horse an' hitch him t' th' democrat. Y'll have t'put th' shafts on first."

As the little man left the room, Kevin asked, "Whatever did I do to make him mad at me?"

"Nothin.' He hates people is all. He had a awful time at home with his dad an' his brothers because they was all bigger 'n he was. Then he come out in th' world to an' even worse time. Maybe I should of let him go years ago, but I keep him 'round just t'make myself feel better. Whenever I act like a prick t' somebody an' feel regretful, I look at his mean little face an' think there is worse than me around. Here, I had a few of them hotcakes left so I threw them in this sack; no use wastin' food an' I don't have a dog. An' here's two loaves of bread f'r Joanne. Tell her if she can't face them, she kin feed them t' th' whisky-jacks, but not t'any ducks as a mouthful of that stuff would sink th' poor creatures like a stone. Oh, yeah, there's also some boiled aigs in with th' hotcakes."

Powers came around from the back of the stable in a buggy drawn by a horse that had clearly passed its youth.

"Here comes y'r stallion; ain't he a peach? That there is real horseflesh, although there ain't a hell of a lot of it left on his bones. I ought t' have m' head examined f'r trustin' a prize like him t' a green horn. Now"—grasping Kevin's hand—"th' best of luck t' both of yez. If f'r some reason y' can't bring th' rig back in, y' just send that old horse back by hisself th' way I told y', an' th' next time I'm out there I'll bring th' rig back myself."

"Thank you," Kevin said simply. "Thanks for all your kindness."

His voice broke, throwing him into confusion.

Seeing his embarrassment, Ed said roughly, "Get on with y'. Y' git on out of here. I got work t' do."

Recovering himself, Kevin climbed into the buggy, waved, and drove proudly off down the main street to the store, where he dismounted and tied up with a flourish.

Fletcher came out on the sidewalk to greet him, offering his hand and a big smile.

"Mr. McCormack! Come right on in. Did you bring your wife with you? That's one of Ed's horses, is it not?"

"No, Joanne did not come with me. And, yes, that is one of Ed's horses. He loaned the rig to me to take out some supplies that we need."

Inside the store Mrs. Fletcher came forward and offered a limp hand.

"I see you are alone. Did your wife not come with you?"

"It was a long walk."

"I am sure it was. She wouldn't be used to that kind of thing. I suppose she is terribly lonely out there."

Immediately on the defensive, Kevin flared back, "She loves it out there."

"There is no accounting for taste. My husband has missed her. Haven't you, Thomas." Fletcher coughed artificially and hastily changed the subject.

"How can we help you?"

"We need a roll of tarpaper and some staples."

"Roof not so good, eh? How many rolls?"

"One will do. We need coffee, flour, syrup, a file to sharpen the Swede saw, some beans, some rolled oats, salt and, if you have them, some potatoes. Would you mind totaling that up as we go? You see, I left most of my money in my other pants."

"That's very odd," Mrs. Fletcher interjected. "You'd be amazed at the number of people who seem to forget their money in the last little while. Why, Thomas had to actually unload a wagon in one case."

"Some people, I understand, have also forgotten their manners," Kevin snarled back. "Mr. Fletcher, we will put nothing in the democrat until this account is settled."

"Oh come now, Jean, I think the kettle is boiling over. Perhaps you had better go and check it."

The list of purchases was not long and soon filled. Seeing the total as it progressed, Kevin was horrified while Fletcher looked distinctly disappointed when Kevin held up his hand indicating a halt. "That will have to do," he said as he handed over the last of his paper money. In return he received forty cents.

Fletcher reached under the counter for a bag of marshmallows which he placed on the top of the goods on the counter.

"What is that?" Kevin asked suspiciously.

At that worst of all possible moments, Mrs. Fletcher reappeared.

"Thomas," she snapped, "that wasn't much of an order."

Kevin pushed the candies rudely off the pile onto the counter, grabbed the roll of tarpaper and started for the door. Fletcher followed with an armful of supplies which he loaded into the buggy.

"Just a minute," he said when the loading was finished. He went back into the store and came back with the marshmallows.

"Take these," he ordered, proffering the bag.

"I don't want the damn things. I don't want any bloody charity."

"Take them," Fletcher repeated. "Any order, especially a cash order, is a boon nowadays, and I am glad to have it. Don't be a bear man. My wife sometimes says things she—ah—regrets afterwards."

Kevin lifted his hands in frustration.

"I said I do not want..." Feeling his voice tremble, he broke off, took a deep breath, muttered his thanks, and drove away, thinking, "Someday I'll come back here with a hundred dollars in my hand. I'll let that woman see them; and then, I'll buy her a bag of marshmallows and watch her choke on them."

As it had not rained for two full days, the road had already dried enough to make the going easy for horse and buggy. The horse was old, bony and slow, yet Kevin felt like a plutocrat as he sat proudly holding the reins. His only regret was that there was apparently no one to see him go by.

As he rode along he thought, "Here am I, a pulpy chemical accident riding along a road leading to another chemical accident to whom I am attached simply by a memory. Two sophisticated and extremely fragile organisms that only the most exact set of circumstances can preserve, and we have virtually no control over the majority of those circumstances. What is the sense of it? Why struggle? Why try to do anything? Then he visualized Joanne, the person, remembered the gentleness of her, and urged the old horse to go a little faster.

15

AGAIN THE DAY DAWNED BLEAK AND COLD. AFTER HER TROUBLED night, Joanne woke deeply depressed, a mood which the grey weather did little to alleviate. She wandered miserably over to the window, looked out and wondered if the sun was gone forever. The silence pressed in on her; not a branch moved in the still air. Untidy clouds still straggled over the swamp, moving slowly, threatening rain.

As she stood looking out the window, she put herself through a familiar discipline that she had established for grey mornings; namely, remembering each reason why the day should be a happy one. This routine might have been called praying if she knew to whom to pray.

There was some food to look forward to as she still had a breast of spruce hen, and in any case another hunting trip was not too unpleasant to contemplate, for her, that is; although the birds might have an entirely different view. Best of all, Kevin might be coming home. So what was the matter with a little grey sky? She wasn't cold, was she? She wasn't sick either, and she did not have to go and make somebody else's bed. She was free.

All her good thoughts cheered her as she turned briskly to the chores for the day. She made the bed, put the coffeepot on the stove, stirred up the fire, swept the floor, washed herself and prepared her breakfast. Once more she set the table and sat down to cold fowl and hot coffee. When Kevin returned, perhaps by some miracle he might bring bacon, or as a special treat, a half dozen eggs. She would have given anything for some toast with raspberry jam, say, or apple jelly—dreams, dreams.

When she went out to get water, there were two drowned mice in the well. By juggling the rope she maneuvered the pail about until she was able to scoop them both out. One was an ordinary field mouse, while the other had long hind legs like a miniature kangaroo. Though she knew it was foolish to feel sorry for two mice out of a possible million, something about their wet fur and stiffened bodies pierced her heart. She decided she would feel sorry for them anyway. Was it hypocritical of her to sympathize with mice while shooting partridges? Would she feel better if she ate the mice? That idea she declined immediately. Did she really deserve to eat at all? She had better accept the fact that she was a predator and, therefore, any pretense of pity was a sham. Nonetheless she did feel sorry for the mice with their sad little faces and water soaked whiskers, and she was hungry.

While the water was heating in the pail over the open fire outside, she tried her hand with the swede saw, only to find that a job which looked so easy when Kevin did it was for her awkward, boring and tiring. Furthermore, while she was sawing she found herself looking at her nose, an instant recipe for nausea.

Once the water was hot, she gladly put down the saw and pulled the kettle from the fire. She was about to go into the house to undress, but then she wondered, why go in? Who was going to see her? So she stripped down, and when she was naked, she looked at her body, pressed her hands against her flat abdomen, and said to herself, even Ed couldn't say I look like a set of deer horns. Maybe her legs were a bit spindly, but the rest of her was, well, nice. Shrugging, she picked up the wash rag and washed herself from head to toe, wishing the while that she had a tub she could get into.

The road was still empty.

Back in the house, she dressed, putting on her hunting clothes. She felt freshened and alive and absurdly happy. She had earlier put a pot of beans on the fire to boil, but they of course would not be ready until late afternoon. Once more she would have to go to her hunting tree if she were to survive.

On the way she stopped at the garden. Weeds were already springing up in profusion, yet there was no sign of anything else until she came to the radish row. There a dozen tiny green plants had just broken through the soil in a thin, wavering row, an unquestionable artifact. She stood there almost crying for joy; and then in accordance with their ritual, she danced a dance of celebration.

First things first, the immediate task was to scare up a few partridges. Once again she made her way to the feeding tree, expecting as she approached to hear the feeding patter. Silence. The remaining birds had fled. Undaunted, she pressed on deeper into the swamp, keeping her eyes and ears open for any sign of activity. Once she heard something heavy break away through the bushes, a fearful sound in a place where bears might abound. After a long sober pause and hearing no more activity, she pressed on again, amazed at her own temerity, to the creek, which at this point was moving sluggishly through the spruces. At intervals it formed pools that were deep enough for a person to wash in. Private bath she noted for future reference.

In one of the pools a lone duck sailed along, peacefully minding its own business. Joanne knelt, propped the barrel of the rifle on a branch of a willow and took aim. At that precise moment a flock of baby ducks came around the bend in the creek. Joanne did not fire.

She stood up, took one step and a partridge rewarded her by exploding from the grass and then, foolishly, landing on a branch a few yards away. This time Joanne got four birds with six shots.

"You're slipping, Joanne," she said aloud. "You"—adressing the rifle—"are to be thanked for firing. You others, you birds, thank you for giving your lives to a good cause." Was it a good cause she wondered. They had become food for two insignificant people whose survival was of no particular importance to anyone other than themselves. How enormously selfish to think that she mattered any more than the partridges in the scheme of things, selfish and egotistical.

After supper that night she took the heavy rifle and resumed her twilight patrol. This time she was careful not to leave the house door open. She also made a careful study of her surroundings in the hope that as darkness gathered she would be able to recognize permanent perils, such as stumps, as distinct from temporary perils like bears making a sly approach.

At ten o'clock she saw something moving away across the meadow on the road from town. At first she was sure it was a moose. She had two alternatives: cut and run for the house or try to bring it down when it drew closer. What would Kevin think if he came home to find a monstrous stack of meat? But hold, if she shot it, she would have to cut its throat and eviscerate it, two operations at which she was not adept and at which she did not wish to become adept. She chose flight, but as she turned she could see that the moose was pulling a buggy.

Now she was really afraid. They had not seen a stranger since they had moved in, and why should anyone be on their particular road unless he were coming purposely to their place since the road went no further? She decided to wait awhile and if it were a stranger, she would back into the house and lock the door. It would not be very hospitable, but she dared not take a chance.

As the buggy drew closer the distant figure stood up and waved; it was

Kevin. She put down the rifle and ran to meet him. As she ran she thought how undemonstrative she had become in their daily routine. They had lived together like two friendly strangers with little conversation and no physical contact. Kevin may well have felt as he always did, but the lack of running water, the constant wood smoke, and the strangeness of their new life made sex seem abhorrent to her. This time she would throw herself into his arms and give him the greeting of a lifetime.

A few feet from the democrat she stopped, breathless and shy.

When Kevin got down, she took his hand and murmured, "The radishes are up."

"You don't say! Hop into my carriage and we will drive in in style."

"Where in the world did you get this outfit."

"Guess."

"Ed, who else could it have been?"

"Could have been Mrs. Fletcher—who sends her love, by the way. Anyway you are right; it was Ed."

"From whom all good things flow. Are we going to keep it?"

"Unfortunately, no. He loaned us the rig just to bring our stuff out."

"Stuff?"

"Tons of things. Ed even sent you a couple of loaves of bread he made himself."

"Bread! I didn't think anyone ate it anymore."

"Don't get too excited; it's pretty heavy stuff."

Then Joanne had an ominous thought.

"How are you going to give him back his rig?"

"Therein lies a tale. He says if we just let the horse loose, it will make its own way home, and he can pick the buggy up the next time he comes out."

"You mean the horse knows its way home?"

"Yep, but I've got a better plan. What say we keep the horse tied up until we have the tarpaper on; then, we can ride back to town in the buggy like two rich ranchers."

"And walk home afterwards?"

"You feel up to it?"

"What I don't feel up to is staying here by myself again."

"Scared, eh?"

"Scared."

"What of mostly?"

"Twilight, semi-darkness, moose, bears, strangers..."

"Enough now! You forgot to mention the mice. By the way, how did you dispose of them?"

"What?"

"The mice. You said you were going to conduct a ravage."

"Oh, that. There has been an amnesty. I found two dead in the well and the rest said they would throw themselves in too if I did not let up. Then the one that sat on my foot made a little speech, the upshot of which is they will leave us alone if we leave them alone."

"Trust them?"

"With my last dollar."

"Too late; that is now in Fletcher's hands."

"Just a metaphor."

Before unhitching the horse, they carried all the groceries into the house. Joanne was secretly disappointed at the meagre load even though she had known they could not buy very much.

"Rolled oats," Kevin announced proudly as he brought in the bag.

Joanne did not like rolled oats.

"Courtesy of Mr. Fletcher and his charming spouse, herewith a bag of marshmallows. Bonus for having made a major purchase."

"If that nice lady had a hand in it, you had better check for arsenic."

"You may play the role of the king's taster."

"All right, but first our last supper—rather, your last supper. I've had mine. You can have bannock and partridge or partridge and bannock, whichever suits you."

"Aren't you forgetting something? What about Ed's leadened bread?"

"Ah Kevin! You mean leavened bread."

"Wait until you have weighed it. Ed said to watch for—agh—I mean —he hopes you enjoy them. He also gave me some pancakes which I ate on the way."

"You've been feasting, you heartless wretch. But then, so have I. I shot seven partridges."

"Seven! Come on now..."

"In the swamp. There were hundreds of them. The gun didn't work very well though."

"Sounds as if it worked very well indeed, and to think it was I who taught you to shoot.

"It was in good hands. Whoops! I had a good teacher."

"Good student. What did you do with them?"

"I ate four, and three are still in the pot."

"Talk about feasting. Now I can tell you, without my conscience killing me, I had eggs and bacon at Ed's. What else did you live on in my absence?"

"Just the birds; the bannock and the remaining flour were ruined by water and mice, a double plague."

They unhitched the horse, removed the harness—taking careful note of how it had to be put back on—and attached a long rope to the bridle. Selecting a spot where the grass seemed adequate, they tied the rope to a stump.

"He can even get his own water from the creek."

"Along with all the bugs he could possibly ask for."

They watched for a few minutes while the horse browsed. Satisfied that it was quite capable of doing without them, they went gaily back to the cabin.

"This time we will take the flour to bed if it starts raining again. Once that roof is fixed we will be okay. We'll have to hit it first thing in the morning because it still looks like rain."

It was their best evening since their arrival. All of Joanne's fears of the previous night had dissipated as the forest receded into darkness. As it was quite cool, Kevin lit the fire in the barrel heater to cheer up the house.

"You know, Kevin, it starts to get dark about eleven, but by two o'clock it is morning."

"You must have stayed up late to find that out."

"Sort of. I prowled around as long as I could because I wanted to be tired enough to sleep the night through."

"And did you?"

"Sort of, although I had a rip-roaring nightmare that woke me up for awhile. I dreamed I heard something break the window."

"Speaking of broken wind, I know why our beans are sometimes awfully hard."

"Relate."

"You are supposed to soak them overnight before cooking."

"Who told you that? Mrs. Fletcher?"

"Nah, Ed."

"I'll try that little trick tonight."

"Not beans again tomorrow!"

Unexpectedly Joanne flared, "Just what the hell else could we have?"

"Beans! Just what I want. I love them."

Later in bed Joanne relented and turned to him in sudden passion, all fierce little teeth, flickering tongue and eager hands.

Just as she was drifting off into sleep Kevin whispered, "I think I should go into town more often."

"You'll have to take me with you."

"I promise."

"Who'll take care of the baby?"

"Lord above, not that!"

"We are all free to choose our actions, but we are not free to choose the consequences, as my mother used to say."

16

THE FOLLOWING DAY WAS AGAIN DAMP AND LOWERING, WITH cloud tendrils writhing amongst the tops of the trees, dampness crushing out the spirit even of the birds, and a total absence of a breath of wind that might clear the skies.

Blundering out of the shack in his pyjamas still half asleep, Kevin urinated, yawned and looked around. If the rain held off for the whole day, he might, he hoped, be able to fix the roof, although where he was to start or how he was to go about it he had no clear idea. The logical method would be to cut the tarpaper in lengths on the ground before applying it to the roof, but he could not afford to make any mistakes as he had only one precious roll.

After some thought, he decided he would take the roll up onto the roof, secure it at the front, which was the high end, unroll it to the edge of the roof at the back, secure it with the appropriate number of poles, and then cut it off along the back edge of the roof. Since he had no ladder and did not want to take the time to build one, he climbed up the corner of the house where the uneven ends of the logs protruded from the walls. Now he had a better view of the situation. He must first remove the top layer of poles, clear them from the roof, and then bring up the roll of paper. He took hold of one of the poles and pulled it loose with a shriek of rusty and reluctant nails. This was the kind of work he enjoyed and he went at it with gusto.

Startled awake by the sudden burst of activity over her head, Joanne jumped from the bed and ran outside.

"What in heaven's name are you doing?"

"Having a bath. Can't you see, for Pete's sweet sake?"

"In your pyjamas for Pete's sweet sake?"

"Holy cow! I forgot; I started out doing one thing and wound up doing another, and in the process I neglected my attire. Well, now that you are out here, how about handing me up the roll of tarpaper?"

"Nix! Come down and get dressed, have a coffee, and act like a human being."

"Oh, very well, but if it rains and we can't get finished, we know who is to blame, and who will suffer the most by drowning."

"Speaking of suffering, how is your old horse?"

"Horse? I even forgot we had a horse."

"Maybe we don't; maybe the wolves got him."

Kevin came down form the roof and went in to dress while Joanne got the fire going and put the coffee on.

"While that delightful brew is brewing I will see to the stallion—that —one-time stallion."

"Make a good title for a book: *One Night Stand by a One-Time Stallion.*"

The animal was in dire straits; in his search for edibles he had managed to get himself so thoroughly entangled in his rope he could scarcely move. Kevin rescued him and led him to the creek for water. That done, he retied it on a shorter leash in another place where the grass was more plentiful.

"Stay there, old horse, and as soon as the roof is fixed we'll take you back to Ed."

After a quick breakfast they returned to their project. Kevin climbed onto the roof and removed the rest of the top poles and the old tarpaper, all of which he threw down at the back of the cabin.

Meanwhile Joanne brought the roll of tarpaper to the back and handed it up, albeit with some difficulty.

"Now what?"

"Can you, when I'm not bothering you to do something else, start with those old poles and drive the nails out—not all the way, just far enough so the tips of the nails are flush with the surface. Meanwhile I'll unfurl the paper."

He carried the roll to the high end, ripped off the cover and set it down. Carefully he squared it with the edge of the roof. Satisfied, he put his foot on it and let the roll go. It promptly shot away, unfurling a black highway down the roof and over the edge, just missing Joanne.

"What happened to the damn thing?" he yelled.

"Didn't you know what would happen? Ever hear of the force of gravity?"

"I never expected it to take off like that. Tiny little slope to the roof and it almost reached the speed of sound. Can you hand me a pole so I can nail it down before it starts rolling in earnest and papers the swamp."

"Very well; this one is ready. You can have it if you promise not to bombard me with any more projectiles."

Late in the afternoon the job was finished, paper down, poles restored and some paper leftover.

"There," Kevin boasted, "now let her rain."

On signal the first drops pattered down, and in a few moments the familiar drizzle began in earnest.

"Hey, you filled the wood box while I was gone. Good Joanne, stay, stay!"

"Where is there to go? Arf! Arf! It was hard work cutting it. Well, not hard, just killingly monotonous. I don't know how you can put up with it hour after hour."

"I like doing it, that's why. By the way, why didn't you bring in the wood I had already cut?"

"I wanted to prove I was made of the stuff it takes to survive in the north."

"Bully for you. We northern boys can put up with almost anything except sass from our wives."

"How much money do we have left?" Kevin looked up uneasily.

"You planning to cut and run?"

"Maybe. How much?"

"Exactly forty cents."

"I may be able to cut, but I won't be able to run very far."

"We have enough provisions to keep us going for quite awhile. We can hang on until the garden comes."

"How long does it take for carrots to be ready to eat, or radishes for that matter?"

"Search me. I don't seem to know anything about anything. It was you who read all the seed envelopes while I was sweating over a hot shovel."

"What we have to do is get a moose or something. I heard a heavy animal run away in the swamp. But even if we got one, how do we keep the meat from spoiling?"

"Dry it, maybe?"

"You know how?"

"Nah. How did the Indians do it? Maybe they smoked it in their peace pipes."

"Bravo! A piece of meat in a peace pipe. Tee Hee, or as Ed would say, 'Baw Haw'."

A trickle of water spilled through the roof, narrowly missing the bed.

They stared at each other in horror. Kevin shouted, "Son of a bitch!" Then he threw himself on the bed, turning his face to the wall. After a moment Joanne quietly took a pot over and placed it under the leak.

"There is only one so far," she said softly.

"I don't give a shit if there are a million."

She went over to the window, leaned on her elbows, her face between her hands, looking out but not seeing anything.

A half hour elapsed before she recovered herself. She went to the trunk, took out the mouth organ and brought it to the bed.

"Turn over. Look at me." He did, saw the mouth organ and said, "What's that for?"

"To celebrate."

"Celebrate! What the hell is there to celebrate about?"

"We both have all our teeth."

Kevin stared at her morosely for a moment. Then in spite of himself, he grinned.

"So we have my love. Come into my arms and we shall dance."

"Something slow."

"'Redwing' of course."

They danced.

For twenty-two incredible days and nights the rain pattered down without a let up; never violently, always softly, on and on. Three leaks appeared in the roof; water gathered in small pools, driddled across the floor and disappeared through the cracks. Several rivulets spilled down the stovepipe, accumulated into substantial drops and fell on the hot stove with the sound of kisses delivered with passion and without restraint.

Sometimes Joanne amused herself with thoughts of Toronto, of running water, warm rooms, flush toilets, of full course meals at restaurants, of people thronging the streets. Then she would look around the shack, thinking things could be a lot worse. She would not let Kevin drift into despair, nor would she let herself. Why get upset over a few setbacks?

During these long days of rain she insisted that Kevin shave even though he protested that there was no sense in it. If he failed to comb his hair, she would comb it for him. She paid particular attention to her own appearance, dressing carefully for each meal. Each day she bathed by sponging herself all over; she kept her nails neatly filed and each night she made Kevin brush her hair. What she failed to do with words, she tried to accomplish by example.

Three days after the rain resumed, they decided that a trip to town was impossible. They would be soaked through before they even crossed the meadow and heaven alone knew what the road would be like. Ed would be worried when the horse did not show up day after day. There was nothing for it but to let the horse go. Kevin untied it, slapped it on the rump and said, "Go and see Ed."

They thought it would gallop away, overjoyed at its freedom. Instead, it stayed nearby for two days before browsing its way across the meadow to the road. That night they listened in dread in case the wolves were after the horse.

A week later Kevin came into the house after a brief foray outside, his face disconsolate.

"The garden is gone."

"Gone where?"

"It is all washed out; it is now under water."

They looked at each other for a long, sober moment, weighing the magnitude of the disaster.

"Will there be time to replant it? I mean is there enough growing time left?"

"What with? We have no seeds left, remember? Besides there is no use fooling ourselves: it is going to go on raining forever."

"You know that's absurd." She came over to sit beside him on the bed. "I'm sorry."

"So am I. What good does that do us?"

"Not much, I guess. Maybe you could go to town again and get more seeds."

"With forty cents? Anyway, as you said yourself, there may not be time for anything to grow even if we had the seeds."

"If we had them, I would surely try again. There is some old saying about planting in the full moon...Say! Who was the guy that Ed said is our nearest neighbour, the one that shoots at the full moon?"

"Fro—Frogman?"

"That's it: Froman. Maybe he has some seeds leftover from his own garden, and maybe he could tell us how to dry meat."

Kevin nodded. "Pretty slim chance for seeds, but you are right about the meat; he must have to do it all the time. I'll go see him."

"I'll come too."

"What for? Oh, you're scared to stay here alone."

"Just say 'reluctant to be left here alone'."

"Okay, we'll go if and when it stops raining. Has it occurred to you that maybe this is another flood like the one in the Bible?"

"Sort of; how about you?"

"You are damned right it has, but with one big difference."

"Which is?"

"God was on Noah's side. Where was the voice calling us to build an ark?"

"He didn't have to; this house is our ark. We didn't have to be told."

"Well, we did something to make him mad."

He began shouting, "We are hoo-dooed, hoo-dooed, hoo-dooed!"

"Take it easy," she urged,. "Take it easy. You are getting all worked up."

He threw his arms wildly in the air, leapt to his feet, rushed from the cabin into the rain and did not come back for two hours.

Joanne was a bit apprehensive about his conduct and about this absence. Reason told her, however, that if the rain did not wash away his sins, at least it would cool him down.

17

WITHOUT ANY WARNING, WITHOUT ANY PRELIMINARY BREAK IN the clouds, the sky on the twenty-third morning after the rain had recommenced was a flawless blue, and not a cloud could be seen in any direction. The birds, reveling in light and new-found warmth, joyfully resumed their summer games while a faint breeze stirred the branches, sending water globules flying.

Joanne and Kevin jumped from the bed at the first sign of sunshine and flew to the door.

"Isn't it just heaven?" Joanne shouted. "Isn't it the most glorious morning ever celebrated on earth?"

"If it lasts. It'll probably cloud up in a minute or two."

"Don't be pessimistic. Now you can see why you were not instructed to build an ark. This was not meant to be a full-scale flood."

"Apparently you did not hear Ed's discourse on bad rice."

"What has rice got to do with it?"

"When things seem to be going well, don't attract the gods' attention by boasting about it. Old Chinese saying."

"Oooh! I guess I put my foot in it. Gods," she shouted, "as the clouds darken on this already dismal day, our first chore must be to dig up some seeds, although we know there s little hope of finding any, and even if we did, they would not germinate."

"'Digging up seeds' seems, somehow to be a reversal of the usual procedure, if you don't mind me saying so."

"Given the present state of our economy, my precise friend, the seeds have to be dug up before they can be dug in. Read 'planted'."

"Or before we can dig into the finished product."

"We shall ignore that. Do not forget it freezes here in August according to Ed. We must have seeds now."

Right after breakfast they armed themselves and set out through the swamp in the direction Ed had indicated when discussing Froman. In a few moments both of them were soaked through from dripping branches, yet since the day was already warming, they did not care. How could they ever have been downcast when it was summer and there was no rain?

Though it was part of their plan to try to shoot a deer on the way, neither of them had the faintest idea of how to stalk game. They floundered from hummock to hummock, crashed through fallen branches, talked loudly to one another, and on occasion even sang. Predictably they saw nothing but a few squirrels who came out to protest their passing, indignant at the intrusion.

After walking about an hour, just as they were ready to admit they were lost, they broke out into a small clearing where there stood the strangest dwelling either of them had ever seen. Having no walls except at one end, it was merely a peaked roof sitting on the ground. It could not have been more than ten feet long, eight feet wide, and seven feet tall at the peak. The whole structure was built with spruce poles. A stovepipe protruded from the middle of the end wall, while at the other end the opening was covered with deerskin serving as a door.

"What in hell do you call that?" Kevin wondered.

"Swiss chalet, depression-style."

"Looks more like a pigsty, farm-style, early Ontario."

"Where the pigs?"

"Where the Swiss?"

Hearing their voices, the occupant pushed aside the door flap and peered at the intruders with watery eyes. Surely the oldest man on earth, he had a tangled grey beard, silvery hair hanging almost to his knees, and a mustache stained brown from smoke and dripped tobacco juice.

"Nice day today," he greeted them cautiously.

"Well—agh—yes, it is a nice day," Kevin answered, recovering from confusion.

"The rain has stopped," he added inanely.

"Since this morning," Joanne confirmed, embarrassing herself immensely.

Kevin held out his hand.

"I'm Kevin McCormack, and this is my wife, Joanne."

"Pleased to meet you sir, and madam. My name is Froman, Hank Froman." Then with sudden suspicion he asked, "Where did you come from? Where are the others?"

"We're from The Spruces," Joanne interjected, thinking it's a home address like saying 52 Bloor St. West. "There are no others, just us."

The old man lifted his eyes and made a slow study along the treeline. Seeing no one, he turned to his guests.

"It's not often I get—not often one gets—visitors. One can not be too careful. Forgive me; socially I am a bit rusty. You will please excuse me. Won't you come in."

He held back the door flap to let his guests pass; then, he dropped the flap and followed them in. The interior of the shack was in absolute darkness except for a thin ring of light around the edges of the door flap, a strip that widened and shrank as the flap stirred in the breeze.

"Sit down—no, right here—lady" guiding her to a bench with a touch on the shoulder. "I'll just light up the lantern." Fumbling in the darkness, he struck a match and bent over the lantern to raise the chimney. In the dim light he looked like Jehovah stooping over a volcano-ravaged dearth.

Joanne stared when the lantern lit up. She thought, my God in heaven he doesn't even have a bed. He must sleep on that pile of skins there in the corner. And what awfulness is that all over the stove? Tobacco as sure as my name is Joanne McCormack.

Kevin's eyes, too, were busy. The only furnishings were the stove, a rickety table and two chairs fashioned from twisted willow branches covered with deer hide, hair side out.

"Will you have some coffee?" Froman asked, slowly wringing his hands in a gesture of uncertainty.

"Really, we just had—" Joanne began hastily.

"Of course you will; I should not even ask. Janie used to say a host never asks; he serves. I've been out of touch and have lost my manners."

With trembling hands he selected two enamel cups from the tumble of dishes, bones, cans, and—inexplicably—ashes on the table. After blowing in each cup to rid it of the ashes, he filled both of them with coffee poured from a rusty pot on the stove.

"I'm afraid I can't offer you cream or sugar; I don't use either one myself, you see, and I do not have guests often enough to—excuse me." He went outside, holding the door flap open behind him, and stood listening as he looked carefully around. "It's all right. What was I saying there?"

"You asked if we took sugar and milk, and explained you didn't have any."

Joanne took her cup, then almost dropped it. Once it had been a light grey colour; now it was stained brown from coffee, she hoped, though around the rim were unmistakable lip smears with shreds of dry tobacco stuck to it here and there.

"Dear God," she prayed, "if I survive this I will never ask for anything again." Then in Biblical terms she added, "Let this cup be taken from me." She lifted frantic eyes to Kevin for salvation.

Neither God nor Kevin came to her aid; she had to sit there with the cup balanced on her knee, completely incapable of lifting it to her lips.

"It must be six months I haven't seen any folks. It seems such a long, long time. I went into town last fall, but I didn't dare stay very long; one has to keep on the move, keep watchful. Fletcher, the storekeeper, pretended to be glad to see me, but I think he is in on it himself. When he said he was glad to see me, I said, 'Glad to see my money, you mean.' You know what he said? 'If you think I just want your money, you can just take those groceries and go. Never mind the cash.' That scared me pretty bad— badly—if he really would let me off without paying, you can bet your bottom dollar he was getting paid by someone else. Don't you think that's about the gist of it?"

As she grew accustomed to the dim light, Joanne began to take notice of other items in the room that had been invisible before her eyes had adjusted to the darkness. Not the least of these was a garrison of gumboots standing casually here and there like a disordered patrol of sad sentinels. Their military appearance was further enhanced by their slack tops which drooped to the side like guards' hats worn at a rakish angle. There were seven of them, and their positions in the room seemed to be quite random.

"Well," Kevin broke a long silence, "did he finally take the money?"

"The money?"

"The money, old Fletcher..."

"Oh yes, he took it all right. Yes, he took it."

"Then everything must have been on the up and up wouldn't you say?"

"Not necessarily. He may have taken it just to put me off the track. On the other hand, he may have been getting paid by us both."

Murmuring, "Jesus!" Kevin glanced at Joanne, wondering how she, so fearfully fastidious, was coping with her cup. Seeing her in disarray, he came to her rescue by raising his own and making fervent slurping noises as if he were enjoying the contents with extraordinary pleasure. Never slow to learn, Joanne there upon lifted hers to within a "long inch" from her lips and slurped even more enthusiastically than her husband.

"Have you been here long, Mr. Froman?"

"Oh, fifteen years, I guess. They passed so quickly I am no longer sure. No, I am lying; they did not pass swiftly at all, not swiftly at all. I am no longer sure of anything. I'm from Nova Scotia, you know. I had a home and a business there, and I could be there yet, but when Janie passed away..."

"Your wife?"

"Yes. It was the flu, all she had was the flu, and she didn't have to die. She just up and died and she had no business to do that. The house was so empty after she was gone. It was thundering with silence.

"They didn't bury her right away—frozen ground they said. They thought I wouldn't leave as long as she—as long as she wasn't..." He wept, pulled himself together and poured more coffee all around, not seeming to notice that his guests' cups were still full.

"I couldn't wait for them to bury her; I had to get away and I did and I've never been back."

"I don't understand. Why did you run away? Why did you come here? Didn't you have family back there?"

"That's just it: I had family all right." He paused, gazing uneasily about as if he thought someone was listening. "I had a son."

"Didn't he..."

"I was already sixty years old, sixty years, and he said I wasn't able to look after myself. Well, he always hated me because I had been pretty mean to him while he was a little boy." He paused in evident distress. "Not just mean—let's be honest—brutal. I beat him and oh my God I am sorry about that. There was no excuse for me. I was just a youngster myself and didn't know any better; I thought kids were supposed to be obedient, I guess. I had such high hopes for him; I expected too much. He always ended up disappointing me.

"Anyway, he wanted his revenge. When his mother died, he thought he saw a way to get even: he would make me dependent on him so he could abuse me and get his own back. Life with him would have been horrible, horrible."

Again he broke down. Suddenly Joanne jammed her cup against her lips and to Kevin's astonishment she actually drank the contents.

"How could he have abused you?"

"You remember the story about the wooden spoon?"

"No," she admitted.

"French Canadian: when the grandfather gets old, they takeover his place—'il s'est donné' they call it—and as the old man grows childish they make him sit by himself and eat out of a bowl with a wooden spoon. So he won't disgrace them, you understand. You can see I don't have much here, just a few old things, but they are my things, and I eat with a fork."

Gently changing the subject, Kevin remarked, "Speaking of food, we were hoping to run into some game on the way across, but all we saw was a few squirrels. Perhaps it is just as well because we don't know how to keep the meat if we do get any."

"I used to salt some in a barrel, but now I dry it all."

"Could you show us how?"

"You just cut your meat into thin strips. Then you hang it over the fire—you make a rack —and under it you make a smudge fire. I will show you my rack outside."

"What do you use to hang it on?"

"Why, haywire of course."

"Ouch, that is something we didn't buy."

"It would give me much pleasure to lend you some."

"And it would give us much pleasure to accept," Joanne responded for both of them. "Do you have a garden?"

"Garden?" The old man mused for awhile, the tip of his tongue flickering from time to time along his mustache, keeping the hairs constantly wet. "No garden, not anymore. I get lots of rabbits and partridges. Old people get too fond of their food. I don't want to be like that. I don't worry too much about what I eat now. So I quit bothering with a garden. Anyway, what I really mean is I have to keep on the move; someone could sneak up on me while I was digging or hoeing."

There go our seeds, thought Kevin.

Froman drifted off into silence. Then, suddenly alert, he said, "I'm sorry; where have my manners gone? You folks haven't had any dinner."

"Oh yes we have," Joanne burst out, too loudly, too eagerly. "We brought a lunch and ate it just before we got here, just at the edge of the clearing." She glanced warily at Kevin before adding, "A big lunch."

"Well that's a pity because if you had known I always have a stew going. When it gets low, I just add to it."

He stood up, went to the stove, took the lid off a much blackened pot, picked up a ladle of sorts, and began stirring the contents. To arouse their appetites he lifted the ladle full of stew and let the mess fall back into the pot. A shape distinctly like a rabbit's head fell back in with a plop.

Joanne retched out loud.

"What is the matter with her?" Froman asked anxiously.

"Her stomach's been upset all morning," Kevin lied. "It must be the water we've been drinking. I had better get her home as quickly as I can."

Recovering her composure, Joanne said weakly, "I'm sorry to have made such a fuss. It's just a touch of the flu."

Kevin looked at her sharply.

"Oh god I'm sorry. It's just a sick stomach. Kevin, we have to go."

Outside in the sunshine, Froman turned suddenly ugly.

"Who sent you here?"

"Nobody sent us. There is no one for miles to send anyone anywhere."

"Did she eat anything on the way over?"

Joanne shook her head.

"Then it can't be poison."

"You mean some person would want to poison us?"

"They would just to get at me. You had better check your pulse anyway; you can always tell it's poison by the way your heart beats."

"It's beating just fine right now. I am not poisoned."

"Well, you can't be too careful. It wouldn't be the first time they tried that stunt. They send a stranger over to see me and try to poison me a little bit so they can take me back. But it backfires on them because as soon as they get here they start getting sick, I suppose because they have been careless with the poison. They come for me on clear cold nights. That is a very dangerous time; that's when I keep a close watch for strangers."

He stopped abruptly and began backing towards his hut. As his back touched the flap he jerked it open and leapt inside.

"Mr. Froman," Joanne called. "What's the matter now?"

"What are we going to do?" Kevin asked. "Do we just walk away?"

The old man peeked out through the flap. "I'm sorry," he muttered. "They wouldn't be that open about it; they wouldn't send you over here in daylight. Give me your hand. I have been rude. Please excuse me. It is getting close to the full moon. I know what it is; it is lunacy—comes from the French word 'lune' meaning 'moon', you know. Not many people know that—about lunacy being crazy because of the moon. I know I am a little bit touched, but it isn't ordinary madness, not at all. It's lunacy."

"No I am sure it isn't ordinary," Kevin replied uneasily. "There is nothing ordinary about it at all. Thanks for your hospitality, and if there is ever anything we can do for you, please feel free to call on us. We will not betray you."

As they turned to go, he turned back, "The hay wire. You said you had some spare haywire."

"Come with me."

Back of the cabin in the deep grass they found several rolls of wire.

"That little roll over there will do you nicely," Froman said. "Now over here is my meat dryer. Simple isn't it?"

"Aha," Kevin agreed. "Even I can fix up something like that. Thanks again."

The McCormacks turned and quickly made their way back into the forest the way they had come. Once out of sight of the hut, Joanne stopped, knelt and rubbed her mouth with wet moss. Kevin sat down, shaking with suppressed laughter.

"Dear wife and constant companion, you beat us out of a nice rich stew with your capers."

"Don't you laugh at me, wretch; I heard you slurping at your coffee, you phony. Know what was in that stew? A rabbit's head. I saw it."

"So did I, and you are wrong; it wasn't a rabbit's head."

"I tell you I saw it; a distinct skull with eye holes and all."

"That wasn't a rabbit, you ninny; you made a big fuss about nothing. It was too small to be a rabbit."

"What was it then, know-it-all?"

"A weasel."

She looked at him suspiciously.

"Oh is that what it was? Are you sure it wasn't a muskrat?"

"About eighty percent sure. By the way, you are in the north now: you must call them mushrats."

"You forgot to ask him about seeds and that is what we came for."

"No I did not forget. He didn't have any seeds. You heard what he said about not bothering with a garden. He doesn't have much of anything. Did you notice his furniture?"

"You mean his chairs? I noticed they were made from deerskins."

"Did you look closely at the deerskin?"

"I was too busy looking at my cup."

"The skins were just crawling with lice."

"Don't tell me anymore or I will throw up again."

"Why did you force yourself to drink that coffee?"

"Because I felt sorry for him."

"Supreme sacrifice."

During the long walk home, they talked of the garden and the talk sobered them. There was no further hope of replanting now.

"There is some good came of our outing," Kevin said to cheer her. "We now know how to dry meat, and we have the wherewithal."

"Except the meat." Though they were tired and depressed when they reached home in the late afternoon, it was good to see their house again even after such a brief absence. In comparison with Froman's shack it looked like a palace or at least a mansion. The ground had already dried considerably; the trees had shaken off the accumulation of a month of rain; the sun was still high in a pure blue sky; they were home.

While Joanne warmed the leftover beans and set the table, Kevin went for water. Fate, of course, had saved the lowest blow of all for the worst possible moment: the well which they had dug so laboriously had caved in.

Kevin stood at the edge of the collapsed hole, sick with defeat. Everything he had tried to do so far had come to nothing: their garden had been washed away; their attempt to repair the roof had not been a success; the well was now useless. He sat down on the gumbo, the water pail between his knees, and he cried.

18

IN THAT STATE WHERE THE MIND, NOT YET WHOLLY AWAKE, drifts in and out of consciousness, Joanne lay in bed half seeing the room. At first everything was blurred and shapeless: the table, the door, the walls themselves were made of foam. As her mind cleared, her eyes began to focus. Sunshine streamed through the window, and through the unplastered cracks between the logs. Overhead she could see light through their newly papered roof, a detail she hoped Kevin would not see on awakening, in case it would ruin his day.

The house was peaceful and secure. On the washstand near the door the pail stood, the level of the water for once fairly high to judge by the distance the dipper handle protruded from the top. The stove was out, of course, and would hopefully remain so until fall if there was no more rain. The wood was stacked neatly in the wood box, although the floor in its immediate vicinity was sprinkled with chips, sawdust and bits of bark. No matter how often she swept, debris would reappear all around the box; there was no containing it. If she could just be sure the weather would remain warm and dry, she could throw the wood out until it was needed again, but the lesson of the rain had been all too clear: the only way to survive was to always be prepared. Looking at her husband sleeping beside her, his arms and legs sprawled all over the bed, his hair long and tangled, she thought: he is nothing but a boy really; he is so easily hurt and discouraged. Whatever he does seems to turn out badly, yet it is not because he doesn't try; he kills himself when he believes he is accomplishing something.

Fully awake now, she felt the familiar pangs of hunger, or at least the pangs of hunger for something different to eat. There were still beans enough, the flour would carry them for some time longer, there was still some coffee—she was playing the endless, hopeless game of inventory without a pencil or paper.

The room darkened abruptly. Always fearing a new onset of clouds, she glanced at the window and gasped in astonishment. Exactly as she had dreaded when she was alone, an enormous prehistoric head stared back at her through the window panes.

"Kevin! Kevin!"

"What is it—hey—what is it?"—opening blurred eyes.

"The window! The window!"

He turned to the window, yawned, and in mid-yawn shouted, "Holy cow!" He leapt from the bed, and as he pulled on his boots. He started yelling, "The broom! The broom! Where the hell is the broom?"

"The broom?" Vaguely it occurred to her that he, too, had seen the chips and sawdust around the wood-box and wanted to clean it up.

"Are you crazy? Don't you see that awful thing at the window?"

"Oh Lord," he squealed. "I mean the rifle, the bloody rifle."

Recovering himself, he grabbed the thirty-thirty from the wall, levered a cartridge into the breach, and plunged out the door with Joanne in pursuit.

Startled by their cries and the onrush, the moose lumbered down the path to the edge of the forest. There he paused just long enough to present a perfect target. Kevin's first bullet clipped the trees far over the head of his target; the second clipped leaves from a tree standing innocently well to the right. The moose departed.

Kevin's pyjamas flapped in the breeze as he ran after his prey. A few minutes later he returned, looking duly chastened.

"I don't see how I could have missed."

"It's too bad," Joanne comforted him. "Just bad luck."

"Bad luck, hell. The animals come up to the very door and beg to be shot, and from three feet away I miss. God hates me."

Joanne started for the house; then, she stopped.

"Let me look at that thing."

"The rifle?"

"No, the violin you are holding in your hand—yes, the rifle for goodness sake. I am going to try a couple of shots myself. Maybe there is something the matter with it."

"It will knock you over."

"Mayhap, but I can't depend on you—I mean I can't depend on you to be here every time I see game."

"You mean you can't depend on me to hit a bull in the ass with a banjo."

That was exactly what she meant.

"Now don't be silly. I have to be able to use it."

"Okay, Mrs. Diplomat. Fire away—so to speak."

She raised the rifle to her shoulder and held it firmly, too firmly perhaps. "What shall I shoot at?"

"Wait a moment and I'll put an old can on that stump. Sixty yards," he added as he paced off the distance.

After a prolonged aim, she squeezed the trigger. The barrel slashed upward, the butt smashing against her shoulder, her clenched right thumb slamming into her nose. Dazed, she lowered the rifle, blood spilling from both nostrils.

"I told you," Kevin cried, snatching the weapon away from her.

"Never mind the 'I told you sos'. Help me stop this bleeding."

"How can I stop it?" he wailed. "I don't know anything about bleeding!"

Helplessly he put his arm around her.

"You'll know a lot about bleeding if we don't do something fast. Come on to the house, and bring that wretched pieceof iron with you."

In the house she wetted a cloth and held it to the back of her neck. Whether it was the compress or the elapsed time, in a while the bleeding stopped. She washed her face and hung up the towel. Seeing Kevin starting to restore the rifle to its nails, she called out, "No, don't do that; I'm going to try again."

"Aw honey..."

"Give it to me."

When they went out, she said, "Where is the can?"

Kevin replied rather sheepishly, "You blew it right off the stump into Kingdom come."

"Put it back up, my boy."

This time she allowed herself to relax before aiming instead of holding it rigidly as before, and concentrated on keeping the barrel down. The shot sent echoes booming around the swamp, setting a family of squirrels off into a storm of bad language. Again the can took flight.

"Not bad," Kevin conceded sourly.

"Now I will try it."

Joanne reinstalled the can. Kevin tried a shot. He missed.

"Try again."

"To hell with it; we can't afford the cartridges. We now have only sixteen left."

"Sixteen cartridges and about as many beans," she said mournfully. "If we don't get some wretched creature pretty soon, we will have to either eat the cartridges or shoot each other."

"If it comes to that, you had better shoot both of us. I don't think I could even hit myself."

"Talk about knowing one's own limitations! Seriously, beloved, we have to find some food or no shooting will be necessary."

"Come on then; let's go right now. You bring the big fellow, and I will carry the twenty-two. If we meet any partridges I will assault them. You can handle the big stuff."

Instead of cutting into the swamp as she had done on previous occasions, they set out across the meadow, following the route into town. This time they continued on the road far past the point where she had turned off before. Once across the meadow, which was still soft underfoot from the rain, the going was much easier and for that reason more cheerful. Here the somber evergreens gave way to poplars in a hilly area. Beneath the trees, which were relatively sparse when compared with the area around their cabin, small brushes grew in clusters, forming a light underbrush through which it was, nonetheless, easy to walk.

"Smell the air," cried Joanne, lifting her face to the slight wind, letting her hair, now quite long, blow free.

"I'm smelling it. I'll swear it is fresher than it is at our place."

"And drier."

"I feel as if a weight had been lifted from our shoulders."

"Let's run and run."

Like two children they locked hands and ran through the bush, each with a rifle and seeming without a care in the world.

"Stop. Let's stop!"

"I thought you were a rugged northern girl. I could run another two miles."

"I've a stitch in my side that would 'save nine.'"

"Just in time then."

In a grassy opening studded with dandelions, they dropped to the ground and lay there breathing heavily. When she had calmed, Joanne remarked dreamily, "I wish we were living here; it's so much less oppressive."

"You do, eh?"

"Hey"—sitting up abruptly—"why don't we come here?"

"We're here now."

"I mean come here to live, ninny."

"Oh sure; that would be just dandy."

"Why not?"

"Don't be silly. In the first place, it isn't our place; it's not part of our homestead."

"Who cares?"

"Nobody right now, perhaps, but sooner or later someone will come and file on it. Remember we have to have a house and fifteen acres under cultivation on our place or we will lose it. Besides, if we moved here, what would we live in, a tent?"

"We could build a new house—all it takes is logs, and we can get plenty of those."

"Be realistic: I couldn't even fix the roof on the one we have now, let alone build a whole new house. You have a loser here, my poor child. A loser."

"Quit saying things like that. Quit saying you can't do things just because we have had a few setbacks. All we have to do is keep on trying."

"Like Bruce's spider."

"Exactly like Bruce's spider."

"Listen, my pet, the first thing we have to do is get through the coming winter and that won't be easy. What we'll do is get a deer or a moose, smoke the meat and stash it away. You can do most of that. As for me, I must concentrate on cutting wood, or we will freeze to death even before we starve—come winter. Next spring if we can find a better site for our house we will think about rebuilding. That is a promise."

They sat side by side, brooding.

At last Joanne nodded. "You're right, old man, we must not make any foolish moves. You cut the wood, I'll smoke the meat, and we'll both go for water."

"Deal!"

They shook hands.

"In the meantime," she said after a moment's thought, "I can at least pick a few dandelions to cheer up the house we now have."

"That is the spirit."

"Wait while I...Hey! Dandelions!"

Startled, he sat up. "What about them?"

"They are edible, that's what about them Edible—you know—chomp, chomp."

"Great Caesar's ghost, we are sitting on a bread basket. What part do we eat? The flowers?"

"The leaves."

"Let's go!"

Together they fell on the plants, pulling them up by the roots or by merely breaking them off, whichever happened first. Kevin stripped off his shirt and they stuffed it full until it looked like a giant rag doll.

"Let me get my arms around it," Kevin ordered. "I'll carry this baby home as if it were a baby."

"That is not a baby; that is a sheaf."

And home they went, singing:
> Bringing in the sheaves,
> Bringing in the sheaves.
> We shall come rejoicing,
> Bringing in the sheaves.

Back home they spread their plunder on the ground. While Joanne sorted out whatever looked edible, Kevin went for water and lit the outside fire. It was to be a feast, and they were not entirely disappointed. The greens were somewhat bitter, yet they were a welcome change. The most important feature of the day, however, was that they had made their second real step in living off the land.

So the days passed: two people alone in the forest, subsisting on partridges, dandelions, wild strawberries, and later on saskatoons, cranberries, a few blueberries, and their meagre supply of staples. By some miracle— for they were not very cautious—they never got ill from anything they ate.

Time after time Kevin convinced himself that he must go looking for work, cost what it might in loneliness or pride. He considered taking Joanne into town with him, but then he thought they would have to rent again, do disagreeable things for disagreeable people, maybe even go on relief. He proposed this plan to Joanne, but she would have no part of it. We are happy here; we will survive. We stay. Because he did not want to go anyway, he discarded the idea each time even though his conscience gnawed at him.

In the darkness he apologized to her for not being a better breadwinner. "You know you would have been better off if you had married one of your old friends."

She turned to him. "Now it's funny you should say that. I was thinking the same thing. I said to myself, as soon as I meet a rich neighbour whoosh I'd be gone. Well so far we have met old Froman, and with all due respect I have to tell you you're stuck with me for some time yet."

So he hugged her and they fell asleep.

19

THE SUMMER ADVANCED. AS IF TO ATONE FOR THE SPRING OF rain, the sun came up morning after dazzling morning in a cloudless sky, and rode the day through with never so much as a mist wraith to cast a shadow. The forest burned dry, the creek stopped running and evaporated until all that were left were a few stagnant pools where the trees stood in deepest shadow. The swamp, which had been quick with the song of birds calling cheerily, fell silent; the leaves of the deciduous trees hung limp and lifeless. The northland slept in sunshine and summer.

For Kevin and Joanne it was a time of dreaming, of long hot days with little to do but sit bemused, each thinking his or her thoughts, seldom speaking. After the failures of the spring Kevin fell into a great state of lassitude. The very thought of digging another well sickened him. He remembered all too clearly the back-breaking effort he had put into digging the first one, and who was to say a second would not end the same way as the first? Sometimes he was tempted to clear a few acres of land, but that too would be futile, for even he could see that the whole quarter section was useless for farming, and how long would it take to clear enough to make a crop worthwhile anyway? Centuries. How would he get it plowed? Where was the seed to come from? Their whole plan had been exactly what his father had said, a pipe dream.

For days he wandered about aimlessly, driving Joanne to the edge of exasperation with his restless pacing, his endless repetition of the question: what am I to do? Finally, in desperation, he took the rifle with him and began strolling through the woods, just meandering along like the creek. There in the heart of the swamp, he fell in love with the forest itself, the hushed solemnity of the trees, the peace, the timeless odour of generations of decaying needles. At the very cen-ter grew two enormous spruces whose branches were so dense no sunlight ever penetrated to their bases. Often he sat for hours with his back against one of these giants, bemused by the scent of gum and lost in meditation.

Then one morning he awoke and took control of himself. He remembered once again Ed's admonition about cutting enough wood for the winter before the snow flew. Here again was the one thing he could do successfully and that would have a purpose. At first he was afraid that the work would be monotonous, but as the pile grew, his old fascination returned in full measure. It became a routine: walk into the bush, select a suitable tree, cut it down, chop off the branches, saw the log into manageable lengths, stagger back to the sawhorse with each one and there proceed to cut it into twenty-four inch blocks. Slowly the pile grew. From time to time he would stack it into a small neat pile before moving his sawhorse to another location.

Watching him, Joanne was at first content; at least he had found something to do with himself, even though to her eyes, there wasn't much point in it since it was clear he had enough wood cut for decades. As the weeks passed, however, it became more and more apparent that there was something bizarre about his preoccupation with his work and his method of doing it. Obviously he was obsessed with what he was doing, and all his actions took on the air of a ritual.

"Don't you think you are overdoing it?" she asked.

"How 'overdoing'?"

"You have become a woodcutting machine. That is all you do or think about."

"I am thinking about you as I do it."

"Look at your stacks. You have cut enough for the rest of the twentieth century."

"No! You heard what Ed said: 'When you are sure you have enough, get down to some serious cutting.'"

"Yes indeed, but be reasonable."

"Leave me alone. I have to keep on; I know what I am doing."

"What about the house? You haven't done anything about plastering it yet, and winter is approaching."

"Don't worry about it. Don't talk about it anymore; it is not worth plastering." Then he shouted, "It's a very old shack—not worth anything. Just an old trapper's shack." A silly smile spread across his face which he tried to hide by bending over the saw.

Deeply puzzled, she watched him for a few minutes, at a loss what to do or say next. Finally she said, "Well, I am going to plaster the house; we don't want mosquitoes inside, and we want the cold kept out too."

"Now you have it; that is why I am cutting wood, the cold is the enemy."

"So be it. Listen, answer me just one question: why are you stacking your wood in small piles like that? Why don't you make just one long pile? The way you are doing it we will have the whole homestead covered with wood by fall."

Turning his back to set up another log, he muttered, "It's better this way—small piles will attract less attention."

"Whose attention in the name of great Caesar's ghost?"

"Just don't talk about it anymore. Just leave me be. I beg of you, don't talk about it anymore."

"Okay if that is the way you want it," she huffed. He put down the saw and took her in his arms. "I am not being nasty, honey. I just can't talk about these things right now."

"Very well; I will get on with the plastering all by my sweet little self."

"That's a real good idea. If you do it, it may turn out all right. You just ask me if you need help with the heavy part, carrying the dirt and bringing the water."

During the long rain she had noticed that the gumbo from the digging of the first part of the well had the plasticity of putty, and should be ideal for making pottery. Now as a prelude to making plaster for the house, she tried moulding some of the stuff into shapes: cups and bowls. Mixing and shaping was easy enough and for a time she thought she had really stumbled onto something. Maybe their homestead would become the pottery cen-ter of Canada. "Visions of sugar plums," she chided herself. People in Toronto, say, or Montreal, would turn over an exquisite piece of crockery, see the signature "Joanne" and know it to be a masterpiece. All dreams ended when with the first baking she was left with a few pieces of cracked and crumbling clay.

So much for that. With the next batch she plastered the front of the house, using a mixture of mud and water that was just soft enough to be smoothed into the cracks between the logs. For guidance she had nothing but common sense, and her tools were somewhat limited: she had to make the mixture in the water pail—and that meant tiresome washing after each batch—she had no trowel, no retaining nails, no lime. After trying fruitlessly to use the pancake turner as a trowel, she called on her husband to fashion one. Several days later the house seemed airtight and Kevin was impressed, although he was ashamed that he had not done it himself.

"Quite a creditable job," he pronounced pompously.

"There you are; next spring we won't have a mosquito in the whole establishment."

"If we are spared."

"Correct, my cheerful laddie, if we are spared."

Three days later the plaster, in the act of drying, began to crack and fall out.

"Just as I expected," Kevin remarked bitterly. "I tell you, nothing is going to work for us. There is no use in our doing anything. We may as well just lie down and let old age set in." Whereupon he went back to his sawhorse where he sawed harder than ever.

There is use, Joanne told herself. If things fail, it is just because we do not know how to do what we are trying to do. We dug the well in the right place by pure luck, but we did not—do not—know how to keep it from caving in. We chose the wrong place for the garden, although we might have succeeded if the rain had not been so copious. We did not know what we were doing—and still don't—when we did the tarpapering. Nonetheless, we shall go on trying until it works; I will never give up.

She shouted out, "You hear me, old man McCormack? I will never give up!"

He yelled, "What?" in an aggravated tone; so she yelled back, "Oh, sheddup."

What was it Ed had said about plaster? She thought back. He said to use moss. To pound it in. She would try her hand with moss; the good Lord knew there was lots of that. Sadly she chipped out all the plaster that had not yet fallen off, and then went in search of moss. For want of a sack of any kind she used a piece of the old tarpaper to carry it in.

Choosing one of the cracks at a comfortable height for her first experiment she began. It soon became apparent that she would need some kind of tool to poke in the moss and hammer it in. Kevin was again called into the fray. "Look here, boss, I want to jam this moss well into the cracks and then I want to hammer it in. Without delay you are to fashion me another tool."

"Nothing to it, Miss."

In a few minutes he came back with a wedge. "Try that for size."

She tried. "No good; it needs to be more tapered. Back to the drawing board."

"Nothing I do or make works; you know that."

"Turn again, Lord Whittington—that's a quote."

"You don't say."

After two more tries they came up with a dandy device and Joanne was on her way. The finished job did not look nearly as neat as the plaster had, but the moss filled the cracks and sealed the walls, much to her satisfaction. On the day it was finished she announced there would be a victory dance that very night.

"Who is invited?"

"Old Froman. Run over and get him."

"Nothing doing. We are getting dangerously close to a full moon."

"I guess that puts you on my card for the first dance."

"Redwing?"

"No, this is a major victory—as I have already pointed out—so we will have to begin with a schottische."

"Then I will put down the saw and practise all day. Do not listen as I wish it to be a surprise."

"No problem, I won't be able to hear it over the roar of the traffic."

In the evening the cabin came alive with joyful music and the shuffle of carefree feet. "Now let the winds blow and the mosquitoes hum," Joanne boasted.

In the early morning the winds did not blow, but the mosquitoes, seemingly undeterred by the moss, hummed with a vengeance. Kevin ducked under the blankets, muttering, "Hoo-dooed."

Joanne, subdued, came up with another plan.

The following morning she went back into battle, this time with her failed gumbo mixture, reasoning that now the moss was firmly in place the mud would cling to it, and she was right. For the first time the mosquitoes sent out only a few patrols in smaller squadrons. "There," she chided her husband, "this time the battle is really over."

Kevin secretly thought that the decrease in mosquito activity was more likely due to the advance of summer, but he wisely kept his opinion to himself.

20

JOANNE WAS DOING HER LAUNDRY ON THE CREEK BANK BESIDE her favourite pool where, by good fortune, some water still remained, although it had an unpleasant odour and was alive with water creatures. Here Kevin had dug out a fireplace and built up a pile of wood for her convenience. She worked in her characteristic fashion, briskly, each movement quick and efficient.

As she bent over the fire, her left hand shielding her eyes from the smoke, she heard a light step and the sound of twigs breaking. Turning abruptly, heart pounding, she saw—just as on the first day—a doe gazing at her with startled eyes. It stood there, ears pricked forward, more curious than wary.

Moving instinctively, Joanne backed slowly, step by step, to the tree where the rifle was standing. Locating it with her hand feeling cautiously behind her, she brought the rifle slowly around, drew back the hammer with a click that seemed to echo through the forest, raised the barrels smoothly, and fired. The deer fell. Joanne dropped the rifle.

"Oh God," she said out loud, "I've killed it."

Hearing the shot, and sure that there had been an accident, Kevin came running, shouting, "I'm coming! I'm coming! Are you all right?"

"I've killed a deer," she told him unnecessarily as he reached her side.

"Well I'll be eternally damned! Well, by crackey, you surely did! Why didn't you answer when I called? I thought the gun had gone off by accident."

"I don't know. I felt—feel—queer."

"I thought you were shot. You didn't answer..."

"I'm sorry. I don't know why I didn't answer, honestly, and I don't know why I shot the deer either. I didn't mean to."

"You shot it for meat, remember?"

"Yes, but what I'm trying to tell you is it just happened—I didn't plan anything."

"Good plan all the same."

"It was so beautiful, so trusting."

"Beauty doesn't fill stomachs. You got a deer, something we have been trying to do for months. Don't feel bad; we have to eat."

"With just one shot," she said, unconsciously turning the dagger. "One shot—it just fell down."

"I guess we will have to butcher it right away." He touched the body gingerly with his foot. "Here, I'll have to cut its throat; I know that much."

"What for? The poor thing is already dead."

"Yeah. Dad always said you have to cut the throat to drain off the blood. Remember the old Biblical injunction: 'All these things shall ye eat, but the blood ye shalt not eat, for the blood is the life'."

"Here is one person who needs no injunctions. The deer I shall not eat at all, no part of it. How can you stand there talking about eating while it lies there, dead forever? It is still a deer, you know."

"Soon," he said callously, "it will be meat, M-E-A-T. Not partridge, but real M-E-A-T." So saying, he opened his jackknife, knelt down and started sawing at the animal's throat. Blood gushed from the gash.

Joanne stood aghast, blanched and sank to the ground as if she were starring in an old fashioned play.

Seeing her go down, Kevin dropped his knife and rushed to lift her up. "Oh honey, please. No more, no more. You go back to the house now. Are you all right? Can you sit up?"

In a few moments she came back to normal as the colour returned to her cheeks. "What happened?" she asked, still bewildered.

He cradled her in his arms. "You fainted, that's all. You fainted when you saw the blood."

"But that was such a long time ago."

"No it was only a few seconds." Then, to cheer her, he said, "Behold the mighty hunter."

"But it was a long time ago."

"'It wasn't twenty years, said Rip/ the story done me wrong/ I slept upon a downy bed/ it only seemed that long.' There, there. Be of good cheer, be your happy self. We have to do unpleasant things if we are to survive; we both know that."

"You seem in good spirits. Here I am practically dying, and you've got nothing kinder to do than recite poetry."

Still trying to bring her out of it, he said, "All the better books agree that girls go snakey over poetry—at least all the arty ones."

After a few moments she freed herself from his embrace and forced herself to watch his amateur butchering. From time to time he passed his hand through his hair, leaving a blotch of blood on his forehead.

Fully recovered, Joanne teased him, "You've got blood all over your head. Try this for poetry: 'Don't shake those gory locks at me.'—Shakespeare."

"Not poetry."

"Poetic speech, nonetheless."

"Furthermore—come hold this leg if you are feeling so chipper—it's not 'gory'; it's 'hoary.'"

"Prove it." "Maybe it's 'horny'. Do you suppose Shakespeare stooped to thoughts like that?"

Since his skill as a butcher left much to be desired, the resultant gobs of meat were not exactly appetizing to behold; nonetheless, it was undeniably food, and once the skin and head were removed even Joanne could tolerate the sight of it. For his part, he was euphoric. As he worked he began to sing:

> There's a pretty little dear
> And she lives up town,
> Her daddy is a butcher
> And his name is Brown.
> Her folks they are
> Of high renown,
> Oh she's the girl for me.

"You know'" he confessed, "when I was a boy, I always thought that was a 'pretty little deer' and I always wished I had one"

"What for?"

"Promise you won't hate me?"

"No promises before confession, or absolution either."

"Well—I can't explain exactly. It was kind of a sexual thing. I guess I had sexual urgings although I could not possibly have recognized them. The idea of having a deer was so I could torture it."

"You don't mean that!"

"But I do mean it, and the worst of it is—well, it was there and what could I do about it?"

"Do you still feel like that, even remotely."

"Don't be silly. At least I told you you would hate me. Of course I am ashamed of having such thoughts, but what control does a boy have over instinct? It was a developing sexual urge."

"What has sex to do with cruelty?"

"More than we would like to admit."

"Men are horrible. What do we do with all the leftovers here?"

"You mean hide and guts?"

"If you must be brutal."

"We must bury them at once. The game warden might spot them and know what we have been up to."

"Way out here?"

"More unlikely things have happened even in my brief lifetime. A freshly killed deer might draw the law like a magnet."

"Especially if the hunter is hoo-dooed."

"Exactly."

"Haven't they said that because of the depression we can shoot for food if we are in dire straits?"

"Don't bank on it. Besides, if I were to plead dire straits, they could have me up for perjury."

"Why?"

"I still have forty cents."

"And a roof over your head."

"Of sorts, as we well know. Hey, there's an idea: if we get caught, they will throw us in the clink. Then they will have to feed us. Lap of luxury!"

"In jail they segregate the boys from the girls."

"Oooh deprivation! I doubt you could stand it. As I said, we had better bury the remains."

"I'll get the shovel."

Before taking the meat up to the house, they buried the remains. While Joanne was preparing supper, Kevin went a little way into the woods at the back of the house, found three suitable poplar trees in a group and there fashioned a platform about ten feet from the ground. He even made a ladder for access. When he had transported the meat to the cache, he stood back to gloat over it. Even as he stood there a squadron of whisky-jacks arrived to sort over the goodies.

"You'll get yours if you hang around here again,"—failing to see the irony in his threat, for even as he spoke they were getting what they thought was theirs.

"What's for supper?" he asked as he was washing his hands.

"For you, steak; for me, greens and beans."

"Some hunter; she can't even face the fruits of her own endeavours. Hunting, that is."

"It seems to me there is a badly mixed metaphor in your remark. If you had seen its eyes, you wouldn't be quite so anxious to pitch in."

"One well mixed metaphor deserves another. Anyway it is none of my business if you prefer beans and greens. More power to you. Lucky you."

In a few minutes the odour of frying venison filled the room. Quietly Joanne dropped a second steak into the pan, a gesture that Kevin, of course, did not miss.

"One is plenty for me," he remarked innocently. "Or is that second one for my breakfast?"

"You had better button up or you won't get one even today, let alone tomorrow."

During supper Kevin wondered aloud. "How are we going to keep it?"

"Keep what?"

"The meat, naturally; we have very few potatoes."

"Well, my sarcastic little man, we'll just have to keep it; did you want to give some away?"

"Flies! Flies! Flies eat meat. Decay. Meat decays you know."

"You are coming very close to getting yourself killed. We will smoke-dry it exactly as Dirty Dick—a.k.a. Mr. Froman—explained to you. Repeat what he said."

"He said make a rack, hang the meat on it and light a smudge underneath it. He gave me the wire for the rack."

"Believe it or not, I remember all that too, even I, a girl."

"All sounds very simple. What I want to know is how we store it afterwards."

"I have a terrific idea."

"Well speak up; this is an occasion."

"One of us should go over to his place and ask for more details."

"One of us?"

"Correct, and since I am a woman he is more likely to help me than he would be to help you. Am I on the right track?"

"Squarely. If you go, I can get on with the wood."

"And I shall arrange my timing so that it will be noon hour when I get there. Free lunch."

"Either that or you could go in the late afternoon and spend the night. Bed and breakfast."

"Plan aborted. There are going to be some plump and happy flies buzzing around here for the next few weeks." Both together: "A few flies never hurt nobody."

So the very next day Kevin built a rack, fired up a smudge underneath it, and began cutting meat into thin strips which he hung on the rack. The meat turned a sickly green at first, but as the heat and the smoke and the sun did their work, the strips turned black, curled up a bit and ended up looking as appetizing as the tongues cut from a pair of worn out hiking boots. To their amazement, when they boiled the finished product, it was not bad at all. In gratitude they said grace halfway through the meal:

Oh some hae meat and canna eat,
And some can eat that want it.
But we hae meat and we can eat,
So say the Lord bethankit.

In the whole episode Kevin did only one thing in which he could take real pride. On the night of the shooting just a she was falling asleep, he felt Joanne nudge him.

"What is it?" he asked, his voice blurred with sleep.

"Do you suppose it was the same one?"

"Was what the same one as which?"

"The deer. Was it the one I saw on that first day we came?"

Then he, the clumsy one, the usually inept and tactless, put his arms around her and drew her close. "I thought of that too, but when I studied the tracks I could see right away they were different from each other. This one had a more pointed hoof."

She wriggled even closer, putting her head on his shoulder, knowing he was lying, knowing that he knew she knew he was lying, and loving him for it.

"I couldn't bear it to have been the same one," she murmured. "The first one welcomed me here."

21

SITTING SIDESADDLE ON THE SAWHORSE, JOANNE WATCHED Kevin work. He had told her she was fulfilling a useful purpose by holding the log in place while he sawed, but the truth was he did not need her there. He found her presence something of a nuisance because he had to ask her to move each time he wanted to advance the log into position for the next block. Although she was supposed to realize that she should move each time a block fell off, she would start dreaming and miss the event.

"The stick's off," he would snap irritably.

"Sorry, I was just thinking—"

"That's just the trouble, you are thinking instead of paying attention."

"While you, my beloved, are so busy working, you don't do any thinking."

"Good, I'll stop. Then next winter when it is forty below, we'll try putting a couple of your thoughts on the fire. That ought to warm us up."

She could not understand where he got his energy and patience. Maybe she was just getting lazy. Getting up, doing a few household chores, and washing seemed to tire her out. Maybe it was a meat diet. If only the garden had been a success—if only—her mother used to say, "If wishes were horses the beggars would ride." What had they missed? What should they have done? Maybe they should not have spent their money on any food whatever; maybe they should have bought turkeys as she had planned. Ed had laughed—cursed rather—at her idea, yet there might have been some sense in it. Sometimes new ideas paid off. Turkeys laid eggs didn't they? One wouldn't have to sell the birds or the eggs; one could simply live off them.

Ed didn't know everything, surely. She dreamed of a plate with two fried eggs on it, all speckled with pepper, and a side order of toast droopy with butter. Ooh, with a pat of jam or a slice of cheese!

"The stick! The stick!"

Her mother always used to serve toast and jam for breakfast with a glass of milk. She had insisted that each child drank a quart of milk each day. "You are too thin," she would say, perhaps with a touch of jealousy. "I'll leave a quart in the icebox, and you drink it, every drop." Oh for a taste of that milk right now. Idea!

"Kevin," she burst out, startling him in mid-stroke. "I've got an idea."

He stopped sawing and stretched his back. "Next time you get one, sneak up on me with it; don't scare the hell right out of me. Out with it."

"We should get a cow."

"Mm hm. And a couple of riding ponies to drag Ed's democrat back to town. How about throwing in a brace of hogs while we are at it?"

"We would have milk; we could make cheese; we would have butter."

"Noble. Where will we get such a fertile beast?"

She stood up, all agog with her idea. "Maybe someone has one for sale. We could offer to pay for it on time..."

"With what? Marsh grass?"

"Don't be so wretchedly negative." Then, thinking it was no time to quarrel, she added placatingly, "Pessimistic, I mean. You can do some trapping come winter and pay it all off by spring."

Slipping the blade back into the saw cut, he sneered, "For God's sake, if you took a piece of cigarette paper and printed on it in block letters with a carpenter's pencil all I know about trapping, you would still have room for *War and Peace* unabridged."

"How can there be anything complicated about trapping? Everybody does it. You just bait the trap, set it and wait for some poor thing to dive into it, hook line and sinker."

"Really? And what would Joanne do when she saw a poor little muskrat all crunched and frozen in the trap?"

"Never mind that; I am not a heartless brute like some men I know. Just think about us having a cow."

Anxious for a rest anyway, he pulled the saw out of the cut and sat down beside her. "You know, I mentioned trapping to Ed, and he said, 'What makes y' think y' know anythin' about trappin? Tell me exactly how y'd go about trappin' a fox.' I answered just about the same way you did, except my phrasing was a little better worded than yours, naturally."

"Naturally. What was Ed's answer?"

"He said, 'Well, y'd not git too big a store of fur that way. What y' got to remember is, a fox never sets down t' eat unless he's sure he's safe. So he won't walk up t' a trap an' just help hisself, because first of all he's got t' make sure no harm is comin' his way. So what y'got t' do is bury th' bait all by itself at th' bottom of a valley. Then y'set a trap on th' top of every hill f'r a mile around. When Mr. Fox goes up th' hill and sets down t' check th' horizon, SNANG y'got him.'"

"Pure science. Now we know."

"All we need is about a hundred dollars worth of traps, not to mention bait."

"Turkeys could have been used for bait."

"Who said there were any foxes here anyway? Have you seen any?"

"Muskrats, then."

"Turkey to bait muskrats?"

"Wood."

"Wood for bait? Oh, I see, for woodpeckers."

"You have all these piles of wood all over the yard. Why not sell some of that? Trade, I mean."

"I thought we were talking about trapping."

"We were. Now we are talking about trading wood for a cow. Don't try to change the subject."

"With you one does not get time to change the subject as it is changed before one gets there."

"Yeah, that is because one is too slow. Now to continue, our nearest neighbours are the Johnstones. Let us try them. For all we know they may have enormous herds of cows eating them out of house and home that they are just dying to get rid of. We offer them wood."

"And since they have only one hundred and sixty acres of trees, wood would be the commodity they need the most."

Kevin resumed sawing, motioning her back to her post. His target was to cut a cord a day if it killed him. He would show Ed what a city boy could do.

"Listen," Joanne went on stubbornly, reseating herself, "please pay attention to me. I know it would be a good idea to at least try. Help me to think what we can do."

Exasperated, he stopped again. "You know very well..." Seeing her upturned face, he was ashamed of his asperity. "You know we don't have anything of any value that anyone would want."

"How about my sewing machine?"

He studied her face. "You might just have something there. But I thought you never wanted to part with it. Your mother..."

"Of course I don't want to part with it; it is the last thing I want to part with—present company excepted—but if it would give us a start, I would do anything."

"Well, it is worth thinking over."

"No it isn't," she bristled. "You always want to think things over and then nothing gets done. Let's try it before we change our minds. Besides, I don't want to do it—sell my machine—so it must be the right thing to do."

"Spoken like a true Christian. Stick!"

"Oh, God damn the stick," she shouted, jumping to her feet. "Do you know why I wanted out of Toronto?"

"Well, you said you wanted..."

"Because I didn't want to be somebody's servant, that's why, and I am not going to be yours either. Sit on your own bloody log."

"Go play in the bush," he answered, not too audibly. When she was angry, he knew better than to try her too far. She could easily go so far as to hit him with one of his sticks.

After she had flounced off—into the woods by a strange coincidence— he resumed his work and his musing. There was certainly enough feed around for a cow at least in the summer time, and he supposed he could cut it for the winter if he could borrow a scythe and learn how to use it. He had never put up hay in his life of course. Still, there could not be much to it if peasants could do it. All that was necessary was to cut it and stack it in a pile after letting it dry for awhile. It might be interesting, too, not wholly unlike cutting wood: rhythmical even though a bit monotonous.

Where would the poor cow stay in the winter time? Stable of course. Oh boy, he would have to try to build one. Yes, and that would turn out like the well he had dug. He was a useless tit if he ever saw one. About an hour later Joanne came back and sat down again, but not on the sawhorse.

"With butter," she resumed stubbornly, "we could fry things without them sticking to the pan. We could also have partridges boiled in milk— like pheasant, you know."

"I'm so sick of partridge I wouldn't like it even if it were boiled in burgundy."

"Pity. That's what we are having tonight."

"Can't I just drink the burgundy?"

"Come and sit beside me."

When he had obeyed, she slipped her arm through his, a gesture that always broke him down.

"Let's try it Kevin. Why don't you go to the Johnstones' tomorrow to try to make a deal?"

Looking uncomfortable, he cleared his throat nervously. "If we go, they may laugh at us, sneer at our ignorance. You know I am not very good at this bargaining business."

"Then I'll go alone."

He shook his head. "It's six miles."

"Some kids walk that far to school. I can do it easily, and I surely do not mind bargaining. I like dickering with people. After all, is that not what marriage is all about, each partner doing what she or he is best suited for?"

It was also true, he mused, that she would get a better reception than he would, she being a girl and a pretty one at that. A wave of relief flooded over him, followed by a backwash of self-contempt. "Maybe you could go one day and come back the next," he suggested weakly.

She hesitated, thinking of Froman: they could be real dirty people. "I don't know about that."

"Let's forget about it then." He would get on with the woodcutting. He had a long way to go yet, and no one could fault him for working. There was no use fighting with himself, he knew if she left it up to him there would never be a cow. She would just have to forget about it.

"I'll do it; I'll go. If I am too tired, I will stay the night—if asked—even if they are dirtier than old Froman."

"I always said you made too much fuss about cleanliness anyway." He would jolly her a bit, make her laugh. What he could not forget was that she was going to do something that was really his responsibility.

"Right you are, I've washed my last pot." She would jolly him a bit, make him laugh, make him forget he was letting her do what was his duty. "Too bad we don't have a dog to lick them clean like they use to have in Irishmen's shanties."

He looked at her. She looked at him. Then without exchanging a word they burst into the same song:

> Have you ever been into
> An Irishman's shanty,
> Where money was scarce
> And whiskey was plenty.
> A three-legged stool
> And a table to match it,
> And the door of the shanty
> Was locked with a hatchet.

Joyfully he scooped her up and deposited her back on the sawhorse. Her fragility sobered him.

"Honey, you are made out of dried twigs and tossed cotton. Where is the meat that was on your bones?" As he set her down he lifted her chin and kissed her, a gesture so rare she burst into tears.

"Did you ever think you might be pregnant?" he asked anxiously.

"Many times. But I am not."

"Are you sure?"

"Of course I am sure. Do you ever look at our clothes line?"

"What's that got to—ugh, oh..."

"What on earth made you think such a thing?"

He shrugged. "Oh, nothing. It is just that you are kind of skinny, that's all."

"Pregnant women get big and fat. Haven't you heard?"

"Well," he mumbled, "they are fat later on, but sometimes thinner at first before they start packing on the bacon."

"Oh sweetheart, how delicately you put that," she said, standing up and adjusting the belt of her skirt.

"I am not about to pack on the bacon. Or pack in the bacon, unfortunately."

By this time he had picked up the saw and resumed the slow easy motion that had become so natural to him. Joanne felt like screaming at him to stop. She would even hear him at night.

When she lay in bed and shut her eyes, she would see the blade easing forward and back, forward and back, now pushing a trickle of sawdust, now pulling back with a thinner spill, while in her head she could hear the "shish, shish" going on forever.

Pausing to inspect the blade, he said, "You know the Johnstones just might have a cow to spare, and they might need a sewing machine."

"Ed said they had about two dozen kids, and that they were a bit shiftless."

"There you are; that's why they had so many kids: they went too often shiftless to bed. Get it?"

She got it.

Left to himself Kevin went on with the self torture. If he went on the errand and was rebuffed, it would stay with him forever. He would automatically hate the people. If he let his wife go in his place he would probably be the laughingstock of the community. He eased the log forward to begin another cut, cringing from past humiliations: asking the teacher if he could leave the room and she ridiculing him in front of the class because he had not gone at recess time; holding himself too long and wetting himself at the desk because he would not ask again, and the kids roaring with laughter when they saw the pool spreading across the floor. There was the time that he took a list of groceries to the store and was turned away in front of the other customers as his father's bill was "too high already"—with other shoppers watching. It made him cringe to think of these things, but they had happened and he could not erase them from his mind. Unconsciously he began to saw faster.

Joanne passed the evening and most of the night in a state of high excitement. In a way she dreaded going in case she encountered dirt and squalor, yet she was entranced with the thought of meeting people again. The idea of the long walk through the forest frightened her, but the picture of her return journey leading a cow more than made up for it—provided they would let her have the cow before she handed over her sewing machine. It would hurt her to lose the machine as it was her prize possession and it had belonged to her mother. Still, if parting with it meant not having to leave their place to go looking for work or staying here alone while Kevin went to work, it would be a small sacrifice to make.

Sometime after midnight she awoke and lay there for awhile too excited to get back to sleep again. Quite apart from the material advantage of having a cow, it would be so nice to have a living creature with them, although she would have preferred a cat or a dog, or even a baby. There would be no baby by the look of things, and she should thank God for that. Anyway, any animal they had would have to pay its way.

Thinking of fecundity, if the cow were bred when they got her, there would be a calf in the spring, a black ungainly creature with wobbly legs and knobbed knees. She decided she would call it Lucy if it were a female, or Lucifer if it were a male. Delighted with her choice, which she felt was most appropriate for the male, she fell to sleep.

22

FOR JOANNE THE WALK TO THE JOHNSTONES' PLACE WAS A welcome change. At first, fearful of every sound, she had been tempted to turn back, but once she had crossed the meadow and had reached the higher ground where they had harvested their first dandelions, the sun dappled the road through the leafy poplars, filling her with joy. The day was warm and bright, the road surprisingly smooth underfoot, and the breezes gentle on her face.

In one place where the wagons had cut deeply into the roadway, she saw a squirrel running towards her in the canyon of a rut, its feet pattering on dead leaves leftover from the fall. Crouching down, she carefully extended her hands, held perfectly still, and let the little animal run right into her grasp. For a second she held its softly pulsing body, rejoicing in the life of it, until for fear it would bite, she let it go and watched it skitter up a spruce tree, chittering with outrage.

"You're lucky I wasn't a lynx," she called after it. "You'd better watch where you are going."

Hearing her own voice, sudden in the silence, subdued her and she hurried on.

After the first half hour she began to grow tired, feeling her legs go cotton under her. Since she did not really know the road, she had no idea how far she had come or how far she still had to go. Every few minutes she looked anxiously at the sun, feeling irrationally it would drop out of sight and leave her there in twilight in unknown country with strange and possibly savage creatures all around her. Why, she thought wretchedly, she had even forgotten matches though she had remembered to bring the twenty-two.

Kevin could at least have come with her, she thought, even if he didn't have the courage to do the talking on arrival. Nevertheless she knew how he felt. If he had come, he could scarcely have left the bargaining to her. The only reasonable way out was the one he had taken: stay home and wait. Sometimes she was infuriated by his timidity when it came to dealing with people, his stubborn pride, his terror of losing face—such thoughts were disloyal. Where on earth could she ever find anyone as kind and gentle as he was, even if he was irritable at times.

Late in the afternoon she reached the Johnstones' place, a house much bigger than her own, built of half-burned logs, and almost hidden amongst a grove of trees far back from the road. Why anyone would choose to build in such a flat, shut-in area when there were such spectacular knolls around, she could not imagine. If it were she and she had a choice, she would have constructed it on the highest hill with all the countryside stretched out at its base, so that when she lifted a window her spirit could go out like the dove at Ararat.

At her approach, a covey of children looked up and scattered like baby partridges into the willows. Two lanky dogs with benign faces bellowed a welcome and came scampering around her, almost bowling her over with their enthusiastic tails.

"Get down," she ordered shakily. "Calm down and shut up until I know you better."

A huge woman with straggly grey hair, weathered skin and enormous breasts came to the door to gaze at Joanne with amazement. "Well, where on earth did you drop from?" she asked in astonishment. As she spoke, she absent-mindedly tucked her breasts back under her housedress, where they hung precariously before working their way out again to peer at the visitor with dumb brown eyes. Joanne concluded they had been drawn out so often to feed hungry mouths, they felt more at home out than in.

"I'm Joanne McCormack," she offered timidly, "from The Spruces."

"Aren't you the tiny little soul to be living away back there in the bush! Come in and welcome. My name is Annie, as Ed probably told you already. He told us you folks had moved back there and we intended to call, but it's a long walk for me and the little kids, and we dare not leave them here alone because you never know what can happen or what they might do. Don't dare. They are good kids, mind, but you can't tell what they might be up to on their own. The Cord family near to town went to a dance one time—just one time—left the oldest in charge and the door locked from the outside, poor little things. It was chinooking when they left—warm— while they were dancing, the weather changed just like that the way it does in this country. They figure the oldest boy he tried to light the stove with coal oil—they were Catholics—place burned to the ground with those poor little mites in it—to death. So I said to Mannie—my husband—we'll never leave ours alone not even for a minute—not that we were likely to go to too many dances anyway—not even for a minute. Of course you don't have any kids yet do you? How in the world could you, you such a wee bit of a thing—justa baby yourself. Ed said you were a real looker, and you sure are real pretty."

The house seemed enormous to Joanne, who already had grown accustomed to their tiny cabin. Along one wall, but moved out enough for benches, stood a long, rough board table. There was a kitchen cabinet with a high back for dishes and supplies, a truly huge wrought-iron stove with silver trim and the word "Queenie" engraved on a plaque on the oven door, a wood-box—empty—and a washstand above which hung a well-used though clean-looking towel. The floor, which must have been built with green lumber, had shrunk, leaving chasms between boards, chasms that mud, water and tramping feet had filled with solid material. Near the stove stood a gasoline drum which, to judge by the tin dipper hanging from its side, was meant for water. In one corner a bitch with wistful eyes submitted passively to the onslaught of six puppies.

Mrs. Johnstone looked her visitor over with candid eyes. "If you aren't the prettiest little thing I've ever seen. But you're all skin and bone. Rabbit meat sure isn't much for fattening a person, although it sure doesn't thin me down any. Watch you don't fall right between the slats on that chair. There should be lots over there in that swamp area. A terrible thing happens to the rabbits every once in awhile, you know, every seven years they say—they get a disease, blister up, die by the thousands. What most people don't know is they are cannibals, eat each other's bodies. Mannie told me that. One comes along, a sick one, eats a bit of bark and dies and then along comes another and eats a bit of him and then he dies and pretty soon there is a great pile of them—sickening thing." She paused, took a deep breath and yelled, "Mannie! Mannie! Where is that man? Excuse me for yelling, but he's so darned quiet I feel I have to speak louder to make up for him. Is your husband quiet too?"

"Sometimes. Other times he talks too much."

"I wish Mannie would talk. He used to, but he quit. I don't know why."

Mannie, a tall, gangling man whose body was a loose assembly of bones and skin, shambled into the room and came forward, stroking his mustache in embarrassment. When she shook his hand, Joanne was surprised that he did not rattle.

"Mannie, this is Mrs. McCormack visiting from The Spruces. Don't shake her hand too hard or she'll fly apart she's so dainty. I'll make some tea for supper and you'll have it with us. You look as if a bowl of spuds would do you a world of good. Do you like spuds?"

"Yes I surely do," Joanne answered, thinking: vegetables at last.

"We don't have a spud in the house, more's the pity. We lost our garden in the big rain. No garden."

"So did we. It just washed away."

"And small wonder over where you are. I asked Mannie to put in another garden at the end of the first rain—didn't I, Mannie?—but he held off, and he was right all along, it wouldn't have come to anything anyway. It would have been a sinful waste of time, because it would have washed out in the second rain."

Throughout the conversation Mannie stood grinning at Joanne, not once taking his eyes off her, his only movement an occasional tug at his mustache.

He has the wet mouth of a born lecher, she thought. What we have here is a passionate walrus. En garde!

Annie galloped to the stove to clatter the lid from a pot and stir briskly. She seemed to have forgotten all about the proffered tea, or else she meant to serve it with supper. Forgetting to put the lid back on, she loped back to her guest. "You'll have some supper with us even though it isn't much: just rabbit stew. Thank God for rabbits."

Cannibal soup, her guest mused, looking about with a careful eye now that food was in question. No chance here to get away with a few slurping sounds. If the food was obscene it would still have to go down the pipe. You are for it my girl. She was however relieved to see that although the house was untidy, it did not appear to be particularly dirty. Whereas a few months before she would have been appalled, she now found it so much better than she had expected she felt almost at ease.

While talking, Annie clattered onto the bare table a seemingly endless row of bowls, cups and spoons; nothing else; no plates, no saucers, no salt shaker, no pepper, no bread, and—Joanne's face fell—no milk.

"You are the first woman we've seen in this house since Mannie's sister came—that was last year, wasn't it Mannie?—and it just does my heart good. A person gets fearfully lonely for someone to talk to. Mannie never talks, do you Mannie?"

Whether it was an attempt to prove her wrong, or just a timing coincidence, Mannie chose that moment to open the door and call in a squeaky voice, "Supper!"

In a moment the children filed in, one after another, in a queue that looked as if it would not end. The final total fell somewhat short of Ed's estimate of thirty-four, but there were eight, and the oldest looked as if that was his age. Each child stopped at the wash stand, dabbled in the water, touched his cheeks with wet fingers, wiped his hands on the towel and trooped to the table, where he sat motionless, looking at but not speaking to their guest.

Mannie took his place at the end of the table, still grinning at Joanne, his mustache wetter than ever. Annie swung the pot from the stove and slowly moving down the table, poured a ladleful of its contents into each bowl. Then she returned the pot to the stove and with the teapot made a second round.

"This tea isn't very strong," she apologized. "You see we have to use the leaves three times over. 'Waste not, want not, pick it up and eat it'. There isn't any milk or sugar either."

So ends my cow, Joanne despaired.

"You come forward now, Mrs. McCormack, and sit right here by me. That's the girl. Now, Mannie, you say Grace like a good man."

"Jesus bless this grub," he squeaked, and all hands fell to.

Joanne tasted gingerly. The word "stew" was an exaggeration; it was nothing but meat and water, rabbit meat. Better not to think about it. How, she wondered, does one simulate gusto without slurping, which is a bit too obvious under present circumstances?

No one asked for or was offered a second helping. As each child came to the end of his noisy bowl, he would lean forward, seize his cup, gulp the contents, and then sit back and wait. When the last child had finished, they cried with one voice, "May we be 'scused?" and at their father's nod they arose and filed out of the house.

"My goodness, they are well behaved," Joanne remarked. "How did you ever train them to be like that?"

"I don't really know. We never had any trouble with them, ever, and we never laid a hand on them. They all took after Mannie, and that's a mercy because he's so quiet himself. Can't say they took after me, although it would have been nice if one had—a girl to be friends with—one that talked. You don't know how much I have wanted one. When I saw you coming up the road there, I said to myself, 'Here she is all grown up, but exactly what I wanted—pretty and friendly.' I think you should stay with us. But there you can't have everything. I don't complain—do I Mannie? Not very much. We never lost a baby either at birth or through sickness. God has been kind to us. Touch wood."

Taking advantage of a moment's silence, Joanne blurted out the purpose of her visit, "I came over to see if maybe you had a cow for sale—or trade, I mean."

Mannie stroked his mustache while Annie slowly shook her head.

"Dear to goodness, no. We don't have a cow on the place anymore. The first year, and up until last year, we had at least one, off and on. In the beginning we had no time to build a proper stable or cut feed. We kept old Floss in a dugout for awhile—it was a fierce cold winter—we kept her alive by digging through the snow and pulling dead grass, but some disease took her off."

"The disease," Mannie squeaked, "was flat belly."

"We had other cows and they would survive the winter, then come spring they would die after the grass came back. I could never figure that one out. Why did they want to die after the worst was over?"

"What about milk for the kids?"

"They don't seem to need it anymore. When they were little, like I said, we always had milk off and on. Seems about the time a new baby arrived we got a new cow that would see the baby through when my milk ran out, and before she up and died. As for Mannie and I, we did what the Arabs do for whisky: without. Cows are awfully expensive, and times have been bad. Often I told Mannie we should go back where we came from, but he just waited. I'm blessed if he wasn't right again, what with all those poor families being burned out by the drought and exploited by the easterners—if we had gone back, we would likely be in poverty right now instead of just hard up. Sometimes I think Mannie and the Lord work hand in hand even though he doesn't go around preaching the gospel or any of that kind of thing, or even go to church for that matter."

If those two are working together, Joanne mused, it will be God who does the lion's share.

Later on as she was helping with the dishes, she listened to the babble from Annie's lips, aware of Mannie's eyes following her every move. She felt bitter disappointment about the cow. Wearied through and through, all she wanted was to get out and go home even though Annie was so very kind to her. If only she would shut up for a little while. From a great distance she heard Annie exclaim, "Mannie, she's passed right out. Poor little thing—pregnant as sure, and her so narrow in the hips—bring the dish rag quick!"

Slowly Joanne returned to consciousness and to an overwhelming sense of peace. Feeling Annie mopping at her face with the dish cloth, she raised herself to a sitting position, murmuring, "What happened to me?"

"You just keeled over like an old pine tree, that's all. You've worn yourself out—I knew that skin and bone meant something. When will your time be up?"

"My time? Why does everyone try to make me pregnant?" Quickly she rephrased it, "Why does everyone want to think I'm pregnant. I am not pregnant!"

"Well then"—obviously disappointed—"you are just worn out from walking and too much excitement. Now you listen to old Annie, you are going upstairs to bed."

"But Kevin—my husband—he'll be expecting me. He'll think the coyotes got me."

"Coyotes never got anybody, honey. They're the scaredest little things you ever saw. Mannie, you go on over to her place and tell her husband not to worry. You can stay the night and bring him over in the morning. You get along now."

Joanne was in a box: if she insisted on going home, Mannie would be assigned to go with her, and then there would be more than coyotes to worry about. She would have to do what she was told and stay the night. In spite of herself, she started to cry. "I'm a boo-suck," she wailed.
"There, there now, you don't need to cry, you'll be with old Annie. I'll take care of you."

Mannie ambled out the door after pausing to kiss his wife wetly on the lips while she held his mustache with both hands.

"Get along with you now and bring that man of hers back in the morning." Coming back to her guest, "If we had a horse we could ride you home, but the horse is long dead now—fell down in the field and couldn't get up. Mannie had to shoot him, poor thing. There seems to be a hex on animals around this place. Except for dogs; they do all right. We came here by car and it's still outside there—what's left of it. Mannie's been taking pieces of it to town to sell although he never seems to get much for them." She disappeared out the door and came back with a ladder made of spruce poles which she stood against the end wall under a trap door in the ceiling.

"Come on now, here are your stairs. You scramble up and I will follow in case you get weak again and try to fall down, but we better be careful because even though Mannie built it the darn thing comes apart sometimes. I don't know how often he's fixed it. Push up on the trap door — that's the way. Now here is the bedroom. I'll put the lamp here where it won't tip."

"I wondered where you slept." The bedroom was simply the space under the roof, without any partitions, windows or side walls. The only furniture was a bed with a tumble of grey blankets on it, an apple box on its side for a bedside table, and at the far end a pile of hay.

"Now," Annie said, "I'll just fix this bed up for you. I could lie about it and tell you the sheets are still on the line, but you wouldn't believe me anyway. There are no sheets; they all wore out a long time ago, and I had to tear one up to make—you know—sanitary napkins. I'm sorry."

"I wanted to ask you about that—I was sort of shy."

"No need to be shy with me. Have you any flour sacks?"

"That's what I've been using. We had one bag. They're awful. Isn't there something better?"

"Well, the Indians use moss I'm told. Hop in now. You swear you really are not pregnant?"

"No, really not. Cross my heart and hope to die."

"Maybe it is just as well. You go to sleep now like a good little girl. You don't need to worry about a thing: there are no bugs here. We aren't very tidy, but we are clean. Put your head down and go to sleep. It's so nice to have a girl in the house—I wanted one so bad you know. If you have to go to the toilet, use that pot over there. I'll empty it now and get one of the boys to bring it bac kup."

"Where will you sleep?"

"Don't you worry your head about that. I'll fix a place downstairs."

Too tired to protest, Joanne lay down and mercifully fell asleep. Once, it must have been late in the evening, she was disturbed by confused noises and awakened briefly to the unforgettable sight of a host of little Johnstones burrowing fully clothed into the pile of hay. Downstairs she could hear Annie talking to the dogs—all sounds distorted by sleepiness and homesickness, tempered with a sense of well-being in response to Annie's kindness.

23

THE TWO HUSBANDS ARRIVED AT EIGHT O'CLOCK THE NEXT morning. Kevin had come in such haste his companion was on the point of collapse, staggering through the door to sink into his chair in a deeper silence than when he had left home the day before. Several times he dozed off, but each time he would jerk awake, his eyes fixed on Joanne.

Scarcely taking time to acknowledge Annie's greeting, Kevin went straight to his wife and took her hands in his, too shy to be more demonstrative.

"What happened?"

"Nothing new or spectacular; I just fainted, that's all. Ladies used to do that all the time."

"Even ladies don't faint for nothing. They had to be too tightly corseted up at least."

"It wasn't for nothing—things were just pressing in on me: I was disappointed about there being no cow. I don't know why I fainted."

"The walk wore her out," Annie suggested. "She's just a little bit of a thing, thin as a rail, and it was too much for her in her condition."

"Condition!"

"She doesn't mean that kind of condition," Joanne reassured him. "I am in no kind of condition."

"I just meant she is skinny and run down," Annie apologized. "She was just standing there talking—I think—and all of a sudden she just sort of slid away. When I had the flu three winters ago the same thing happened to me. Plunk down I would go and there was Mannie frightened out of his skin wondering what ailed me. 'It's nothing,' I told him. Maybe it was something Joanne ate."

"More likely something she didn't eat. She probably has partridge fever: too much partridge and not enough vegetables."

"Rabbits," said Annie. "You had better try rabbits. There is more nourishment in one rabbit than in a whole flock of partridges Mannie says, don't you Mannie?"

Mannie did not say.

"Come and have breakfast, you men. Your wives have already eaten."

Kevin was introduced to the stew pot and the recycled tea.

"Mannie, why don't you take Kevin out to see the farm while we do the dishes?" Annie suggested, busily gathering up the bowls.

"Nothing to see."

"Well now, there isn't too much to see at that; the man is right again. I guess you two have seen your share of bushes and trees at your place, though this place is a bit better than your own—even if I say it who shouldn't—yours is all swamp pretty near. Why in goodness name did you settle there?"

Kevin answered uneasily, "They told me there was a house on it and..."

"They are a bunch of government easterners to tell you a thing like that. Why it is just a trapper's cabin and they said it was a house—letting innocent people get sucked in like that! Still you have to forgive your enemies the way the Bible tells you too. Those clerks never get out of their chairs long enough to see what a place is like. Town people! If the government was any good, they'd give those plush jobs to men like Mannie who really knows the country inside out. You'd make them sit up and take notice, wouldn't you Mannie?"

Mannie was already sitting up and taking notice—of Joanne.

The McCormacks left before dinner, partly out of the desire to be home and also out of the desire not to face anymore rabbit stew. At the door Annie put her arms around Joanne, hugging her with real affection. "You be careful now," she began, and astonished herself by starting to cry.

"Now look who's blubbering," Joanne teased, blubbering herself. "Thank you for being so kind to me. I am sorry you didn't have a cow for sale, but it has been a lovely visit."

"Aren't we a pair now? Remember you've a long hard winter ahead of you. Oh, something I forgot: have you any jars for preserving?"

"No we..."

"Mannie, get those jars from the shed. They are no use to me at all. We have dozens of them, but the kids eat the fruit as fast as it comes in the house so there is nothing left to can. You could maybe put down some saskatoons if you can find some."

"None left," Mannie squeaked.

"None left! Where did they go?"

"Traded to that guy passing through. Twenty-two shells."

"Well we needed shells; I can't deny that. I'm sorry, Joanne. Everything I do seems to go wrong, but we still have our health unless Mannie has traded some of that too. The man is ingenious."

"Good-bye and thank you again for your kindness. I am sorry about the jars, but we will make out."

"Never mind a few old jars. I wish you were going to stay with me for good. I wish you were my daughter."

In spite of their disappointment about the cow, the McCormacks started for home in a happy mood; Joanne, because she was on her way back to her own place, and Kevin because nothing had happened to her.

As soon as they were on the road he said, "Have I ever got a surprise for you!"

"Good or bad?"

"Good, of course; otherwise I wouldn't tell you."

"Come on then, out with it."

"You will just have to wait until we get home, and don't try to weasel it out of me because it won't do any good."

"You found a cow."

"Be reasonable, I am not a magician."

"You started to dig another well."

"You can't guess. You'll just have to wait."

"I don't want to know anyway; so there. By the way, what did you think of them?"

"The Johnstones?"

"No, the prime minister and his followers."

"She was very kind to you, Mrs. Sarcasm."

"That she was, bless her. They are even worse off than we are in some ways. They eat nothing but boiled rabbits, they have no cows or horses, they lost their garden, and they don't even have beds for the kids."

"Cut it out."

"Gospel. The kids just burrow into a pile of hay like little squirrels."

Kevin grinned. "I am not sure that squirrels do burrow in the hay. You can't be serious."

"Never more so in my life. I saw them. They don't even undress."

"He looks like a lazy devil, old Mannie."

"Not so much lazy as discouraged."

"Neither lazy nor discouraged in bed apparently. He looks horny to me, just plain hog-out horny. Did you see the way he stared at you and licked those lecherous lips?"

"I saw. I don't think he meant anything by it though; he just isn't used to seeing other women."

Kevin snorted. "All I can say is—and I may live to regret this—if ever you see me looking at another woman the way he looks at you, you had better get the rifle out."

"Why the rifle? I could do what needed to be done with the butcher knife and save ammunition."

"With me on the dead run?"

Faltering at the end of the third mile, Joanne called time out. In a little clearing by the roadside she sank down, and there, lying on her back, in a bliss of fatigue, she looked up into the deep blue of the sky. She found that with her face in shadow the sky changed from a blue-black abyss into a sea filled with a thousand swimming things. The air that normally seemed so pure was troubled with flying tufts of cotton, wispy threads of silk, nameless white spots, and—incredibly—a spider riding a fragment of web torn away by the wind. She slept.

Not having the heart to awaken her, Kevin kept watch by her side until quite late in the afternoon. Lying there in the sun, Joanne looked so fragile it worried him. Of course he had noticed before how thin she was, but he had not been particularly concerned about it, reasoning that anyone would lose weight on an almost strictly meat diet. He had noticed that whenever she was away from him for a few hours she always looked smaller than when he saw her again. This time he would swear that she was smaller.

At four o'clock feeling he could wait no longer, he put his arms around her and called her name. Instead of waking, she stirred, smiled a broken smile and went on sleeping. Something in Kevin's chest burst, filling him with remorse and an overwhelming sense of responsibility. It was not enough to love somebody, one had to cherish and care for the one he loved. God knew he had cherished her, but he had not cared for her enough perhaps. Yet what had he not done that he could or should have done?

A little later she awoke and smiled again. "I had such a lovely dream."

"What was it?"

"We were in some beautiful place together—in a forest—the sun was shining and we had fruit, great red apples that we were gathering to put in bottles."

"Now where do you suppose that dream came from? I'm the one who should have dreamed of bottles; my arms would have been two inches longer by now if Mannie hadn't sold them. By the way, do you suppose he really traded them for ammunition?"

"What else would he have traded them for?"

"Moonshine, of course."

"Do you think he drinks?"

"Nothing else could make a man so lethargic?"

"I thought boozers were hot to trot."

"Only when on the intake; the aftermath is one of torpor."

"You speaking from experience?"

"You know better than that. Here, let me help you up."

"Let's not overdo the invalid bit. I am as fit as a fiddle now. Annie was right; those rabbits are a powerhouse of energy."

As they drew near their homestead they could see the house snug amongst the trees, waiting for them. The piles of wood, the sawhorse, the axe driven into the chopping block, all seemed dearly familiar.

Joanne—feeling she had been away at least a month—took Kevin's hand. "Can you believe I cried the first time I saw this place?"

"You feel like crying now?"

"I feel like shouting with joy. Tonight you will play the mouth organ in the moonlight."

"No moon."

"Don't be a killjoy."

"I'll play by starlight, how's that?"

"Better. This is the first time I have come home to this place after being away overnight."

"Don't say you never get out. I did take you all the way to Froman's."

"Oh, that was just for part of a day, a few hours."

"How does it feel?"

"It feels like home, what more can I say?"

"I know, that was the way I felt when I came back from town with the horse."

"I could eat the face off that horse right now."

"Oh, that's too bad; I was going to offer you some fresh venison."

"Don't I wish I had some."

"We have," he said casually.

She studied his face for a second, "This is no time for jokes. What you have here is a starving lady who has eaten nothing but two bowls of rabbit stew for..."

"Come," he ordered, leading the way to their tree platform. "Behold."

It was stacked with fresh meat.

She said, "I'm blessed. Did Mannie get it?" She bit her lip and added, "Fox paw."

"No, Mannie did not get it; I did. Believe it or not, it came right up behind me while I was sawing wood. All I had to do was go in quietly, pick up the rifle, and shoot." He hesitated. "It wasn't much of a shot. Point blank as a matter of fact."

Recovering confidence, he did a little jig. "One shot! Me! Old boar's tit himself!"

"I can't leave this place for a minute..."

"And that isn't all: this time, if I get at it tomorrow, I will do the smoking. Mannie gave me some new ideas—fired up my ambition."

"Now you are taxing credibility. The man can't talk."

"He can't, eh? Sometime I want you to get him away from Annie's crossfire and he'll talk the leg off you."

"There is still something does not match up: if he knows how to smoke meat, why doesn't he do it at his own place?"

"Says he prefers rabbits. Rabbits can be snared—by the kids of course—so he doesn't have to do it. It's a cinch for him; the kids do all the skinning and cutting up, and there is no need to smoke the meat because they catch a meal at a time. In the winter if a moose or deer comes knocking at the door like they do here, he may condescend to shoot it. In the winter, you see, the meat freezes and there is no need to smoke it. It is called rolling with the seasons. Mannie is not lazy, he just leans on the side of efficiency."

"Falls. Leaning would take effort."

"He apparently conserves his energy for under blanket maneuvers."

"At which he has a great measure of success."

Although his preparations for smoking the meat made for a smoother operation than Joanne's had been, the problems were a little more severe. This was now fly season and all through the process he battled swarms of small houseflies with sticky legs, and bloated blowflies whose insolence enraged him. He made no mention to his wife of the times he had to wash fly-blows off the meat, nor did he tell her of his suspicion that some of the meat, towards the end of the job, was already on the turn as he cut it into strips. The whole process was hateful to him, and he resented the time taken away from his wood sawing.

The evening the last of the meat was processed they sat, or rather crouched, around the fire holding a counsel of war.

"We might as well face it," Kevin began, "we won't be having flour, beans, other vegetables or milk this winter. We have the smoked meat, and later on, with any luck at all we may get another deer or even a moose. By that time it will be cold enough to keep it without smoking it. In the meantime we can go on nibbling on whatever greens or berries we can dig up. After that?"

"Don't forget I plan to dry a few berries if it can be done without sugar. We just have to get vegetables somehow. Or can we survive on meat alone?"

"Scurvy."

"What did Cartier and his boys do?"

"Spruce tea at the end after most of them had kicked the bucket. Spruce tea—I don't even know what it is. Boiled gum? Horrible! At least he had the Indians to advise him."

"Any hope of scaring up an Indian? What about the Johnstones? They seem to be surviving."

"I don't know about that," Kevin mused. "They are on rabbits right now, but for how long have they been in that shape? I get the idea that things have just gradually gotten worse for them, and they haven't paid the piper yet."

Without consciously doing so, he drew a sketch of a house on the ground with what they called "the stoking stick."

"As I see it, here are our alternatives: stay here and take a chance on starving: go into town together and look for work; try for relief; or beg my father to cough up a dollar or two. Does that about sum it up?"

Neither spoke for a few minutes, each running through the familiar questions in silence. Eventually Joanne stood up straight, gathered a few sticks of wood, threw them on the fire and resumed her place.

"First of all," she began, "let us look around us. There is old Froman, who is three times our age, surviving nicely, although I suspect he has more money than he knows what to do with. The Johnstones, as you pointed out, are hanging on there with a battalion of children. All we have to worry about is ourselves, and we are young. To answer your four-point summary, we really have no problem at all in making a decision because taking one still leaves the other three options open if we fail. I say we stay right here and do the best we can. If things don't work out, we can try one of your other choices. All we have to do is make sure we have a happy time."

"Just one thing, we must not get caught here in a situation where we can't get out if we have to. Above all we can not let ourselves run down to a point where, like Mannie's cows, we die of flat belly. You are already pretty skeletal."

"If things don't work out, as I was saying, can you bite the bitter bullet? Can you beg for relief or grovel for your father's favour? Are you capable of doing that?"

"For myself, no. But I will do anything on earth if it is the only way to save you. Anyway, that was quite a speech. Let us hang on, then, as long as we can. You have said just what I hoped you would say."

"Just one last word before we have our singsong by the fire. Being here is not a sacrifice for me; it is a joy. Remember that. This is the happiest time of my life. Now get that mouth organ."

The next morning Kevin returned to his sawhorse.

24

ON THE FIRST DAY OF SEPTEMBER, JUST AS SUMMER WAS DRIFTING into autumn, eighteen inches of heavy wet snow crushed down on the unprepared land. Deciduous trees bent low under the weight, arched into a praying stance, or in some cases came crashing to the earth, while the evergreens became, in a few hours, old-fashioned Christmas cards. The meadow, normally a rolling sea of hummocks, smoothed into a tundra region, white and still.

Summer birds, not yet ready for migration and caught by the sudden cold, flocked to every available shelter. They huddled under the spruce trees whose low, curving branches formed a natural tent, under the eaves of the house—wherever there was a trace of warmth—and there they died by the dozens, miserable little bundles of feathers quickly brushed over with snow.

It was the McCormacks' first taste of a northern winter and its sudden impact frightened them. The abrupt plunge from summer was as unbelievable as it was unexpected. When he came out on the first morning, Kevin blessed the time he had spent on the woodpiles, thinking how much more difficult it would be to try and find wood when the snow really came down.

From the storm he learned one lesson, and relearned a second: one, that his clothing was totally inadequate for cold weather; two, that in the future he must be doubly sure to put away his tools at night or he would lose them under the snow. Shivering in his summer weight windbreaker, he took over an hour to find the axe where he had dropped it the night before instead of driving it into the chopping block as was his custom. In searching he very nearly panicked. What if he could not find it at all? How would he spilt kindling or what if he had misjudged and there was still not enough wood for the winter? That was a sobering thought.

Coming in from the cold, he stamped the snow from his feet at the door, put the axe in the corner, and in a sudden burst of light-heartedness, danced Joanne around the room. Far from depressing him, the cold and the new problems it brought invigorated him, filled him with new ambition. He felt that the waiting was over and the real battle had been joined.

"Let me go, you idiot," Joanne cried, pretending to be angry. "What have you got to be joyful about? Methought you would come in all trembly and full of dire warnings."

" I found the axe, for Caesar's sake. I feel good because winter is here and I am full of beans."

"You are a tad late for that, the beans ran out sometime ago, remember?"

" So they did. I nearly lost the axe—forgot to put it in the block."

"Now it wants to live in the house, I see."

" You are lucky the saw hasn't moved. Fortunately for us it hangs very conveniently on the sawhorse in plain sight where it belongs."

"As long as someone remembers to hang it there."

"I'll remember now all right. A scalded cat fears hot water."

"Then why not remember to leave the axe in the chopping block. This is a house, not a tool shed."

"But. . ."

"But me no buts as Mother used to say."

"All right, all right. This establishment is sliding into female domination. I'll take the damn thing out, and then I'll go live with old Froman."

"I never saw an axe in his house unless it was covered with tobacco juice in a corner somewhere."

"Do you think winter is here to stay?"

"Nobody told us it would come like this without warning. Summer is supposed to drift into the autumn. You know the poem:

'As imperceptibly as grief
the summer lapsed away,
Too imperceptible, at last,
To seem like perfidy.'"

"Where is the imperceptibility, I ask you?"

"Precisely. Winter coming at this time is just about as perfidious as you could hope for."

"And what would a psychiatrist say of a dream, 'How do you feel about it?'"

"'Cribbed, cabin bound, confined. . .' and desperately short of warm clothes. The jacket is like a handkerchief, and my feet are soaking wet." He lifted her high in the air, set her down on the bed, took a place at her side, and began taking off his oxfords which were, indeed, soaked through. "First of all, I'm going to shoot some unhappy beast whose hide will make me a pair of moccasins something like yours except mine will go right up to my knees. Also we will have to make me a windbreaker. How are you at tanning hides?"

"There are times when I wouldn't mind tanning yours. But apart form that little operation, I wouldn't know where to start."

"Or stop, for that matter. When you were going to school, why didn't you take courses suitable to wilderness living? You wasted too much times on things like the three 'R's', nasty paws?"

"Is that so? Well, you get the hides and I will hit them with my sewing machine, and then you will see where my real talents lie."

"Don't count your stitches before they are sewed."

"The sewing is the easy part. You will have to shoot, skin, scrape, and chew away at the end product to make it flexible."

"You got that part of it wrong; it is the Eskimo wives who make the moccasins."

The cold spell lasted for three days. On the fourth day the sun came out and the snow disappeared almost as quickly as it had fallen, leaving the meadow grass flattened like licked fur. The creek burst into timid life briefly, and then subdued. Day after day the sky remained a clear, deep blue, with never a cloud sailing across it. At night the moon rode silently, flooding the swamp with silver light. It was an Indian summer, the loveliest time of the year.

On those nights when the moon was at or near its fullest, from away across the forest in the direction of Froman's place came, on several occasions, the sound of gunshots, an ironic link with civilization.

Now as the nights grew colder and the flies were gone, they reasoned that their meat would keep without drying it. Kevin resolved therefore to devote his whole time to hunting. By now he realized that he would never see animals by stumbling at random through the trees. Not only would the noise scare everything away, but also the law of averages was against his being in the right place at the right time unless he kept reappearing at the right place. Each morning at six he arose, dressed, took the rifle and followed a fixed route through the swamp in a circle that led across their own homestead to the adjacent one, and eventually made its way back to the starting point. On each sortie he made little marks on the trees so that he would always be able to follow the same route. Soon he grew to love these early morning excursions with the sounds of the forest all around him: snow birds picking at the trees, squirrels letting their motors warm up in short bursts, dead leaves rustling underfoot and sometimes a coyote or two exchanging comments. Hunting was even better than cutting wood.

On his fourteenth round of hunting his patience was rewarded. In the late afternoon of a day when he had delayed his departure until mid-afternoon, less than a mile form the house, a moose stepped out on his pathway exactly as he had planned. For a second they stared at each other, equally surprised; then, Kevin raised his rifle and fired. The moose staggered up again and crashed off into the bush.

Having levered another cartridge into the breach, Kevin ran forward, hoping for another shot. There was blood on the ground where the beast had fallen and spattered drops on the dead leaves where it had fled. For a half of an hour he floundered after his prey, never actually seeing it, but hearing the branches crashing ahead of him. Darkness came quickly now, and soon the chase was obviously hopeless. Disgusted with himself and cursing his luck, he turned for home.

Although the light form the window welcomed him, his homecoming was spoiled as he thought of the moose, probably in agony in the darkness, alone and doomed.

"Kevin?"

"Yep."

"I thought I heard a shot way off. Did you get anything?"

"No. I hit a moose, but it got away. Just call me old boar's tit one more time."

"Are you sure you hit it?"

"Yes, and I wish I hadn't. There was blood all over the place."

Joanne pictured it: the animal stumbling through the forest, mortally wounded, with the long night of agony settling around it.

"What can we do?"

"Nothing tonight. I will go as soon as daylight to try to find it. It may be dead by then, but if it is not, at least I can put it out of its misery."

"All right. I wish as much as you that it hadn't happened the way that it did."

Early the next morning they set out, he with the thirty-thirty, she with the twenty-two. Starting from the point where he had shot the moose, they followed the bloodstains deeper into the forest. In less than fifteen minutes they came upon a moose lying in a willow thicket. At first they thought it was dead, but as they approached, the animal turned his massive head, menacing them with pain-dulled eyes. It struggled to get to its feet, and then fell back.

"Here," Kevin whispered, handing his wife the rifle. "Give me the twenty-two and I will finish it off with that. No use wasting the expensive cartridges."

When he fired, the shot sounded small, flat and ineffectual. The moose merely shook its head as if a bee had stung it. With fumbling fingers Kevin ejected the spent shell, slipped another cartridge into the breach, snapped home the bolt and aimed again. The gun failed to fire; the moose leapt to its feet and charged. With a calmness she could not afterwards believe herself, Joanne fired the thirty-thirty at point blank range, slamming the moose back on its haunches.

Stunned, the two people stood there, she with her rifle still at ready, until they were sure the crisis was over.

"You sure did it that time," Kevin marveled. "How on earth did you think and act so fast? If it had been I, we would still be standing here wondering what not to do."

"Oh no we would not; we would both be pancakes. As for giving me credit for fast thinking, I did not think at all. It was exactly like the time I shot the deer; the gun just up and fired. Maybe I am a born killer. Maybe I will have to be locked up."

"Well, I have long suspected you should be locked up all right; I can't deny that. Nonetheless, it was a bloody good job you were on your toes that time or the coyotes would have had something to howl about tonight."

"Looking at it another way, if I had not asked to come along, you would not have tried to use a popgun to torture the poor thing with."

"All my error, not yours. Never again do I take a popgun on a serious hunting trip."

"Never send a boy on a man's errand, as they say."

"Nah," he said with disgust, "nor a man either. Girls seem to have everything in hand around here."

She approached the body gingerly. "You know, I don't now feel as bad about shooting the moose as I did the deer."

"Born killer developing; first partridge, then deer, now moose—what next?"

"Men?"

"Or women. How about Mrs. Fletcher for openers?"

"Too late; I am not mad at her anymore. Now I am going home while you do your grisly bit with the knife. Please do not start hacking or chopping until I am out of sight and sound."

"Born killer," he jeered

"All right, I will stay."

The butchery was worse than expected. He had never dreamed there could be so much blood in one animal, nor could he believe how monstrous the beast was. The hide was tick infested and his knife was hopelessly dull. "You are saved, Joanne, can you tear yourself away long enough to go home for the axe?"

She was able to tear herself away.

It took two days to complete the butchery and bring the chunks of meat back to the cabin where they put it up on the rack. The head they had left at the slaughtering site; the hide they dragged wearily home, a heavy and unpleasant business.

As it turned out, they might as well have left the hide with the head. The following day they stretched the skin out on the back wall of the house, and in the gorgeous fall sunshine they scraped away, or tried to scrape away the flesh that remained on it. "How do you know this is the thing to do?" Joanne asked.

"Adventure books. I learned the whole thing. Just keep scraping and you will soon be clad from head to toe in soft leather."

It was an idle boast. Not really knowing what to do, they simply left the hide to dry. After a week or so they took it down, found it as hard as a sheet of plywood, tried to cut it, failed and wound up by carrying it far back in the woods and covering it with debris and moss.

"Let's have a look at your moccasins," Kevin demanded. "Maybe we can whomp something up with a piece of blanket since leather is out of the question."

"Easy on. We have exactly four blankets."

While he was examining her left moccasin, he noticed a neat hole through the toe and out of the sole.

"Hey, how come this hole in your moccasin? I never noticed that before."

"Shows how much attention you pay to the way I dress. I don't think you love me."

"I do so, although I'll admit I am more interested in how you undress. Seriously, how did that hole get there?"

"It happened, dear man, months ago the day you were whooping it up in town. On that occasion I shot a hole through it with the twenty-two."

"What in the name of all that is holy—no pun intended—were you doing shooting holes through your moccasins?"

"What I was doing was trying to shoot a blasted partridge. When I pulled the trigger, as usual the damned thing didn't go off. I lowered the barrel and was just on the verge of drawing back when the fool thing did go off."

"That's impossible!"

"It may be impossible, but that is what happened."

"Are you sure you didn't recock it and pull the trigger without thinking ?"

"I am absolutely sure. I lowered the barrel and whap!—the bullet went right between my toes; otherwise, I would have gotten gangrene and you would have to saw my leg off."

"This is no joking matter."

"Why not? You love sawing, don't you?"

"I told you to never point the gun anywhere but at the ground when you are not actually aiming at something."

"That's were my foot was, on the ground. Do you think I was standing on my head?"

He sat looking at the hole, turning the moccasin over and over as if he could find an answer in the mystery of the misfire.

"You know, it must be the ammunition, just as Ed said. But he never mentioned any delayed firing—must be a slow burning cap if there is such a thing. Seems to me he also said something about a firing pin. He was going to look at it. Did it ever happen again?"

"Ed cursing?"

"No, smart Alec. Did the gun ever do it again?"

"Nope. It often refuses to fire, but it has never gone off by itself on any other occasion."

"If Ed ever shows up, we will ask him if it ever happened to him. It certainly did not happen when I was using it."

Following through on Kevin's suggestion of making a pair of moccasins out of one of their blankets after the dismal failure with the moosehide, Joanne made a windbreaker instead. Although the results would not have earned much acclaim for styling, the jacket was a bit warmer than his shirt and seemed quite serviceable. The solution to his footwear problem, they found, was already in their hands, or to be more precise—on Joanne's feet: her moccasins, in which her feet were quite lost, were big enough for him.

"Now we are all fixed up," she said. "All we have to remember is not to go out together when the snow flies."

"And keep the gun always pointed away from our feet or the moccasins will be riddled with holes long before spring."

Having solved the clothing problem, they turned their attention to the final preparation for winter. For food they had a full rack of moosemeat, a box of deer meat, all of which should keep indefinitely. The house, thanks to Joanne, was well sealed, and Kevin had a few winter clothes, sufficient they hoped for short outdoor sorties. There was wood in plenty, and they still had a gallon of coal oil as they had not used the lamp very much throughout the summer. All in all they felt they were well fixed.

After stock-taking, Kevin said, "Well, there we are honey, you are now invited to a hunkering-down party."

"Where do we have that little caper?"

"In the bed, of course."

"Will there be guests?"

"Not unless we invite old Froman."

"Oooh! Persona non grata!"

"After what I saw walking on his chairs and in his hair, I would say there would be all the 'grattage' you could ever wish for. That is French and probably way over your head."

"You mean all over my head. Get out the mouth organ and play something licentious to suit the occasion."

25

WINTER DESCENDED, NOT ABRUPTLY AS IT HAD IN SEPTEMBER, but slowly, growing colder day by day as the ground hardened with frost, and the remaining pools in the creek glassed over with an ever-thickening layer of ice. No trace of the marsh odour remained; the air was clear and sharp. There was an atmosphere of melancholy about the bare trees, and sadness in the fallen leaves even though they scampered about in the slightest breeze. There was a sense of waiting, a hiatus before the storm.

On November the fourth when she awoke in the morning, Joanne felt vaguely uneasy; something had changed. Then it struck her: in a place that normally was silent, the silence was now absolute: there was no stirring of wind, nothing.

"Wake up, wake up, it's snowing!"

"Snowing? Oh yeah, snow. Well, it was bound to come." He rolled over on his stomach and buried his head under the blankets.

"Oh no, you don't. Get up and make the fire. I would myself if I were not so tired."

"So am I," he mumbled. "Besides, I am at that stage of life when over-exposure can be dangerous. You had better do it."

"Coincidence. I am at the same stage."

"Three years younger at last count, and women live longer than men. Do you want to hang on for years and years after I am gone? You are elected to make the fire."

"I decline the post."

"Get up or I'll tell your mother."

"Tell her and smell her and kick her down cellar, as we used to say."

Reluctantly he swung his feet to the floor. "Murder! Winter is here for sure now. This batch won't melt off."

While he fiddled with the stove, his better half sat up with blankets draped around her to watch him work.

"We'll be cabin bound for sure now. At least I will, since you used the blanket for a windbreaker. What I mean is we can't both go out at the same time. Moccasins—one pair—people, two."

"No decent socks—two people. I've been thinking about that: there are some strips of blanket left; what say we try wrapping them around our feet and legs—you know—like puttees."

"A noble thought. We'll have to try it. That is, you'll have to try it, because by the time you get that stove going, your feet will be frozen right off."

"One just fell off."

"And listen: what in the world are we going to do all winter? There isn't anything to read; cooking is a little too simple to keep a great mind active; there is no need to cut wood, and no real housekeeping to do. Maybe we should stay in bed sleeping all winter like the bears."

"Well,"—coming towards her with an exaggerated leer—"there are worse ways of passing the time."

"I said sleeping, not romping."

"Anyway, we have no rompers, so I guess I'll stay up."

"And make coffee."

"Don't I wish I could."

"Even that cup has been taken from us, as someone has already said."

"Whoever it was who took the cup might as well have taken the pot too." With his back to the stove, which was now rapidly heating up, he gazed idly about the room. "What are we going to do with that snare wire Fletcher gave us?"

"Gave? Catch rabbits. Wasn't that the idea?"

"Sure. You going to eat them if we do?"

"Not likely. Why, man, we have enough meat to keep us going all winter. What we could do is learn how to cure skins. Ever hear of rabbit fur?"

"Well if it is a fur coat you covet, just ask old Kevin—aka B.T—he has already demonstrated his skills with the moosehide."

"Perhaps—and here is an original phrase—'practice makes perfect'."

"One thing I will have to start practicing this very morning is bringing in the snow to melt for water. The last time I drew a pail, the ice had almost reached the bottom of the pool."

"At least the melted snow will be clean, depending on where you get it of course."

And so the winter days began, each the same as the other: make the fire, gather snow, boil the meat, bring in the wood... Almost every night the coyotes howled far away or close at hand. Owls took time out to threaten with their mournful cries. A few snowbirds brushed the willows and once a weasel came to visit. He was a long, sinister creature with no desire to be sociable in spite of Joanne's attempts to befriend him. If there were any other animals hard by, they left only tracks and some contemptuous excrement. The McCormacks were alone.

Then Joanne fell ill. For two long weeks she lay in silence, sleeping fitfully in restless bouts or lying there staring at nothing with eyes from which all sense seemed to have fled. Often she cried out or fought off tormentors that only she could see. Gazing upwards from her bed, she would cry out, "I am afraid of the high, afraid of the high!"

Desperately Kevin tried to comfort her. "There isn't anything there, honey; there isn't anything there."

"It's on the roof! It's on the roof! Oh close the window; don't let it in."

Having had no experience with illness, Kevin was frantic with helplessness. When she was cold, he bundled the blankets around her and stoked up the stove until the pipes glowed red. When she was hot, he put cold cloths on her forehead. There was nothing more he could do. They had no medicine of any kind, not even aspirin. He cursed himself for being so unprepared. He forgot to eat, but remembered how to pray, and then felt guilty for praying only when things had gone wrong. His prayer never varied: "Let her get well. Let her get well."

Several times he almost went for help, yet he dared not leave her alone even for a few hours in case of fire, or in case the fire went out as it surely would before he could get back. It would take him at least two hours at the best of times to reach the Johnstones' place, but with the snow on the ground, he had no idea how long it would really take. The round trip could easily take five hours, five hours in which anything might happen. Even if he did go, what could the Johnstones do to help them anyway? It would be better to stay home and do what he could to comfort her.

And the snow sifted down, layer upon layer.

In the midst of this horror, the coyotes grew bolder, approaching ever closer. One night when the babble was particularly near at hand, he went out, and there they were in the moonlight, circling the meat platform as if they were working out a plan to help themselves. Completely losing his head in his resentment, he grabbed the axe and charged the circle. Of course they fled, leaving him standing there with the axe, feeling more than a little foolish.

The following morning Joanne awoke, dreamy still, but clear-eyed and peaceful. She drank a little of the broth he brought her before falling into a deep sleep. In another three days she was up and about, though still very weak.

As soon as Kevin was sure she could look after herself, he prepared to go once more into town. He was convinced that her trouble was their pure meat diet, and that a few vegetables would put her back in shape. Of course he had no idea of what he could do when he did reach town unless Ed were back home; that part he would have to resolve once he got there, but something had to be done; no longer could he just sit waiting for fate to dispose of them.

His preparations for the journey were not particularly elaborate. First he took the remains of the last pot of meat and put it in one of the paper bags Joanne had insisted on hoarding since their arrival. His plan was to tear a page out of their old *Chatelaine* and use it as a wrapper, a plan that was promptly vetoed since the magazine, although already dog-eared from reading and rereading, was the only written material they had. He put on his socks and the moccasins and wrapped his legs with blanket remnants. Over his summer cap he pulled another strip of cloth and tied it under his chin. Then, cursing, he took it off as his new windbreaker had no buttons and it had to go on first. Back on with his hat and he was ready to go.

"You look like Little Orphan Annie, only bigger."

"Just so long as I am warm I don't care if I look like John the Baptist."

"Take one of the remaining blankets just in case."

"And what would you do?"

"I have the stove and scads of wood."

"Don't worry about me now. You should be all right too. I've stacked wood in the house, as you can see, and there is a full pail of water. You need go outside only for snow or to empty the pot. Wear my old shoes; they are not much good for anything but dancing though."

"Oh, hooray, can I really go dancing?"

"Now I know you are back on your feet. I'll stop at Froman's and ask him to pick you up."

"I thought you said a homesteader's life was a tough one."

"Are you going to be afraid?"

"All I will ever be afraid of again as long as I live will be falling sick. I'll keep the door locked, and what is to get in anyway."

"Mannie."

"Oooh!"

"Now I am on my way. I should be back the day after tomorrow. Be very careful with the fire."

In a rare gesture of open affection they kissed, and he went out the door pretending not to see the tears on her face and hoping she did not see the ones on his.

Although it was seven o'clock in the morning, the moon was still quite high in the sky. The snow sparkled in the light; the air was cold and invigorating. Where the road wound through the trees, the snow was comparatively shallow; only in the open spaces had it drifted enough to make his passage difficult. In slightly over an hour and a half he reached the Johnstones' place.

At first he thought he would simply hurry on by, but his feet were now so cold he knew it would be folly to take a risk. His hands, too, were freezing in his pockets. Whatever time he lost would be more than compensated for by the new strength he would gain from resting. Furthermore it would be wise to let them know that his wife was alone, in case his plans went awry and he was not back by noon of the day after tomorrow. He also nurtured a secret hope that by some miracle he would not have to go any further. There was always the possibility that their circumstances had improved and they would volunteer—volunteer what? A few rabbits, he thought sourly.

Annie had the door open and was calling to him long before he reached the door. "Well I'll be a corker if it isn't Kevin. Come on in and shut the door. You look iced right up and for a minute I thought you were an Indian coming into scalp us or whatever. Then I said to Mannie, 'That's Mr. McCormack or I'll eat my shirt,' is what I said. Eat my shirt, because I recognized you right away. Where is your little lady?"

"Well, I am sort of on my way into town to get some stuff and...."

"Oh why couldn't she come?"

"She—that is I couldn't—she..."—his voice trembled.

"Out with it man, for God's sake what happened?"

Recovering himself, he went on carefully, "She has been most awfully sick, awfully sick. I thought she was leaving me. I couldn't leave her to come for help—anyway she couldn't—she hasn't ...."

"There, there now. What hasn't she got?"

"Annie," he said, capitulating, "she couldn't have come anyway, because she has no warm clothes. I even had to wear her moccasins."

"Oh, the poor little thing, the poor little thing. As soon as you get back we are going to make her—I'll do it while you are gone partly. I'll start right away making her a pair of moccasins out of rabbit skins—if there is one thing we have plenty of it is rabbit skins; the stable is snide with them. No moccasins. No jacket either, I'll bide. Oh I've got the loveliest idea: when you come back, you send her over to me and I'll deck her out like a northern princess. I can do these things."

"You are awfully kind."

"Here's Mannie at last, just getting up. You sit here Kevin,"—placing a chair in front of the kitchen stove. "Put your feet in the oven. Mannie, help him take off those leggings and I'll heat up a bowl of stew. It's a wonder you didn't freeze your feet and hands—rags for socks and no mitts."

"I'm just fine," Kevin replied hastily. "We tried to cure a moose skin, but it just hardened up."

"Mannie could have shown you how to do it, couldn't you Mannie? He's a natural born tanner—used to be while the moose and deer were still coming around. We haven't seen a hide for a long time around here, other than rabbits."

All the time this conversation was going on, Mannie sat staring at their guest with an air of benevolence, his only sign of life an occasional tug at his mustache. As soon as Kevin began to thaw out, this gazing bothered him. Christ, he thought, is he after me now?

"You picked a pretty cold day to go gallivanting," Annie cautioned, putting a bowl of stew in his hands. "Twenty below."

"Really? There is no wind and it hasn't been bad at all as long as I kept moving. I thought I was being a real hero at first. I told you that Joanne has been ill. I think it is the pure meat diet; she needs something else."

"Didn't I just know it was going to happen? Her so thin. When she told me she wasn't pregnant, I knew right away, didn't I Mannie, didn't I say she was probably eaten out by cancer? Didn't I say that? I said right off the bat—or tuberculosis maybe. Meat wouldn't hurt anybody any more than it does us. Galloping consumption, that is probably what she has the poor little thing. It can't be menopause."

"No," Kevin agreed. "It can't be menopause."

Annie's first diagnosis should have frightened him to death, but the second two following so rapidly took the sting out of it. As a physician Annie clearly lacked some measure of credibility.

"She is even thinner now than when you saw her."

"Sure sign. It's all up to God now."

"If I wait around for God to do something, we'll starve to death for sure," he answered, then he shut up abruptly, thinking he sounded as if he were asking for help. When she had been ill, he would have done anything to get help, but now that she seemed to be recovered his pride got the better of him once more.

"If you're meant to starve, you will starve—not a thing you can do about it. I used to go after my poor Mannie to shake things up, silly me. He knew all along when to sit back and let things go their own way, didn't you Mannie?"

Turning again to her guest, "Mannie should be in the government."

"You could be right," Kevin replied dryly.

"You folks getting many rabbits?"

"Nope. I got another deer though. Did Joanne tell you she shot one last summer?"

"Good gracious me! I'd have thought the rifle would knock a little thing like her galley west."

"She is small, but she is tough, and she is a way better shot than I am."

"Bless me."

"Oh yes, we got a moose too."

"I must say you are lucky. Mannie gave up hunting because nothing ever came his way, It was just a waste of time. Besides the kids keep us in rabbits, and all it takes is a few snares and their slingshots. No wasted cartridges around here. None at all, not that I mean you wasted cartridges. No, I didn't mean that."

Kevin stood up and stretched, reluctantly leaving the fire. The first six miles of his journey had been much easier than he had expected, yet he was tired and the temptation to relax a little longer by the fire was hard to resist, until it occurred to him that maybe that was how Mannie had begun his slow drift into perpetual lethargy.

"Thanks for the stew and the fire; I have a long trip ahead of me yet. I'll just rewrap and hit the road."

He was tempted to add, "If I am not back by tomorrow night, will you look in on Joanne?" Such a comment might have sounded too dramatic, and furthermore Mannie would be only too glad to comply. He settled for a simple, "Good-bye."

Another two hours of somewhat harder walking brought him to the highway, where the gods had a small surprise for him. If he had stayed five minutes more at the Johnstones' he would have missed a ride. As it was he had just stepped on to the main highway when along came a taciturn homesteader with a cutter and a snappy team of horses.

"Going far?"

"Town."

"Get in."

Neither of them spoke again until Kevin let himself down at the store.

"Thank you very much."

"Don't mention it."

Kevin walked up and down the street to unstiffen his legs before he entered the store. Fletcher was stunned. The last time he had seen him, this customer had been reasonably well dressed. Now he looked like a bundle of rags, and several days of not shaving did not improve his appearance.

"For goodness sakes," Fletcher burst out, coming around the counter to shake hands. "I hardly recognized you."

Opening his mouth to speak, Kevin lost control of his voice—why he did not know—and hastily turned his back, making a great show of warming his hands while he tried to regain his composure.

Seeing his distress, the storekeeper busied himself behind the counter,while his customer brought himself under control. Then he bustled forward.

"Well, then, thawed out a bit now?"

Kevin nodded.

"Come in for a bit of shopping, I'll bet."

"In a way. First though I will have to find Ed."

Fletcher shook his head.

"You'll have a hard time doing that; he has gone to Edmonton to help his sister whose husband just died. Do you know Powers, the dwarf at the livery stable? He's looking after Ed's business. Perhaps he can help you."

Kevin's face fell. "Oh..."

"You need a place to sleep, I guess."

Kevin nodded, his disappointment manifest.

"We've no room out back, but I suppose—if you want to, you can bed down here on some bran sacks after we close. Tomorrow we can fix you up with whatever you need. You don't really need Ed for a place to sleep."

Kevin swallowed, summoning all of his courage. "It's more than that—I wanted to ask—well—Mr. Fletcher—the last time I was here..."

"Yes, I remember that,"—coldly.

"You said if we needed help, to come and see you."

Fletcher's face hardened. "Yes?"

"Well, we are a bit down—I mean..."

"You mean you are out of food and you are broke. You want me to give you credit," looking at his customer over the tops of his glasses, his hawk-like appearance disturbing Kevin more than anything he said or how he said it.

"We just wondered—a few necessities..."

"How and when would you pay?"

Gritting his teeth and fighting to control himself, Kevin spoke through stiffening lips. "I'll clear some land—crops—next summer..."

"Sure you will. How will you get the land broken? Do you know how much land you would need for a paying crop, even if it succeeded, which it likely would not? Where will you get seed for this hypothetical crop? More credit?"

"I've cut wood..."

"Every homesteader within fifty miles of here has cut wood, which they can bring and stack in my backyard. Man if I took every stick of wood I have been offered, I'd have a pile long enough to reach kingdom come. You haven't got a team and you live twenty miles away. Even if I wanted wood, how would you get it in here. Grow up."

Kevin put his cap back on. "I don't know. All I know is that Joanne is sick from eating nothing but wild meat. I have to get food somewhere. Is there any work yet?"

"You knew the answer to that before you asked. If you are that desperate, I will give you a few things, but let's call a spade a spade: it will be charity and we both know it."

As Kevin moved blindly toward the door, Fletcher intercepted him. "Look here now, don't go storming out of here thinking you've been hard done by and that I am a heartless bastard. What do you think I am? A millionaire? I'm just a one-horse storekeeper in a one-horse town. I'm trying to make a living like everybody else. I am not a missionary; I can't feed the whole world for Christ's sake. You are not the only one, you know. There must be fifty people a month come in here begging."

Kevin raised his hands in a gesture of helpless agreement, unable to speak without blubbering. "I know," was all he could say.

Fletcher went on in a calmer tone, "Look here, why don't you try for relief first? They will maybe give you a dollar or two. Stay here tonight and try at the government office tomorrow morning."

Slowly recovering himself, Kevin finally took hold of the door knob, paused, and with a degree of dignity that surprised even himself, spoke very carefully.

"It was credit I asked for, not charity. I would have paid it back even though it sounds ridiculous right now. I have never owed anyone anything I did not pay back, and I would not have started now. If you can't give me credit, then forget it. You are out of the picture as of now. I do not want your charity or any goddamned relief. I will die, and I will see my wife die before I beg again."

He stumbled out into the darkened street where he trudged up and down in a helpless turmoil of emotion, his mind racing over the scene in which he had just participated, while he tried to concentrate his thoughts on what he could do next. Not that he had many alternatives to consider. The most sensible thing to do was telegraph his father and ask for a loan. To go begging again so soon after Fletcher's rebuff sickened him, although this time he would not be pleading face to face. His decision made, he turned about and strode towards the telegraph office which he had seen earlier while he was walking the steet. He was too late: the door was closed and the lights were out. Ever since coming to the store he had been too pre-occupied to notice that darkness had closed in. To send a telegram he would have to wait for the next day. Having spurned Fletcher's offer of bran sacks, he would have to go to the livery stable, dwarf or no dwarf.

Minutes later he was standing in the office of the livery stable warming his hands at the stove.

"What do you want?" Powers asked, his litle pinched face soured even more by the authority vested in him during Ed's absence.

"I'm stuck in town and I need somewhere to pass the night."

"So get a hotel room."

"That is out of the question."

"You'll smoke and set fire to the place."

"I don't smoke."

"Nobody smokes when they are bumming a night in a barn."

That did it, Kevin, the quiet and the gentle, had had enough. "Listen," he said, grabbing the little man by the shirt front, "it's twenty below, I'm twenty miles from home, I'm broke, and I am tired. On top of that, I am a hell of a sight bigger than you are. I am going to stay here, and I don't give a shit whether you like it or not."

"Let go of my shirt. You can sleep in the loft with a horse blanket. I hope you freeze your ass off. Give me your matches."

"I told you I do not smoke."

"Give me your matches or go find a snow drift."

"Whatever you say. Where is that blanket?"

"Matches first."

"Here, take them. Where is that blanket?"

"What have you got in that paper bag? More matches?"

"It was my lunch. Moose meat if it is any of your business."

"You shot a moose?"

"No I cut a steak off as he weht by."

"You shot a moose. Wait here while I go get the cops."

"Away you go, but before you get out the door, the charge will be mur-der."

"That's crap. How could you murder me if I am on my way to get the cops?"

"Try it, my dear little man. I think I'll kill you now anyway."

Kevin awoke once in the night and lay there in the sweet straw with a not-so-sweet horse blanket wrapped tightly around himself. He thought of their cabin with the firelight flickering through the damper of the stove, Joanne sitting on the edge of the bed—home, a sheltering place from the cold outside, a refuge from the tongues of men. Whatever it cost him, they must retain that place and find a way to survive there. The first and most immediate step was to get food enough to carry them through the next few months of winter.

As he lay there he began to see his conduct for what it was: Ed had called him stiff-necked and proud, and had warned him he would have to bend if he were not to break. He had boasted to himself that he would make any sacrifice to protect Joanne, but what had he done? He had cut a lot of wood, and helped her to get a little meat, efforts that had cost him nothing. What he had done was shelter himself from what he feared most: rebuffs and refusals.

Well, he lived in the world of men and men were not always kind or accommodating. To survive, one had to ask and risk refusal. He knew now what he had to do and was almost relieved that he had to do it the very next day and get it done with. There was much of the night left for the most refreshing sleep he had ever experienced.

26

ALTHOUGH IN THE COLD LIGHT OF MORNING HIS NIGHTTIME resolve seemed more painful to implement than it had in the dark, Kevin's determination did not waver. To his surprise, Powers the Surly, slapped a bowl of porridge on the table together with a cup. "Get your own coffee," he growled, pointing at the pot on the stove. It looked as if it were going to be a pleasant day.

At the store Fletcher greeted him with a curt, "Good morning."

"I have come back to apologize for my outburst yesterday," Kevin began, involuntarily removing his cap and standing with it in his hand like the caricature of a Welsh coal miner waiting respectfully for his pay. "I understand your position. You can not run a business by giving away your stock to people who can't or won't pay. On the face of it, I am in no position to pay for anything as you so frankly pointed out last night."

Fletcher had the grace not to reply.

"You said you were prepared to give us some groceries."

Fletcher nodded. "Some essentials."

"If the offer still stands"—he took a deep breath—"we will be most grateful for them. My only reservation is that I intend to repay you at my earliest opportunity. You may believe that or not as you wish."

"Have you thought about applying for relief?"

"I have to get home. My wife is sick, and if I am away much longer she might get worse. She may not even be able to tend the fire. I just can't fool around any longer. And there is this: when I am in a position to repay you, rest assured I will, however preposterous that may seem to you right now."

Now that it was said, now that the begging was done, Kevin forgot how saintly humility should make him feel; instead he loathed himself. God had let him down. Why give a man the gift of pride and then force him to grovel. He had, in Ed's words, 'kissed ass', and he did not like the taste.

"Very well," Fletcher agreed, his face showing contempt. "There is no point in picking and choosing; I will gather up what I know you will need. Go find something to do while I do what has to be done."

In spite of an attempt to walk with dignity out of the store from which he had effectively been dismissed, Kevin felt that he scurried. For Joanne's sake he had done what he had to do; it was almost over. Nothing worse could ever befall him, unless—the thought shattered him—he had to do it again sometime.

On his way out of the store he noticed the post office in a small building directly across the street. Neither on his first trip to town or up until that moment on the present trip had he given any thought to mail. There could possibly be a letter from his father, for even if they had not parted on the best of terms, they were not enemies. The old man may have sent them a magazine or two, and he knew who would be pleased to get them.

"Anything for McCormack, K. McCormack?"

"McCormack? Oh yes. We thought you were never coming in, but Mr. Fletcher said you would be back sooner or later." She handed him a roll of magazines, another roll of newspapers, and two letters.

Delighted, Kevin went back to the livery stable, made himself comfortable by the stove and prepared to browse through his bonanzas. The letter post-marked Toronto was obviously from his father. It was not a very thick envelope, but he could not complain since he had not written himself. The second was a local letter with his name on it in block letters as if scrawled with a carpenter's pencil. His curiosity piqued, he opened the second letter first:

Kevin,

Open that wallet. This time something is going in instead of out. I meant to come see you but my sister's husband died and I have to go away for awhile. The railway gave me a contract for 400 telegraph poles. Pick out as many as you can 20 to 30 feet high, at least 8 inches in diameter at the butt, and straight. No snakes mind. Mark them but don't cut them till I get there. The deal is you cut them and we haul them to town. You get 50 cents a piece. Here's a money order for 40 bucks in advance. Don't molest no women whilst in town. That place of yours has got a bad enough name along those lines already.

Ed.

A roaring started in the back of Kevin's head and his stomach turned to sloshed acid so that his body wanted to fold in the middle. It was Christmas morning! It was all his birthdays rolled into one! It was an "A" on an exam! It was summer! It was food, mitts, ammunition, medicine— and he had just accused the gods of being unjust. Above all it was vindication: he could pay his bills, and their place was worth something. So the dumb city boy had not chosen such a hopeless homestead after all. Shutting his eyes, he gave thanks for what Ed had done. Oh bliss! Oh Fletcher!

After he had calmed down a little, he slipped the money order and the letter into his shirt pocket; and then, he opened his father's letter:

> Dear Kevin,
>
> It will soon be Xmas and I have not heard from you once since you left. You must still be mad at me, and I suppose I deserve it. To tell you the truth, I've had a change of heart and am actually a little proud of what you were trying to do. At least you tried to do something, which is more than can be said for many. While I am in a repentant mood, I must also admit that I was jealous of you taking Joanne away from here. I miss her as much as you would have. Anyway, because it is nearly Xmas, because I have had a little luck at my job, and to show you are not forgotten, enclosed is a money order for fifty dollars. I wish it could be more. I thought money might be a bit more useful than the traditional red mitts and peppermints.
>
> Dad.

"To him that hath shall be given," Kevin rejoiced, falling back on a borrowed phrase since he was too dumbfounded to think of one of his own. If only his dad could have known that three minutes ago the red mitts and the peppermints alone would have been deemed a blessing. It was too much for him; he put his head in his hands and wept.

At that moment Powers came in, threw off his mackinaw, saw his visitor in tears, and muttered, "What next?"

Kevin looked up, still dazed, and stared at Powers as if he had never seen him before. Then as a slow grin spread across his face, he rose, picked up the little man, and danced him around the room.

"Let me down, you harelipped asshole."

"Don't spoil things. Today is a day of miracles. Why, even you were almost civil this morning." His emotions were again too much for him, sending him into a foolish jig around the stove.

"City people! If they ain't blubbering, they're dancing around. It's sickening. Why don't you go home?"

"You're getting mean again," Kevin cautioned. "Oh, I'm going home all right; I'm going home rejoicing, my sad little man."

Yanking on his wretched cap, he strode down the street armed with a new kind of pride, tempered by an immense sense of gratitude. Whereas his recent prayers had consisted of an endless plea for his wife to get better, he was now pestering heaven with repeated inner cries of, "Thank God." Then the sly old doubting nibbled at his conscience, "God or gods? Or luck?"

After collecting his money at the post office, he went first to the telegraph office to wire his father ten words of gratitude. Finally he strolled over to the store to be greeted by a restrained, "Your goods are ready."

"Thanks," Kevin replied casually. "I'll check it out as I am sure there are a few things we need that you can't have known about."

"Now you listen to me..."

"It's all right, Mr. Fletcher; it's all right. Look at this stuff" —extending his hand with the bills in it.

"Money..."

"Yes, money, the stuff that pride and dignity are built on. Without it a man is a dog, something to be castigated and whipped and debased." Sobering, he added, "Don't get me wrong. I am still more than grateful for the help you were willing to give us. I won't forget that. Let us just be glad together. Hey, I'll bet this is the fastest repayment of credit you've ever experienced."

"Relief?"

"No, thank God, it is not relief money, although it is a distinct relief to have it. One other thing I would like you to know: part of this came from the products of our homestead. That, to me, is the best part of all. Let us now go over the entire order. Do you have any wool?"

"I do," replied a somewhat subdued Fletcher. "Heavy stuff?"

"I guess so; it's for mitts and socks, and maybe sweaters. Needles to match, of course. I want another pair of moccasins for Joanne because the ones you sold her fit me."

"You will want a winter cap."

"Nix, we don't want to go crazy here. My wife can knit me a toque."

While he accumulated the order, it occurred to the happy customer that he was once again faced with the problem of transportation. Obviously he could not carry the stuff, and it was doubtful that he could borrow a horse with Ed out of town.

"Try Powers," Fletcher suggested.

"I am not that rich. Besides if he came with me I might have to kill him."

Fletcher withdrew into a deep study, obviously wrestling with his conscience. "I must ask my wife about the yarn and the needles; she'll know what to give you better than I do. Be back in a moment." He needed time to think. It was, after all, a substantial order at that, and this young man might turn out better than anyone expected. Also he seemed like the kind to remember a good turn. He might well be worth cultivating.

A few minutes later he came back. "I'll tell you what we will do. I'll lend you one of those big toboggans there. It will run on the loose snow a lot better than a sled. There is a chap in town this morning who will be going out your way—well, part of your way. He could take you and your stuff as far as the turnoff. He lives farther along the highway. You should be able to drag the toboggan in from there, although I am glad it is not I who has to do it. You can bring it back later on if you do not want to buy it. Try not to scrape it up too much."

"Say, that will be the cat's meow."

"Maybe you won't think so by the time you are a few miles on the road. It will be the devil's own pull. There are potatoes, carrots and turnips in the order. If it does not get any colder, and you travel like the Dickens you may get them home without freezing them. As I said it will be the devil's own pull."

And the devil's own pull it was. Of the long trip home he was to remember very little. At first, when the farmer let him off at the junction, his new elation bore him along on wings, but as the day progressed his joy faded into fatigue. His head and his body seemed to become disconnected in a bizarre manner so that his mind was detached and unaware of a body which had become a machine that had no purpose but to put one foot down after another. Strange fantasies drifted before his eyes: the curved bole of a tree was, for a second, a woman's leg encased in a black stocking. Bells rang all around him, not loudly but steadily, tiny gongs struck with a monotony that was hypnotic. Scraps of the song "Button up Your Overcoat" floated eerily about, somehow nauseating him. Several times he fell asleep as he was walking along.

Early in the morning of the following day he reached the cabin, floundering through the last few yards of deep snow, at the end of his resources. When Joanne opened the door, he staggered across the room and collapsed on the bed.

"I am going to sleep for two weeks. You can have the joy of unloading the goodies. The vegetables must be brought in at once and pray they have not frozen. When I wake up, we are going to have a dance—a big one."

27

IT WAS THE HAPPIEST DAY OF JOANNE'S LIFE; IT WAS THE LONGEST day. All the while she busied herself with the joyful task of unpacking goods she was consumed with curiosity. Time and again she checked Kevin out to see if he were still sleeping, and each time she was a little disappointed to find out that he was. Happily there was plenty to keep her occupied. First, in her methodical way, she put on a new pair of the heavy socks that had arrived on the mysterious load and pulled on the new moccasins, which fitted this time. Then she started unpacking. As she could not drag the toboggan into the house—she could not move it at all—she had to keep going out in the freezing cold. She thought of waking Kevin up long enough to take off his windbreaker for whatever protection it would give her, a temptation she resisted as she could not be that inconsiderate. Who cared about the cold when the pot once again steamed on the stove, filling the cabin with the glorious scent of coffee? She made bannock, using lard for the first time in a long, long time; she brought in the bag of carrots and turnips as well as the flour; and she put some beans on to soak—how could they ever have gotten sick of beans? When all the groceries were stored away, she sat down to bannock and jam with a generous cup of coffee laced with canned milk.

Her next task was to undo the rolls of papers and magazines, flatten them, and lay them under the bed in order. Each day, she decided, they would open one paper exactly as they would have done in the city—civilization was not all bad—the news would of course, be long out of date, but that did not matter for, after all, what difference did it make if an earthquake took place a month ago or yesterday? That thought gave her pause, necessitating a moment of reflection helped along by more coffee. The hypothetical earthquake, then, had no reality until Joanne McCormack read about it. The death of the persons killed had to be postponed until she was informed. What would have happened if she never received the news? There would have been no earthquake.

The magazines would be more strictly rationed: each week they would read one article or story aloud—one story, no more—and they would work their way through the issues in order as they did the newspapers. Thus they would have something to read for a long time to come.

Where in the world had Kevin gotten all the goodies? Credit? She doubted that Kevin would ever have the courage to ask for credit and even if he had she was sure Fletcher would never have given it to him. The most likely explanation was that Ed had outfitted him or loaned him the money. Perhaps he had stolen the whole works—that was ridiculous—and it was blasphemy to their marriage even to have thought such a thing. It had to be Ed once again.

Late in the evening she began to worry about Kevin for he had slept for hours and hours without stirring, and now his breathing, which had earlier been quite sonorous, was now barely perceptible. Frightened, she put her face close to his to make sure there was still life in his body. Feeling no breath, and not hearing any, she put her face even closer still.

"Back off, you sloe-eyed temptress," he warned.

"You are awake!"

"Have been for the last half hour, hoping for coffee without having to beg for it."

"I thought you were dead."

"There were times I thought I would be for sure, that I would never get back. It was just walking and walking and pulling that damned—blessed—toboggan, and it flipping over and getting jammed in the snow. It was also cold, although that part didn't bother me as much as I thought it might. Thank goodness for the new socks and mitts and for your old moccasins and your homemade windbreaker. By the way, it—the windbreaker—may not be handsome, but it is surprisingly warm.

"You know, good spouse, the whole scene we painted for ourselves is grossly exaggerated. The darned trip and so-called hardships were not awful at all—I enjoyed at least ninety percent of it. Either that or I really am a rugged northern boy; you are lucky to have me."

"Why did you lie there pretending to be asleep if you were so full of beans?"

Drawing her under the covers, ignoring the fact that she was not dressed—read undressed—for the occasion, he murmured, "I just wanted you to make a fuss over me; I remember the last time I came back from town. Also I was counting our new-found blessings."

"Where did all these blessings come from?"

"From Ed and—hold your breath—from Dad. As soon as you drown me in coffee I will show you the letters."

"Oh, I thought we had some unfinished business."

When that business was attended to and the two of them lay side by side with steaming cups of coffee, Kevin pulled the letters from his shirt pocket. "You can read these in a moment after I have told you the first part. I went to see Fletcher just as soon as I got into town to ask him for credit. He was snotty—I blubbed. He sneered at me and told me he would give me some food, but that we both knew it would be a gift, not credit. He said our homestead would never be any good for anything and that we had no way of ever paying off a debt. He, in a word, humiliated me."

"In front of anyone?"

"No, I was spared that, thank God. But, as I said, I made an even bigger ass of myself by blubbering. Anyway, when I pulled myself together, I expressed myself in very clear terms—without recourse to profanity, either theological or scatological—and marched out of there with my head held, if not high, at least at half-mast."

"Well? How then did you hit the jackpot?"

"There is more to come."

"*Raconte.*"

"I slept on the straw in the livery stable attic with a horse blanket that stunk to high heaven; that is I slept for a time until something woke me up. As I lay there it came back to me what Ed said that first night around the campfire at the spring. He said that in this country—any country I guess—one must not be too stiff-necked about it. One has to adapt, and in adapting bend a little or one will break. It was something like the old Biblical cautionary about pride. I saw that what I was doing was exactly what he told me not to do. It was my epiphany. When I admitted my fault to myself, I knew what I had to do and I resolved to do it the very next day. Man, how I slept after that."

"And then?"

"Yesterday morning I went back to the store and I bent, all right. I bent right to the floor. I did what had to be done, I kissed ass. It was sickening. Fletcher said he would throw a few things together for us, gifts, and ordered me out of the store."

"Why did he do that?"

"Power and glory. One does not get to whip a dog everyday. Anyway, I went to the post office and the letters will tell you the rest."

First getting out of bed for yet more coffee, she sat down with the letters.

Kevin sipped his coffee. "Ah, Kevin. Whatever did we do without it?"

"Oh my dear, my dear, my dear. What a marvellous thing to have happen. I hope you thanked Ed and wired your dad."

"I did not thank Ed; he was not there. Why else do you suppose I slept in the stable? And yes I did wire Dad, and I do not know what I am the most grateful for in his case, the money or what he said about you."

"That was nice."

"You are rather quiet, my old serpent; I thought you would be whooping and hollering. Do you know what this means? It is not just the money, although right now that means a great deal indeed. Do you realize what it means? It means we are actually going to make something—a living —off this place. At last there is a purpose in being here besides just hiding and having fun. Fletcher says Ed sometimes gets contracts for railway ties and maybe we can contribute to that too. It means the worst is over; we have survived."

"I realize all that," she replied in a low voice, "even more than you think, and of course I want to 'whoop and holler'. Who wouldn't?"

"Then what is the matter? For goodness sake 'whoop'."

"It is only that—it's as if—you know, as if God, or fate if you will, is playing games with us."

"How do you mean?" She bit her lip. "Maybe I am being foolish, but it looks like some kind of a cruel cosmic game: first we nearly starve, then I get sick, then you go to town. It is as if my getting sick was to force you into going. Why could you not have gone to the post office first? Why did you have to go through a kind of baptism of humiliation? Someone out there is playing with us."

"Ho ho, hold it, honey."

She had struck a nerve. He stopped and then rephrased what he was about to say. "I know exactly what you mean." He hesitated in some embarrassment before forcing himself to go on. "I never spoke about this before because it was kind of nutty. You remember last summer and fall when I was cutting so much wood?"

"Do I ever."

"Did it ever occur to you I was getting a bit strange about it?"

She nodded in brisk agreement. "Yes I saw you were obsessed, and— perhaps I shouldn't say this—I also saw you were doing it to keep yourself from having to do other things you should have been doing."

"Agreed. Anything else?"

She studied his face. "No," she lied, after hesitation. "No, I don't think so." Suddenly she smiled. "I am lying; I did see something else."

"Out with it."

"Why did you make a whole bunch of small woodpiles instead of one big one as any sensible person would have done?"

"Ooh!" He sipped at his empty cup to give himself countenance. Then he burst out, "Since this seems to be our hour of major truth, it was a way of saying 'bad rice'."

"Oh that."

"Yeah, remember Ed said when a Chinaman had a good crop coming along, he would stand by the field and yell 'bad rice' to keep the gods from getting wind of it?"

"I know. Do you still think ...?"

"Aw, hell, I don't know if I do or I don't. The idea stuck in my head and I couldn't shake it out; I didn't want to take any chances—bah, I begin to sound like old Froman."

She touched the tip of his nose. "I know," she murmured, "I know. I was pretty worried for awhile there: I thought you were going a bit squirrelly. Only listen to me," she cried in sudden anguish, "since my sickness, I am no longer sure you were wrong." She burst into tears.

"Take it easy. Take it easy." In trying to put his arm around her, he managed to upset her coffee. "To hell with it," he said. "Let it rip. Have a good cry; I've had mine. Cry and then we will have supper, and after that we will dance. Why are you crying anyway? Everything is all right now."

"I don't know," she wailed. "Maybe we are like Kinney's cows: starve all winter and then when the grass is green again, we die."

"Aw, come on my honey, maybe we are both just boo-sucks"—hugging her to show what he really felt. "Maybe that's wrong too. Be nasty to me; don't let the gods think we mean anything to each other."

"Please don't say anything more about the gods."

"Yes"—with a sniffle —"that's it. And that is it. Let us forget about all the fates and gods and stuff and go back to being happy. Know what? We have something to read, and a daily crossword puzzle."

"Hey, we can do one each every day."

"Nay! Now you listen to me: we are not going to do what we did at first. We won't eat up all our store of food at once; we will let the meat carry the major load, and we won't lap up all the papers and magazines like Eskimos after a seal. We will ration everything so that we won't run out in a few weeks. That also applies to coffee after tonight. *La messe est dite.*"

"Correct. This place has to pay for itself. Now back to the gods for just one minute: there is really only one enemy out there, and that is our own ignorance. All the 'bad luck' we had came because I didn't know what I was doing, and worse still, I was too proud to ask for help. That won't happen again. Old Johnstone is useless around his own place, but he can and will show me what to do and how to do it. He knows how to crib a well, how to tan skins, how to plant a garden. I shall prey on his mind, to coin a phrase. He is my well; I am going to pump everything he knows out of him whether he likes it or not. You can help by turning on the charm when he is around just to soften him up."

"Would you like to rephrase that last sentence?"

"Don't be dirty. There is nothing can whip us now; we have made it through."

That night the wolves howled.

28

COMING, AS IT DID, ON THE HEELS OF KEVIN'S BONANZA, Christmas turned out to be something of an anti-climax; they had already had their Christmas. They nonetheless did what they could to celebrate the occasion. Kevin prowled their property—he no longer referred to it as the swamp—in search of a suitable tree and found a multitude. Unfortunately the best were the tallest, and when he felled them, the branches splintered off in the bitter cold. "One hundred and sixty acres," he lamented, "and I can't get a decent tree. We would be better off trying to log off Bloor Street West."

"What would we use for money even if we were there?"

"Barter; I'd trade myself off to a rich widow for a five-footer."

"Might as well do it right; I'd trade myself off for a ten-footer already decorated."

"There are very few ten-footers even in the army, and of them only a handful were decorated."

"Extremely funny."

"Anyway, I will go back into the woods and try again."

After another long search, he cut two small shrubs to bring back for approval.

"Excellent," Joanne enthused. "I asked for a tree; I get two buggy whips."

"What you need is two buggy whippings. How would you like to flounder around up to your ass in snow trying to find something that isn't made out of glass?"

"Love it. Give me the windbreaker and the gloves."

"No sir—read madam—science will now triumph where nature has failed. Watch this operation closely." Whereupon he tied the two trees together. "How is that?"

"That will have to do. There is also one consolation: if you had found a decent tree, there would have been no room in here for people."

"Even as it is, there is still not a hell of a lot."

"There will be a little more in a minute because you have to go out again."

"What for?"

"Using bad language for one, and to gather some decorations for another."

"Oh sure. What would you like? Crepe paper? Tinsel?"

"Rose haws or hips, whatever the right name is. I've seen them still hanging on the vine here and there."

"I wish it were here instead of there," he complained, putting his mitts back on.

For once he did a lot better than Joanne expected. He brought back not only the rose haws, but also some Spanish moss—looking more like whiskers than snow, which it was supposed to represent—and some frozen cranberries that were still on the branch. Except for the cranberries, which fell off as soon as they thawed, what he had brought served the purpose. Strung together on some of Fletcher's twine she had religiously stored away, the haws made a more or less colorful chain when draped about the tree. As a final brilliant touch, Kevin tore a piece of tinfoil from a tea box he had used to bring the groceries on the toboggan. The foil they fashioned into a few tired stars.

"Would you say it was resplendent?" Joanne asked, looking at their finished product.

"Resplendent," Kevin agreed. "It relates, perhaps more to the pagan than the truly Christian concept, but then who ever read about a Christmas tree in the Bible? And, for that matter, did they have conifers in Bethlehem? What I am trying to say is it smacks of the pagan primeval, n'est-ce-pas?"

"Let us just hope the devil keeps his nasty paws off it. Pun intended. Yes, I know, we've used it before. What's next?"

"Presents? Start bringing them in."

"There is a dearth."

"A void, rather. Did I not bring you back a sleighful of goodies a short time ago?"

"That you did, my fine laddie, that you did. Who could ask for more?"

Shortly after his glorious trip to town, Kevin had re-established his hunting trail, realizing that if he left it too long untravelled and the snow got much deeper, he would have a difficult time breaking trail. As he found out on his first circuit, it was already almost too late since in the fresh snow it was more a question of floundering than walking. To make matters even more difficult, he had started carrying both rifles so that he could deal with birds as well as bigger game and the additional weapon made for awkward progress. By Christmas week the trail was restored and he had bagged four fool hens to substitute for turkey.

One new inconvenience now came to light—or, rather, failed to come to light—he had not been sufficiently generous when he replenished their supply of coal oil, and it was immediately apparent that from that time on for the rest of the winter they must save it for emergencies only, leaving the cabin in darkness most of the time. In one way his omission proved to be a blessing since reading time was thus strictly limited and, therefore, their supply of reading material would last even longer than anticipated. For entertainment after dark, they now had only the mouth organ and Joanne's voice. If either one of them felt low in spirits, the other went out of his or her way to be extra cheerful as they both recognized that joy requires effort.

On Christmas Eve nature took a hand in the festivities when in cold, clear moonlight, a lone wolf sang a Christmas lament, without accompaniment, in memory of all his companions who had died by gunshot, trap, or poison. Though it was a chillingly melancholy song, the primitive beauty of it was more moving than any carol either of them had ever heard. While he sang, Joanne and Kevin held hands in rapture; when it was over, no creature dared respond.

They stayed outside in spite of the cold to listen for an encore. The entire world, their entire world, was awash in moonlight so bright it made every detail stand out like carvings. But it was not the visual stimulation that was so stunning; it was the total lack of sound. It was as if the frost had stopped the motion even of the molecules, and time itself had paused. The trees stood frozen in moonlight and so, it seemed, they would stand forever. For Joanne, in particular, the experience had an undertone of déja vu, since during her illness she experienced a recurring nightmare in which she was a speck of consciousness that floated in avoid where it had always floated and would float forever, a spark without substance, an eternal awareness without reason. That night both she and Kevin felt a breath of the meaning of eternity.

In a hushed voice Kevin asked, "Do you realize how alone we are?"

"Yes," she answered even more softly. "It is exactly like being at sea."

Although they could not know it, away to the northeast the storm was already gathering and their little ship was in for a rough ride.

On Christmas morning Kevin awoke early, got out of bed, lit the fire and put on the coffee. "Here you are, my pet," he offered. "Early morning service for the beloved. And to add to your joy, old Santa seems to have brought you a tiny little present, unwrapped of course." He handed her a brand new deck of cards.

"Kevin! Holy smoke! Now we can play cards."

"As long as the light lasts."

"When did you get them?"

"Last trip in to town, when else?" She reached under the pillow and handed him a wrapped package.

"What's this?"

"Something you said you wanted." It was a shiny mouth organ, a far better one than the one he owned.

"Now where in heaven did you get this? You haven't been anywhere."

"I stole it from old Froman the day we visited him. I've spent hours and hours trying to get the tobacco stains off it."

"Come on, where did you get it? It is brand, spanking new."

"Major truth: remember the night we had supper in the Chinese cafe? Well you saw it and wanted it, so the next day I went back and bought it. You do not know how often I came within an ace of giving it to you, but all along I reminded myself of this day."

"You know what? I think I'll keep you after all. What will you have?"

"Why 'Hummerskew' of course." And 'Hummerskew' it was.

"Now we shall have music all the time, won't we Kevin? All the time, and we won't get sick or sad."

Without warning, something or someone knocked on the door, a sound they never expected to hear again. Kevin hesitated, then went to see what it was.

"Froman! Well what in the deuce..."

"Merry Christmas folks. I thought maybe you people might like a little treat on Christmas morning. Here, take and eat this." He handed Kevin a plate of what seemed to be pancakes. "They are sourdoughs. I keep the same mash brewing all year round."

"Well this is very, very kind of you; come on in."

"Oh no thank you. I just wanted you to have these. I didn't mean to butt in."

"Oh come now, come on in for a minute at least. I have to give you back your plate."

"Well, only for a minute. Merry Christmas, Mrs. McCormack."

"Merry Christmas," she responded, wrapping the blanket tightly around herself. "Do you mean you walked all that way over here just to...I mean, to bring us a gift?"

"Yes of course. I hope you like them."

"Joanne," Kevin cut in, "absolutely adores anything made of sour-dough. She was saying just before you came in how she wished she had made a mash herself. Right, Joanne?"

"My very words. Sit down Mr. Froman—on the bench there. Get him some coffee, Kevin."

Froman looked around uneasily. "I am not dressed for visiting—I ugh, agh—do you have a comb?"

"A comb," Kevin blurted, looking at Froman's long dirty hair, thinking of the type of beast that grazed therein.

"You deaf?" Joanne prompted her husband. "Give the man your comb."

Froman took the comb over to the washstand where he proceeded to comb vigourously with much of the residue flying into the water pail. Then, instead of sitting down, he handed the comb back to Kevin, took the empty plate and without a further word disappeared out the door.

"Well I guess that is our Christmas visit. Joanne, I am going to trade combs with you before replenishing our water supply. Why in hell do you suppose he wanted to comb his hair?"

"Maybe that was the real purpose of his visit. Maybe he has no comb of his own."

Shaking his head, Kevin threw the water out and went outside for more snow. When he came in Joanne was already up.

"Here is your breakfast, husband"—placing a plate of the pancakes on the table. "Merry Christmas."

"Listen, wife, on Christmas day I just can't sit here making a pig of myself while outside the birds are suffering. If you don't want them your-self, can I give them to the whisky-jacks?"

"Who am I to discourage altruism. Even so, feed the birds."

When he returned, they both stood at the door waiting to see what would happen. No birds came.

"See what I mean, we are alone, we are drifting in the ocean of silence."

Late in the evening the first wave shook the house as wind and then snow—snow as they had never seen it—slashed across the province. On the following day the wind died down, but the snow still came sifting down, sifting down, and the house sank slowly in the rising tide.

Two days later the horror started again for Joanne. For a week she tossed and turned all night long while Kevin prowled the house in an agony of helplessness. When she was quiet, he hoped; when she cried out, he despaired. His endless silent prayer began again: let her get well and come back to me.

Eventually she calmed, but she did not come back to him. Day after day she remained motionless either in the bed or sitting on it. Sometimes she slept, but more often she just lay or sat with her great blue eyes fixed on him with an expression of pleading or of condemnation. Later she began silent weeping, hour after hour, and nothing he could say or do had any effect on her.

And the winter went on. January slipped into February, and at last came a break in the weather. While he was gathering wood in what felt like forty below zero, Kevin felt a puff of summer air. Looking up, he saw that the sky was turning green. A few hours later he heard it coming, a great roaring in the evergreens, and bursts of summer wind with the smell of the sea upon it. In one day the snow was stripped from all the trees, and, freed from their burden, the branches lifted and tossed in the wind.

Now, at last, provided he could break trail fast enough, he could go for help. First thing in the morning he would stoke up the fire, damper it down, and make his way to the Johnstones'. How they could help he was not sure unless Annie would come and stay with Joanne while he went on to town. There he could get someone with a sleigh to come and get her.

All within one hour he heard the roar of the north wind, the awesome battle overhead, the south wind pushed back, the fearsome cold clamping down again. There was no way he could go for help since he had to be there to keep a fire going night and day. Furthermore who knew what she might do when she found herself alone?

The nightmare resumed. By day he prowled the house, stoking the fire, trying to keep occupied with nothing real to do. Joanne now slept most of the time or lay in a trance, he did not know which. When he adjusted her covers, he was afraid even to turn her, she had become so frail. By night he dozed by the fire, while mice, emboldened by silence, scampered across the floor.

One evening, in desperation, he stepped outside and emptied the rifle into the sky, hoping Froman might hear and recognize it as a distress signal. There was no answer. Another day he floundered through the snow for two miles on the way to the Johnstones', grew panicky at his slow progress and retraced his steps. While he was gone, the fire had already burned down and the house had chilled. Joanne was awake, and in her eyes was a look of terror he would not forget.

Most hurtful of all was his own strength which seemed to grow as Joanne weakened. He had never felt more physically fit in his life. If she had been well, he could have spent entire days outdoors exploring the homestead, choosing the trees for the telegraph poles and marking out a route where he could cut the road when the snow melted. Pacing the tiny room, he flexed his muscles, longing for action.

In desperation one morning, he sat down on the bed, opened a magazine and started reading it out loud just to hear his own voice. To his astonishment Joanne began to pay attention. It was miraculous. With each day that passed her condition improved. He read to her each day, acting out what he was reading, coaxing a smile from her from time to time. He washed her, groomed her and played the mouth organ. After a few days she could sit up and move about a little. Though she seldom spoke, she no longer cried, and at rare intervals even offered him a sketch of her old smile.

March brought some alleviation of the cold, although the wind was bitter still. One last snow storm piled up massive drifts, a huge disappointment to Kevin who thought winter was over for good. It was, however, winter's last fling; each day it grew a little warmer until soon the whole forest was filled with the tinkling of melt water. Sticks began to show through the snow while here and there bare patches appeared. At twilight time the sounds of thawing calmed down as the frost fought for domination, but in the morning spring returned and the creek slowly began to fill with water.

Joanne, whose mood brightened as spring blew into the house, sat for hours in the doorway, watching the snow recede and listening to the glad sounds of oncoming summer. Meanwhile Kevin threw himself wholeheartedly into his pole project. Each morning as soon as breakfast was over, he crossed the swamp to the higher ground on the far side where the pines grew. There he selected and marked the trees which he felt met Ed's specifications. At noon he came cheerfully home, at first to prepare lunch and eventually to eat what Joanne prepared. Slowly joy was coming back into their lives.

"I'll be starting the road as soon as the snow is all gone," Kevin explained. "I thought that Ed would have come while there was still snow for hauling the poles out on sleighs, but I guess he knows what he is doing. In any case, as soon as the ground has thawed, I will dig a new well. This time I will line it with a log cribbing, although I will have to entice Mannie to guide me in that. He will also have to help me dig it, poor man. How is that for joyful news?"

Joanne nodded wistfully, not taking her eyes off the empty meadow. The memory of the winter was still too acutely with her. Kevin could not possibly know the awfulness she had been through, the grey hopelessness of the days, the aching melancholy that struck at twilight and never left her until daylight came again, or of the sleepless nights of tossing and turning, and always the nameless terror. The worst part of the ordeal was that she could not explain it because she did not have words for it. All of it was still with her to a degree although it was passing now, the shadows receding— unless the beast sprang again.

About one thing she was right: Kevin really had no idea of what had happened to her. He thought only in terms of physical sickness. He was aware she had lost her joie de vivre, and that she was in some kind of mental turmoil, but such things were, he was sure, the result of malnutrition. Sunshine and fresh vegetables would surely put her back on her feet. It was up to him now to see she got what she needed, and he was ready to do whatever had to be done to bring her back to her old cheerful self.

"Cheer up, Joanne; it will soon be summer."

"And then the rain will start again."

"No, it won't do any such thing. Ed said some years were wet and some were dry. I promise you this will be a dry one. There will be no problems this time. I will do better this year because I have learned to bend."

"Did you bend?"

"Right to Fletcher's floor."

"I broke."

"Please, please do not talk like that anymore. Do you want to leave this place?"

She shook her head. "No, I will not be leaving this place. If it does rain, what will you do about the roof?"

"Don't worry about that; Ed will be here soon, and I'll be making lots of trips to town—we'll be making lots of trips to town. We will get a load of boards and some new tarpaper, and this time we will do it right. Besides," he chided her, "we had fun even when it rained. You were happy all the time."

"Yes," she agreed sadly, "I was happy then."

29

AS SPRING EXPLODED AROUND HIM, KEVIN THREW HIMSELF INTO road making, becoming just as obsessed with the work as he had been with the woodcutting the previous summer. The physical exercise was a joy after the long inactivity of winter, and he had the added stimulation of having a financial return from what he was doing. Although he looked forward each day to Ed's arrival, he really wanted to have his task completed first so that he could show he was capable of operating on his own.

With the sunshine, Joanne began slowly to emerge from the shadows in her mind, even though she was still woefully thin and so weak she could scarcely spend an hour on her feet. Most days she passed on the doorstep soaking up warmth, watching the winter fade away. The nights were still terrible for her, particularly at the time of twilight, but Kevin's cheerfulness was infectious: she could not sit forever moping in the face of his enthusiasm.

It was a Sunday morning. After the dishes were washed Kevin sat beside Joanne in the doorway, longing to get on with his work, yet feeling he should spend a little more time with her. There were no leaves yet, no sign of green except along the edge of the marsh where the pussy willows were emerging and April flowers were thrusting their ugly heads through the sod. Crows, the first summer birds to return, quarreled raucously in the poplars far on the other side of the meadow.

"Kevin."

Startled from his reverie by her voice, he turned to her eagerly. "Yes— you want something?"

"Do you ever think of the first days we were here?"

"Well sure. Often."

"Were you really glad then or were you just putting on a front to please me?"

"I would like to be a hero and tell you I was thinking just of you, but being an honest man, I was never so happy in my life. Mind you, I was a little scared—afraid I would not be able to cope. That was my only reservation."

"There was a bit of that in me too. Looking back, though, those were the best days of all. Already it seems so long ago, so long since I felt joy in anything."

"It has been a long winter for you. It is all over now and you must forget the bad parts."

"Let's go down to the creek, down to my laundry place. The water will be running again."

Joyfully he got up to help her to her feet. It was the first time in months she had shown any real interest in anything. She was on her way back.

"Wait one minute; I'll get the twenty-two. Maybe we can scare up a partridge. We haven't had any since Christmas." At the edge of the creek they sat on a log, side by side, arms about their knees.

"See, there is the pool and my fireplace just as I left them last fall, abandoned and desolate."

"Did you think it would get up and run away?"

"What I mean is it seems strange that things exist when you are not there to see them—at least I think they exist. When I was sick, I sometimes got this queer feeling that outside the cabin there was nothing—as if only the inside of the house existed in a sort of void. It was horrible. The only way I could fight it was to fix my mind on something I knew must still exist outside, like the sawhorse, or more often this fireplace."

"Sounds weird, yet maybe I was feeling something similar: I felt as if I were high, high in the air looking down on our place, and I saw it as an island in solitude."

A chickadee, teetering on a willow branch, called with its spring voice, "Phoebee! Phoebee!"

"There is the place where you sho...saw the deer." He got up to stretch. "It's all right now Joanne. It's all right. The time of aberrations is over. It is soon to be summer; the worst is over; we have won!"

Apparently the gods were listening. Two partridges whirred in for a landing on a tree just behind Joanne.

"Don't move," Kevin warned, jumping to his feet and grabbing the twenty-two. "There is our supper."

He pulled the trigger. The gun did not fire and the birds took flight.

"Look at that," he said furiously, swinging to his right. The gun fired. For a fraction of a second Joanne stared at him with astonishment; then, she fell forward.

"Oh God!" he cried, flinging the gun aside, and gathering her up in his arms. "It's all right," he whispered. "It's all right. It's all right"—adding inanely, "It's only a little mark on your forehead—nothing at all." With giant strides he ran with her to the cabin where he lay her on the bed. Blood seeped from the hole in her forehead. He grabbed the towel from its nail, dampened it and hurried back to the bedside. When he touched the cold cloth to her forehead, she sighed, gave him one slow sweet smile, and then she slipped away.

He placed his face close to hers, could feel no breathing and cried out her name. When she did not respond, he clutched her by the arms and shook her, his single act of violence toward her in all their time together.

He stood there looking down at her while the afternoon faded into twilight, while twilight drifted into night, while tiny rivulets eating through the last late patches of ice outside froze and fell silent.

As the room darkened, knowing how she dreaded the darkness since she had fallen ill, he lit the coal-oil lamp and put it near her. The coal oil was almost gone. Once a mouse, perhaps sensing something unusual in the silence of the cabin, hurried across the floor on quick little legs, stopping to look up at him with its whiskers twitching. Suddenly it seemed unbearable to him that the mouse—possibly the very one that she had rescued—should still be there, should still be living, while Joanne was gone. In a blind burst of rage he lashed out with his foot, sending the mouse soaring across the room where it struck the wall, fell back and lay still.

In the night a strong wind came up and resumed its relentless fretting of the loose tarpaper. As Kevin stood vigil it seemed to him that over the roaring of the wind there was another sound, the sound of desolation. He began to understand that there was no point left in anything. If he went for help, it would not bring Joanne back to him; if he went on living in the cabin, he would become another Froman. He could not go back to the city leaving Joanne without anybody even to mourn for her. They had started their great adventure together, and everything they had done was for the two of them, not just for one. He had killed her; he had to pay the price even though it had been an accident. He would not go on without her.

Just as the sun rose over the meadow, he took the thirty-thirty, sat on the bed beside his wife, and stroked her face one last time. Then he put the barrel in his mouth and pulled the trigger.

For a few seconds after the sound of the shot the swamp was stunned into silence. A great gust of wind snatched a piece of the tarpaper from the roof and sent it soaring across the meadow. The sounds of spring stirred back into life, and in a little while the thaw resumed its work as the day began to warm.

Ed found the bodies about a week later, and it was he who informed the police, who—to his disgust—insisted it must have been a murder suicide even though they could not find the twenty-two. For a time there was a flurry of interest in the community, but since no one knew the McCormacks, it soon died down. And then there was no more talk of Kevin and Joanne.

The End